Praise for the Marla Adams Series

Marla is impressive and a strong female protagonist that sucks you into the story and won't let go. I was very impressed with how the author kept the suspense throughout the book making you wonder what will happen next.

La Mar A., Amazon Review

This book had me hooked from the first page! Marla Adams is the kind of protagonist I love—fierce, flawed, and unstoppable. The tension was relentless as she dove into a case that felt chillingly real, and I found myself holding my breath more than once. What really stuck with me was how personal this investigation became for her, forcing her to face both external threats and her own past. The mix of medical intrigue and suspense kept me glued to the pages. If you love thrillers that make you think while keeping your heart racing, this one is a must-read!

Samantha Thatcher, Amazon Review

If you like edge of your seat suspense, you won't want to miss this! What a page turner! I was kept guessing until the very end!

You will not be able to put this book down. Way to knock it out of the park!! Highly recommend!!

Tonya, Goodreads Review

The story follows Marla Adams, a formidable DEA agent whose relentless pursuit of a notorious criminal mastermind leads her through a maze of dangerous encounters and ethical dilemmas. Hanford's writing style is fluid and engaging, with a knack for creating vivid imagery and complex characters. His portrayal of Marla Adams as a multifaceted protagonist is one thing I particularly enjoyed. She is more than a law enforcement officer. She's a woman who is battling her demons while striving for justice in a murky world. This depth of character adds a significant layer to the narrative, making the reader invested in her journey.

Literary Reviewer, Goodreads

Whether it's illegal drugs, human trafficking, murder, or mistreating cattle, this story revolves arounds the Adams' efforts to apprehend the culprits and see justice done. I could hardly put the book down-- thoroughly thrilling and chilling.

TK Hagen, Bookbub Review

Patrick Hanford delivers a gripping finale in the Marla Adams series. Set against the sunny façade of South Padre Island, this thriller blends coastal charm with dark undercurrents of crime, corruption, and environmental mystery. Special Agent Marla Adams faces her most complex case yet—unraveling the link between drug overdoses and a dead tiger shark in a story that crackles with suspense and unexpected twists. A sharp, atmospheric read that pulls you under and doesn't let go.

Challengeer007, Amazon Review

Get ready to be immersed in the deceptively calm world of South Padre Island, a place where beautiful beaches mask a shocking secret, in this suspenseful thriller. The novel weaves together crime, suspense, and environmental intrigue, drawing you into Special Agent Marla Adams (a powerful and engaging lead character), increasingly complex mystery. With a fast pace and an eerie, atmospheric tone, this beach-town mystery is surprisingly gripping.

CAC, Amazon Review

This book takes the calm, postcard-perfect setting of South Padre Island and turns it into the backdrop for a sharp, unsettling mystery. From the very first pages, you can feel something is off beneath the surface—and not just in the water. DEA Agent Marla Adams is a strong lead, and her investigation pulls you deep into a world where drug overdoses and a dead tiger shark might be two sides of the same sinister coin. The pacing is tight, the tension builds steadily, and just when you think you've figured it out, the truth hits harder than a wave.

Sivan Kish, Amazon Review

The Depths of Marla Adams is the fourth and most captivating book in the Marla Adams series. The author has made DEA Agent Marla Adams her best yet: sharp, fearless, and navigating emotionally treacherous waters. With live and dead sharks, live and dead people, Marla plunges into the case, leading her into questionable alliances, family secrets, and a predator more dangerous than anything in the Gulf. I love the vivid scenes, tight plot and action. The author pushes the protagonist into a more complex heroine. If you love high-stakes crime thrillers, I promise The Depths of Marla Adams delivers. It's a must-read.

Windy&dry, Amazon Review

This is a thrilling ride that blends coastal charm with chilling mystery. The twist involving a beached tiger shark adds a unique and eerie element, making the story stand out among typical crime thrillers. It delivers suspense, strong pacing, and a setting that's as haunting as it is beautiful. A great conclusion to the series!

Marilyn from Mo., Amazon Review

The Depths of Marla Adams

Patrick Hanford

SAVOY
HOUSE

Savoy House Publishing

Cover design by KJ Waters Consultancy (kjwconsultancy.com) and Jody Smyers Photography (JodySmyersPhotography.com).

Second Edition 2026

ISBN: eBook 979-8-9856939-8-0

Paperback: 979-8-9856939-9-7

"We provoke a shark every time we enter the water, for we forget: The ocean is not our territory, it's theirs." Peter Benchley

South Padre Island and Laguna Madre

Ranch Brand

Chapter 1

Near the coast of South Padre, Texas, the waters of the Gulf of Mexico rarely revealed their secrets, a dangerous territory of blinding reflections and shimmering blue from millions of sunsets. Alone, a human head bobbed in the ebb and flow of the sea.

In the dark green water, a tiger shark glided with ease, like a predatory machine. Its lifeless eyes hunting for prey. Its rough skin blended in the ocean depths, and its fins cut through the water as if it were born to do so.

A fishing boat rested forty-seven feet below the surface, its hull tilted. A trickle of gasoline seeped from the stern. The waters allowed no sound and offered no second chances. Twenty feet away, crabs and sea worms fought over a piece of an arm, and their movements were anything but coordinated. Six ankles shackled to a deck rail, with the remains of the legs still attached, swayed in the current as if they were metronomes set to the tempo of death. The shark rocketed toward its prey, biting into a thigh and tearing muscle and sinew with sheer strength. The water exploded in a frenzy of blood as a second tiger shark entered the fray from the darkness. One snap of its jaws tore into the last lower leg, crushing bone and leaving a spiraling vortex of crimson.

◆

DEA Special Agent Marla Adams surfaced from the deep end of the heavily chlorinated waters of a swimming pool wearing full scuba gear. She lifted the mask off her face, pulled the mouthpiece away, and took a long breath.

A high-pitched whistle blew. The scuba instructor called out to his five students. Everyone to the shallow end, please. Long golden hair flowed past his ears, giving him that perfect beach vibe even though he lived in San Antonio, Texas. He strolled over barefoot to the far side of the pool and settled down on the concrete side. "Since everyone completed the training sessions successfully, I will certify each of you."

When they all clapped, Marla felt a twinge in her partially amputated right little finger.

The instructor grinned. "Good luck to all of you on your Caribbean trip next week."

One couple in their thirties high-fived each other and a second couple in their fifties gave each other a peck on the lips.

Marla stood alone and rinsed her mask in the water. She was clearly the odd woman out and not ready for any other man in her life.

Across the county, Cassie was hard at work on Marla's ranch, tending to over a hundred cattle. She not only managed ranch duties, but had become a proficient chef and her boss's spur-of-the-moment travel agent. She surprised Marla with a week-long Caribbean trip, hopping the islands from Saint Kitts to Saint Lucia.

Marla needed a break. After Crosby, her husband, had died, she dug into work seven days a week at the DEA and the ranch for over a year, but that was not enough to breach the loneliness. Forgetting the world on a distant island should help, but she had to time her vacation perfectly with calving season for her herd starting soon.

Though still the newbie at work, no one called her that anymore after single-handedly finding hundreds of pounds of heroin in a South Texas County Commissioner's new two-million-dollar home. The number one rule in drug trafficking is don't show your money, and with the official's taxable income last year of one hundred twelve thousand dollars, something didn't add up.

But life could jump in your face, and vacations rarely happened as expected. Before she could even kick off her vacation plans for a week of diving and snorkeling excitement, Special Agent in Charge (SAC) Davies abruptly rerouted her to the Gulf Coast instead.

The blazing midday sun beat down on Texas from above while South Padre Island basked in its glow; a salty breeze carried the scent of sunscreen and coconut oil through the air. This was no Caribbean paradise, but better than scrub brush, dirt, and wind.

The South Padre Police Department sought assistance from the DEA after two more young adults had succumbed to a new and deadly drug wreaking havoc in the community. The death toll in the town reached five in just thirty days.

Medical circles once considered fenethylline, a substance combining amphetamine and theophylline, benign. Created in 1961 under the name Captagon, and initially promoted as a treatment for narcolepsy and fatigue, by the 1980s, its highly addictive nature and lack of accepted medical benefits led to its classification as a controlled substance. Now, it was back, and with a vengeance.

Marla drove her double-cab pickup to the outskirts of the city and parked near an isolated beach house, with a weathered beige front door that almost disappeared against the undeveloped sandy landscape stretching northward, with sand dunes creating soft golden waves. The intense sun's reflection off the windows was almost blinding in its brightness.

Unlike the vacation rentals in the area that boasted swimming pools and volleyball nets, this particular place stood starkly unique and devoid of those summer amenities. The website images of the property exaggerated the reality by showing flowers and large patios that didn't quite align with reality.

Her truck bed held scuba gear, with a rigid plastic tonneau cover hiding it from sight. Her mouth watered at the thought of plunging into the blue sea depths. Diving deep, finding solitude, yet not complete isolation from the world. Even after his death, Crosby was always with her, in her thoughts, if not in body. In her mind, her soul, he never told her to come to him, but each day, she sensed that yearning to be with him again. Submerged, removing the mouthpiece would be simple. Would he be waiting for her in the depths?

Festus, her border collie, barked beside her, snapping her back to reality. "Right," she muttered as she brushed off a sense of weight from her chest that had clouded her thoughts momentarily. She pushed open the door of her truck and watched as her enthusiastic dog swiftly hopped over her lap and bounded onto the beach. When Marla followed suit, a distinct scent in contrast to the usual seaside surroundings hit her.

The DEA office in San Antonio booked the seaside cottage on the edge of town to steer clear of hotels and tourists, but a sudden incident threw a wrench in the works. A sixteen-foot female tiger shark carcass had beached just seventy-five feet from her front door. The sight of the decaying predator felt like a metaphor for her life, once fierce, now hollow and abandoned.

When the National Oceanic and Atmospheric Administration (NOAA) conducted a necropsy on the beach, they found a human shoulder with an orthopedic joint among the shark's stomach contents. The area evolved into a hub of activity, a grotesque attraction drawing reporters and spectators alike.

Festus sniffed the rancid air before rushing toward the dead animal. A flurry of seagulls took flight from the decaying mass as onlookers snapped pictures. Marla whistled sharply, and the dog turned, bounding back to her side.

She stood clad in her work attire: white button-down, long-sleeved shirt, black pants, black shoes—and a holster clipped to her belt with a pistol inside. She raised the tonneau cover and slid her baggage out, but left the scuba gear before unlocking the beach house door, then felt a sudden urge not to enter. Shaking the thought out of her mind, she motioned Festus to stay, then pushed the door open. A salty, musty aroma mixed with stale sunscreen engulfed her, and at once she realized the DEA had overpaid for this place. The interior temperature was stifling, even in comparison to the humid outside.

The small room had a bed, a living area, and a kitchenette, with a closed bathroom door off the side. Her luggage held the usual fare of button-down shirts and black pants, but she added cargo shorts and a Jimmy Buffett T-shirt for personal flair. With a thud, she dropped her travel garment bag and a small carry-on suitcase on the bed. She rubbed the stub of her right fifth finger where the pain had once throbbed but now only lingered as a strange numbness.

Two dim bulbs flickered to life when she flipped on the light switch, casting a weak glow over seashell, crab, and shrimp motifs embedded in the faded indoor/outdoor carpet. Two lumpy pillows rested on a too-small bedspread. In one corner stood a round dining table with metal legs bolted to the floor, topped with a vintage 19-inch television, its remote controller chained to the table—an odd precaution for anyone wanting to pilfer a three-decade-old TV remote.

The bathroom was a throwback, featuring a slender, circular mirror suspended over a pink porcelain sink, with only a small square of soap and a two-ounce bottle of shampoo as amenities. Marla shifted her attention to the front window of the building, peering through the sand-speckled glass, which lent a hazy ambiance to the beach outside. She turned on the air conditioner, and the motor roared to life, struggling against the oppressive heat.

Festus didn't mind the noise. Marla snapped her fingers, and he leaped from the doorway onto the bed, his tail wagging as if everything was perfect.

A sliding glass door led to a small concrete patio enclosed by a two-foot-high wrought iron fence painted bright turquoise. A pair of plastic Adirondack chairs beckoned guests to unwind and soak in the beach vistas. But something dead marred the view lying a short distance away.

Two hundred yards from her new residence, surfers rode the waves while high tide lapped against the wet sand, retreating back to the mysterious depths. Windsurfers skimmed over the surface, and scattered clouds raced across the blue sky above them. Marla's thoughts darkened as she settled into one of the plastic chairs, inhaling a mixture of a cool, salty mist and the reek of decay.

More than a mile south, the midday sun reflected off buildings while parents and grandparents hunkered under red, yellow, and green umbrellas stuck in the ground. Children ignored the heat while building sandcastles and chasing the tide. Teenagers, ignoring everyone else, rode skimboards over the wet sand. But beneath the surface of their carefree laughter, those sun-kissed faces might hide secrets tied to the drug that had claimed lives in this beach town.

The thrill of a vacation had evaporated, replaced by the weight of her mission and the darkness of the unknown.

Festus padded to the dead animal, nose twitching at the rank air. Seagulls scattered in a flurry of feathers as he approached. He retreated when Marla whistled sharply to call him back and gestured to the north end. "Go entertain yourself." The dog charged past the shark toward the undeveloped area of the island and disappeared behind sand dunes in seconds.

Marla caught a glimpse of a white Ford Bronco with an emergency lights bar on the roof and South Padre Island police markings on the door. It rolled to a stop in the sand beside the beach house. Instinctively, Marla brushed her hand over the holster on her right hip, a reflex born from years in the law enforcement field.

The driver's side door swung open, and a female police officer appeared, her brown short-sleeved uniform hugging her athletic frame. Aviator sunglasses shielded her eyes, and a broad smile as bright as the midday sun broke across her face. She strode toward Marla, hand outstretched. "Good day, Agent Adams. I'm Sergeant Standish."

The weightlifter-sized biceps and forearms didn't escape Marla's notice as Standish gripped her hand in a firm handshake.

"Nice to meet you." Standish loosened her grip and turned their clasped hands. "Got part of a finger missing."

"Right." Marla pulled her hand away. "Call me Marla, please."

"Got it, Marla. Most people just call me Standish. Glad you're here." She nodded toward the dunes, her expression shifting. "Was that your dog I saw running off?"

"He loves any place where he can stretch his legs," Marla replied, a hint of affection softening her tone.

"Had a dog like that years ago." A touch of nostalgia rose in Standish's voice and then she peeked at the scuba gear in the truck bed. "Diver?"

"Beginner. I just passed my certification. And you?"

"Long time. There are a few good places to go to. I'll take you if we find the time."

"Thanks."

Standish placed her hand on the truck bed. "How's everything else so far?"

"The view's fine—except for that," Marla pointed to the carcass.

Standish grimaced as her smile faded. "It's a beach; it happens from time to time."

Marla pointed toward the small house. "And this direction."

"Right." Standish's brow furrowed. "I just found out you were coming this morning. No one from the DEA briefed me on the specifics."

"But here you are," Marla said with a touch of sarcasm. "You found me."

"It helps when you're a cop, and you've lived here most of your life," Standish said. "I know most businesses in town. Only a handful of decent hotels along the beach, and when I saw no one had registered with a government rate, I contacted local Airbnb and Vrbo owners. I found your listing here. This spot is usually a college hangout for weekend parties. The owner is an elderly lady who moved almost twenty years ago and hasn't updated a thing inside. The kids don't care as long as they have a place to crash at night and surf in the morning. Someone pops by every few days to restock toiletries and change the sheets." She pointed southward. "A little ways down is the Margaritaville Hotel. It's nice."

Marla scanned the beach. "Thanks, but I prefer the peace and quiet."

Standish gestured toward the shark and the gathering crowd. "Not too quiet right now."

"True," Marla conceded. "Any updates on the victims?"

"The last ones were grad students from an in-state university. We did a hotel search and found their belongings. Forensics are processing everything."

Marla turned serious. "And the human shoulder joint found inside the shark?"

"Do you think there's a connection between the shark and the overdoses?"

Marla shrugged. "Could be a coincidence."

"Well, since you asked, there's a complication. The serial number on the joint has a large scratch across it—probably from something like a serrated shark tooth. Most numbers are unreadable. We contacted the manufacturer, but they're reluctant to release information without a written release from the owner. I'm guessing that's not happening anytime soon."

Marla nodded, processing the information. "How many days does NOAA estimate the shark has been dead?"

"Need to ask them."

Marla looked back at the carcass and asked, "And the shark? Will someone drag it off the beach, or is this my new work-cation backdrop?"

Standish sighed. "Budget cuts. Since it's off the beaten path and not during spring break, the city council voted to leave it be. Apparently, removing a rotting mass isn't a priority."

"Isn't it a health hazard?"

"Depends on who you talk to. But trust me, it's all about the money. They need a front loader and a dump truck to remove it, which is expensive. The council isn't keen on spending tax dollars on anything that doesn't align with their pet projects."

"So, how long for nature to do its thing?" Marla inquired.

"Probably about a month. Wild animals, crabs, seagulls—all are quick when they're hungry. We can gather the bones and remaining parts and haul them to the dump. Nothing new about letting nature take its course out here." Standish pointed to Marla's cap. "What's the logo?"

"My ranch in Hildebrandt. It's a heart with the female symbol in the center."

"Ranch? Nice." Standish motioned for Marla to join her. "Let's head back to the station and see what we have on the overdoses. Do we need to track down your dog before we go?"

Marla waved her hand toward the undeveloped beach area. "No, Festus is smart. When finished sniffing around, he'll return and lie down on the porch."

"He'll find the house after only being here a few minutes?"

"He's got a good nose," Marla smiled. "Let me get my wind-breaker." After closing the tonneau cover and locking the truck and front door, she dropped her cap on the porch. "He'll smell it and wait for me."

Chapter 2

The Bronco turned off the beach and onto a side street. Standish spoke with a mix of pride and enthusiasm. "There's so much to do here! Great restaurants, of course—fresh fish caught right out of these waters, not like the stuff shipped in from who-knows-where in the center of the country, or on the other side of the world. It's on your plate within minutes of being caught. Ever had seafood that is so fresh it's practically swimming?"

Marla smirked. "Does miniature frozen shrimp in an enchilada count?"

Standish scoffed, rolling her eyes. "Definitely not. We have outdoor festivities every night, with fireworks at dusk and live music ranging from hip-hop to reggae to blues. You might try to enjoy the island while you're here, if you give it a chance."

"Thanks. We'll see how it goes."

Standish turned the Bronco into the parking lot of the police station. The single-story rectangular brick building stood in stark contrast to the colorful establishments around town. Unlike their vibrant exteriors adorned with palm trees and murals of dolphins, this was a solid white structure, with POLICE DEPT printed in bold letters on the glass doors.

Marla pushed the door open and stepped into the empty lobby, a ten-by-twenty-foot space with scattered chairs. "We don't get many visitors," Standish said.

Behind thick Plexiglass, an officer acknowledged them, and the wooden door to the main office buzzed. She opened it, revealing a large room filled with desks and busy officers. Marla caught herself with a fleeting image of her hometown police station crossing her mind and the resulting images of a serial killer terrorizing the town's citizens and her family.

"Are you okay?" Standish asked.

Marla turned her head and forced a smile. "Sure."

The chill of the air-conditioned room enveloped her as she surveyed the surroundings. Fluorescent lights buzzed above, illuminating officers who moved between desks and up and down hallways. Most were indifferent to her presence, except for one man sitting two desks away. His fixed gaze followed her every move.

Standish's loud whistle stopped the chatter in the room, and all eyes were on her. "This is DEA Special Agent Adams. She's here to assist with the investigation into the new drug." She turned to Marla, a questioning look crossing her face. "What's it called again?"

"Fenethylline."

Standish nodded and continued, "She has full authorization to discuss the case with anyone here. Feel free to assist her."

Most of the officers greeted her cordially but with a polite distance—all except Officer Ricky Roberts, who remained seated, glaring at Standish. "Why do we need the Feds here?" he challenged Marla. "You don't think we can handle this, do you? We deal with drugs almost every day."

Standish's expression hardened. "Ricky, show some respect. She's smart. You're talking to the officer who cracked the Hildebrandt serial killer case."

Just then, a young officer who looked fresh out of high school swaggered behind Roberts and mussed his hair. "Ricky here caught the trash can kicker all by himself! Tracked him down on his bicycle and handed him a fifty-dollar fine last month."

Roberts swatted the hand away, irritation flaring in his eyes. "Shut up, Rhone. What have you done besides driving around and ogling at bikinis all day?"

"Enough," Standish interjected. "Special Agent Adams is here to help, not to take over."

"Yeah, right," Roberts scoffed. "We can manage anything that comes our way. We don't need any help."

Marla stayed calm. "Appreciate your loyalty to the police department, but given that fenethylline is the drug of choice, the DEA was called in, so I am here to help."

"Let's go to my office," Standish said, motioning for Marla to follow.

As they entered the office, Marla closed the door behind her and sat in a threadbare chair. "You introduced me to everyone except Chief Womack. Where is he?"

"Currently at a nursing home. He and his wife were in a car accident a few weeks ago. He walked away without a scratch, but...she's been through multiple surgeries and is barely hanging on."

"Sorry to hear that," Marla replied. "What's the story on Officer Roberts?"

"Pay him no mind. His wife left him last week. He's always been a pain in the ass, but now he's Mount Everest over the top."

"Is she still in town?"

"Last I heard, she went back to Nebraska. Seems she preferred cornfields and flat land over the ocean and nightlife. Who doesn't love sand, water, and a beautiful sunset every night?"

Standish sat behind her desk. "But seriously, why you? Why are you the one here?"

"Excuse me?" Marla raised an eyebrow.

"I know about your past." Standish leaned back in her chair and crossed her arms. "Your father was the serial killer..."

Marla slapped the desktop, her voice sharpened. "Hold up. If you're handing out my biography, get it right. He wasn't my father. He kidnapped me as a child. Stole me from my real parents."

"Fair enough, but still," Standish pressed, "why you and not someone with more experience?"

Marla inhaled slowly, releasing the tension in her shoulders. "All the other agents were tied up, and I was set to go scuba diving in the Caribbean. My boss's boss called me in after my boss had already left for his own vacation. I want to wrap this up ASAP so I can still get some diving time in before heading back to San Antonio and checking on my cattle at the ranch."

Standish nodded, taking in the information. "You have free rein to use any open computer or phone at the station. Is there anything else you need right now?"

"Do you have the full toxicology report on the OD victims? And I'd like the NOAA necropsy report, too."

"Sure thing." Standish picked up the phone and dialed an extension. "Bring me the drug folder...and the shark one, too."

Moments later, Officer Roberts appeared at the door, leaning in to hand the folders to Standish without a word.

As he turned to leave, Standish called after him, "Hold on." She opened the folders and held out several pages toward Roberts. "Copy these and give them to Special Agent Adams."

He shot Marla a guarded glance before replying, "Yes, ma'am."

"Anything else, Marla?" Standish asked.

"Anyone else I should know about at the station?"

The question intrigued Standish. "Meaning?"

"Do I need to watch my back with anyone besides Roberts?"

"Don't get the wrong idea about him. He's just stewing over his ex, and right now, he's not liking anybody—especially himself."

Roberts reappeared, dropping the papers on the desk before exiting again.

"I have a couple of errands to run," Standish said. "Take your time reading. Just remember, you can keep the copies, but you can't take anything else out of the building."

Once Standish left, Marla closed the door, then cracked it open. The bustling station filled her ears while perusing the police files. Roberts was the only person to glance her way, and he did it repeatedly.

When Standish returned, she knocked twice and smiled at Marla. "Got what you are looking for?"

"So far."

"Good. If you need anything else, just let me know. Want a ride back to your beach house?"

"No, thanks. I think I'll walk around a bit and grab something to eat before heading back."

"Don't forget about the fish. Caught fresh every day. What about your dog? You sure he's going to be okay?"

"Festus can take care of himself, but I'll swing by and pick up some dog food. Oh, one more thing."

"Sure. What?"

"Where's your shooting range?"

"Four buildings south of here on the boulevard. It's a privately owned store. That store allows shotguns, rifles, revolvers, and pistols. Show your badge, and the time is free for law enforcement."

"I don't like being given anything. Never know when that could come back to bite you."

"Don't worry. The chief is half owner."

As Marla wandered the streets, surf shops lined her path, each offering the same trinkets and T-shirts. She stopped at a leather store and reached for an address book. Her fingertips brushed over a heart branded on the cover—strikingly similar to the one Crosby had made for her on their wedding day.

Marla's stomach growled as the late afternoon sun sank toward the rooftops. She stopped at a small restaurant with a parking lot full of automobiles. If it was that busy, the food should be good.

Inside, the wall displayed a panoramic view of Hawaii, with palm trees and sandy beaches. Fake green grass covered the floor. Scattered dried salt latched onto the large picture windows outside, with a small collection in the corner of each windowsill. Marla squinted at the burning western sun, casting flickering speckles of brightness through the window.

At the cashier's desk, a young girl asked her if she was by herself. When Marla said yes, the girl smiled and led her to a table for two. Every person in the restaurant wearing vacation clothes stared at the woman walking between tables wearing a white button-down shirt, black pants, and shoes. The half-zipped windbreaker concealed the pistol in the holster.

Five seconds after she sat down, a boy said nothing as he placed a small bowl of salsa and a basket of tortilla chips near her, then disappeared into the kitchen. Mexican restaurant or not, you should get chips with every meal in Texas. A large blackboard hung on the wall with Today's Specials, each starting with the word—fresh-caught.

A middle-aged waitress, past the sun-kissed phase of life, had a multitude of non-specific tattoos over leathered skin. Her arms were rail thin.

"What'll you have, darling?"

"I'm from out of town. What's good?"

"Kinda guessed that from your, uh, attire. Not much beach wear there."

"I'm here about the recent drug overdoses. Did you know them?"

She raised the corner of her lip. "No. They were tourists, like ninety-nine percent of the population in town."

"Know anything about the drug?" Marla asked.

"Not me. I've been off all that stuff for a decade. You ready to order?"

"What do you suggest?"

With a vacant smile and a stitch in her forehead, she peered at the blackboard. "If you like blackened fish, you'll like the number two. Yellow rice, coleslaw, and jalapeno hush puppies come with it. Good with that?"

"Sure."

"Something to drink? You look like a sweet tea person." She waved her pencil up and down her customer's outfit. "No, no. Moderation. Cautious. You like half and half, right?"

"Perfect."

After eating her allotted fish for the day, Marla paid her bill and stepped out past the door. A convenience store sat next to the restaurant, and she remembered Festus needing dinner. A high-pitched electronic ding-dong sounded when she opened the glass front door. An overweight man with a scruffy beard, shaggy hair, and a tie-dye T-shirt sat on a stool beside the register, holding his phone while his elbow rested on the counter. He nodded once at her as she headed for an aisle.

"Have any dog food?" Marla asked.

"Only canned. One more aisle over."

Passing by an aisle of extra salty or sugary infused snacks in bright colors begging for anyone's attention, Marla found what she wanted in the corner. After sliding a five-pound bag onto the counter, she said, "Found this. Didn't have a price on it."

"Didn't know we had that." The guy put his phone down and checked the price with a hand-held barcode scanner. "Eight-ninety-nine. You here because of that shark?" He rang up the purchase. "Cash or card?"

She slid her card into the reader. "No. Something else."

"But you're a cop, right?"

"DEA. How'd you know?"

"Inside the windbreaker, there's a bulge on your belt, and you don't look like a cartel member. DEA, huh? Going to a big drug bust? Where?" He put the bag in a plastic sack and stuffed the receipt inside.

"No. Nothing tonight. I'm going to feed my dog and then wait."

"Wait for what?"

Marla smiled and grabbed the sack. "Thanks. See ya 'round."

She wandered down the sidewalk toward the beach with tall overhead streetlamps shining down every forty feet, leaving long shadows stretched across the shore. The sun had disappeared, leaving remnants of orange streaks under clouds. The clean ocean air felt invigorating. A rhythmic tide rumbled every few seconds and lay a carpet of water over the sand, only to be sucked back in. She stopped and counted the waves. Rumor was that every seventh wave was bigger. Fatigue and the tail end of the day caught up to her; she lost count several times before catching a pattern. The only thing she was sure of was that she could easily fall asleep listening to the white noise all night.

Marla stopped near the beach house and heard a bark several yards away, then another. Festus bounded out from behind the dunes, his fur matted with seawater and sand, and his tongue lolling out of his mouth. Marla dropped the sack on the sand, knelt on one knee, and waited for him. The dog didn't stop but ran circles around her until she laughed and called out, "Festus, stop!" The dog halted with his tongue hanging to one side of his mouth. "Good boy. Did you find any new friends?" She rubbed his head and noticed her front door partially open.

Chapter 3

The heavy, salt-laden air clung to Marla's skin, amplifying her uneasiness. Something moved inside the house.

"Festus," she whispered, "stay." Marla left the bag of dog food on the sand and stepped onto the porch, her eyes glancing left and right.

A flashlight beam skimmed inside the house. The hair on her arms quilled. As she reached for her gun, she eased the door open with her other hand. She bit her lip as the creak of the hinges broke the silence. The light turned off. The dim interior revealed someone had trashed the place.

She glanced at Festus to make sure he stayed before scanning the room, her eyes darting among the overturned furniture, clothes scattered along the floor, pillows torn apart, and the mattress pulled off the bed with the bedspread tossed aside like a hurricane had passed through. The door to the bathroom stood ajar. She remembered closing it before leaving.

A faint noise from behind the disheveled bed caught her attention, a figure hunched over, half underneath the mattress.

"Police!" Marla's voice sliced through the tense darkness like a knife before she flipped on the light switch.

The intruder whipped around, surprise etched on his face. It was a kid, a skinny teenager, wearing a dark hoodie pulled tight. His eyes widened with panic, then shifted to a calculating stare as he assessed his situation.

Marla gestured with her gun. "Get out from there and step back!"

He hesitated, then lunged over the mattress toward the window.

"Stop or I'll shoot!" Marla yelled as she positioned herself between him and the door.

"Just let me go, lady," he growled. "You weren't supposed to—"

"Doesn't matter!" she cut him off. "You've broken into my place. Why?"

The kid's gaze skimmed across the room, calculating his next move.

Marla could see the tautness in his face, the desperation in his eyes, the young age of the kid. "You got five seconds to explain."

"Easy," he said, raising his hands higher. "I'm just looking for shelter. Got caught out here with no place to go."

A lie she wasn't buying. "Counting down. Four."

"Listen. I didn't mean no harm."

"Three—Festus!" she shouted, banking on the dog to unnerve him. "Get in here!" Marla caught the slight twitch in the kid's shoulder.

"Who's Festus?" he spat.

Before she could answer, the sound of a low growl echoed from the doorway. Festus' stance was defensive—teeth bared, ready to protect her.

"Back up! You don't want to mess with the dog."

The intruder stepped back, but then snatched a nearby lamp and swung it at Marla.

She ducked, letting the lamp crash against the wall behind her, scattering shards of porcelain and plastic across the floor.

Festus barked fiercely. He had never attacked anyone, but the intruder didn't know that. "All I have to do is say one word, and the dog will rip you apart. Why are you here?"

The intruder stumbled backward in fear as the dog continued barking at him. "Look, I don't want no trouble. Let me go and just leave it at that."

"On your knees."

His eyes widened. "What? No."

Marla seized the moment, moving to flank him as he stumbled. She grabbed his thin arm and twisted it behind his back. Festus stopped barking.

"Let go!" he shouted.

"Not a chance," Marla replied, locking her grip tighter. She needed handcuffs, but didn't have any. "You're going to stay right here until the authorities arrive." With her hands full, she couldn't use her phone to contact the police, and was too far away for anybody to hear the scuffle. Firing her weapon was not an option, so she pulled him up and made him sit in the corner.

A loud thud echoed at the front of the house as she reached for her phone. Her stomach dropped.

"What now?"

The kid took advantage of the distraction, shoved Marla aside, and bolted for the exit.

"Festus, no!" Marla yelled, but the dog was already in pursuit, barking as the intruder dashed past her and into the night.

Marla charged out the door just in time to glimpse at the boy disappearing into the shadows.

"Festus, stop!" she shouted, but the night swallowed her voice.

The dog returned, panting but still on high alert. He pressed his body against Marla's leg as if sensing her turmoil.

A dead seagull with a broken neck lay on her porch, its body still warm. It had collided with the glass and died on impact. But why would a bird do that at night? After holstering her gun, she stepped inside, her heart pumping, the room chaotic. Her mind raced with thoughts of how bad things could have gone.

The kid didn't kick in the door, so he had a key. After checking her belongings, she realized this wasn't a random break-in. Her cap and the DEA's directive to locate the drug fenethylline were missing. At least he left the remote control attached to the chain.

A deep breath later, the weight of recent events settled firmly on her shoulders. She couldn't shake the feeling that this was only the beginning.

She had to call SAC Davies, her boss, concerning the recent action. After lifting the mattress back onto the box springs, she called out, "Festus?"

The dog ran into the house and jumped on the bed as if nothing had happened.

The intruder was rude enough to turn the A/C unit off. She picked up her clear adhesive tape dispenser on the floor, tore a strip off, and covered the fingerprint from the air conditioner OFF button, hoping he wasn't smart enough to use a knuckle and not the tip of his finger. After retrieving the fingerprint, she pressed the MAX AIR button, and the motor roared like a chainsaw. She rushed to check her pickup, and relief washed over her when it was untouched. Thank God her scuba gear was in the truck bed and locked under the tonneau cover.

Darkness had fallen, allowing the nightly fireworks to illuminate the sky above the ocean. Their brilliance masked the unsettling tension around her. Should she try to search for another place tonight? No. Whoever ransacked the room was likely watching from somewhere along the shore. She felt it in her bones—this was bigger than expected.

After returning inside, Marla secured the entryway by wedging the chair under the door handle, but the window was the real problem. The raging air conditioner located under the glass and near the sleeping quarters prevented her from hearing anyone outside. An easy target, especially now that someone knew the layout of the room. Sleeping in the truck was not an option, so she propped the mattress and leaned it against the window to obstruct any external views and decided not to change clothes in case she had to make a run for it.

She turned off the lights, gathered the remaining torn pillows and bedsheet, then settled on the opposite side of the box springs. With the remote chain stretched from the table leg, she pressed the ON button, lighting the dark room like an actor on stage and the audience in the shadows. They could see you, but you couldn't see them. She switched it off, squeezed the torn pillows together, and tugged the sheet over her shoulders. Festus nestled beside her, his warmth a minor comfort in the growing unease.

◆

Marla jolted awake when Festus jumped on all four paws, stared at the door, and gave out a low growl. In the pitch-black room, Marla drew her pistol from the holster and placed a calming hand on the dog's back. "Easy, boy." She got on her knees behind the box springs and aimed straight ahead. "Someone out there, buddy?" Festus stood like a statue, then eased, sat, and licked his lips. Marla glanced at him. "Everything good?" The dog turned and licked her face once. "Let's see what's up."

Marla removed the chair from under the door handle and stood to the side. When she pushed the lever down and opened the door, nobody rushed in. Festus fidgeted and whimpered.

She slapped her leg. "Go."

Festus sprinted out the door, and Marla knelt to a firing stance in the doorway. Nothing was amiss. She eyed the pencil-thin moon floating high in the inky sky. A cargo ship's row of round lights illuminated the darkness several miles out in the ocean. A sound similar to the tide crashing on rocks filled the air, but the shoreline was flat and sandy. To the left, sixty or seventy feet away, the dog barked several times. Marla trudged across the sand. "Festus, sit." The dog ignored her, bounding forward and backward. "Festus."

Marla froze in place and stared at an object while the dog's barks became more insistent. She pulled out her phone and dialed a number.

"911, what is your emergency?" asked the operator.

"This is DEA Special Agent Adams. I am at my rental house on the island's north side, and I need you to contact Sergeant Standish right now."

"May I have your address?"

"I don't remember that. Standish knows what it is. She was here yesterday. Get her on the phone."

"Stay with me while I call on another line."

Moments later, Marla's phone clicked, and a voice mumbled, "This is Standish."

"Marla Adams, here. You need to come to my place right away."

Standish's voice cleared. "Why? What happened?"

"Not sure, but you have to do something before the sun comes up. No lights, no siren, no need for it."

"Okay. Be there in a flash."

Marla sank to the sand, anxiety gnawing at her while Festus leaned against her. After what seemed like longer minutes than expected, two bright headlights swung onto the beach. Festus ran to the shoreline.

When the Bronco came to a stop, Standish lowered the window. "What happened?"

Marla stood and gestured toward the water. "Turn your headlights that way."

Standish turned the vehicle north and found Festus sitting and staring at another beached tiger shark. "Oh, man. This is bad. Two? The news media will have a field day."

Marla swept her arm across the ocean's width. "How many more dead fish are coming?"

Chapter 4

As the sun peeked above the ocean, police officers blocked off the area with yellow crime tape while NOAA employees methodically inspected the beached shark. A few early morning vacationers hung around, filling their curiosities, while others went about their routine closer to the hotels, sipping coffee or mimosas under umbrellas. Barefoot joggers splashed water under their feet with each stride while trying to ignore the mandated detour. The officers politely encouraged them to continue their runs in a different direction.

Marla's day-old, long-sleeved white shirt and black pants stuck to her skin while Festus stepped closer, a silent sentinel at her side. She stopped near the second tiger shark and waved at a man sitting on top like riding a horse. "Excuse me, sir?" Marla flashed her badge toward him. "Excuse me, may I speak to you?"

The man slid off the top of the fifteen-foot fish and brushed the front of his orange plastic overalls with gloved hands before smiling. "Yes, ma'am. What can I do for you?"

"I'm DEA Special Agent Adams. I'm the one who found it this morning."

"Nice to meet you. I'm Dr. Horatio Hernandez, veterinary medical officer for NOAA." He slipped his gloves off and gestured back at the animal. "I was taking skin samples."

"Glad to meet you, sir. Did you perform the necropsy on the first shark?"

"I did."

"Have you heard any additional info on the human remains?"

"That was an absolute surprise when we opened the stomach, but nothing new since yesterday. No word on the serial number, and because of the extensive human skin, muscle, and bone damage, DNA testing is impossible."

"No DNA? Why?"

"Shark stomach acid can destroy just about anything."

Marla nodded once and pursed her lips. "Hmm, right. With the history of the first shark, I need a big favor."

"Sure, if I can?"

"Could you provide tissue samples for me to send to our crime lab?"

"What do you want?"

"A couple of tubes of blood, a chunk of the liver and kidney."

He chuckled. "I suppose we don't have to worry about patient privacy in this case."

Marla didn't laugh.

"Sorry. A little medical humor there. But, yes, easy enough. I'll get that for you."

"Oh, and one more thing," Marla said. "I'm not sure what the protocol is, but could one of your employees slice open the stomach and check for any human body parts while I'm here?"

Hernandez glanced at the first decomposing shark less than a hundred feet away. "Makes sense, considering they both died around the same time."

"What do you mean? This one looks worse."

"Right. It's much more decomposed than the first one. My guess is they both died close to the same time, but this tiger shark probably sank to the ocean floor and sat a few days until internal decomposing gasses floated it to the surface, and then the tide brought it in. Days apart on the beach, both dead around the same period. We found tags on both. Let me get the samples for you, and I'll have a tech open the stomach right away."

Marla and Standish stood nearby as a technician approached the shark's belly. With the point of the knife, the tech punched a hole in the stomach, and in one quick slice, several smaller fish and a part of a human leg with a significant portion of the skin gone spewed out onto the sand with an overpowering stench of old vomit.

Both spun away from the gruesome sight. Marla gagged. "Okay, same song."

Standish waved her hand toward the police officers. "Widen the perimeter! Another fifty feet out all the way around." She called the station. "I need an enclosed box truck to transport a body."

"What about an ambulance?" the dispatcher said.

Standish gestured with her hand as if the person at the station could see her. "Way too late for that."

Marla called out to Standish, "I need to make a call." She tracked through the sand toward the beach house, with Festus following close by, and contacted SAC Davies' private line.

"Davies, here."

She plopped into a plastic Adirondack chair on the patio. "This is Adams, sir. I'm going to need help down here."

"Give me a rundown since you got there."

"I checked in yesterday, met the sergeant, and she took me to the station and introed me to the staff. Afterward, I walked the shoreline, ate dinner, then returned to the beach house. But when I got there, it had been ransacked. Someone knew I'm DEA and snatched the case file."

"So, we have contact. It's always good to have that as long as you survive."

"There's more."

"More? As in more contacts?"

"Yes and no, sir. I made a few small buys, probably heroin, all of which are at the Brownsville office, but unfortunately, no fenethylline yet. Last thing. Early this morning, my dog jumped up and barked while I was sleeping."

"Barked? Dogs do that."

"Not my dog. He only barks when a calf is down. I went outside to check the area and found another shark beached."

"Another?"

"Yes, sir. NOAA is there now performing a necropsy, and the vet is gathering samples for me. I'll send it to our lab. Thought it was odd that two dead tiger sharks were less than a hundred feet from each other, so I asked him to open the stomach. Didn't expect another orthopedic shoulder joint, but just wondered what more coincidences there could be."

"And what did you find?"

"A leg, waist to knee. Can't get a visual ID since...no head, and most of the skin is gone."

"Gone where?"

"Not sure, sir. The vet says shark stomach acid."

"Listen, Adams. I'm up to my ass in alligators in the office. Too many activities with the OCDETF. (Organized Crime Drug Enforcement Task Force) And by the way, thanks for delaying your vacation to help."

"You're welcome, sir." Marla shuffled a shoe over the sandy patio with no idea it wasn't obligatory.

"I'm glad you did, but to help you, I would have to pull an agent off their case. Can't do that for at least another week."

Marla stood and turned around before leaning against the short metal fence around the patio. "Do you think the task force should be involved?"

"Not yet. You need to gather more intel before I ask for that. Since Borland is on vacation for two weeks, I'm putting Samuel Tillman in charge of the San Antonio office until he returns. Borland texted me, and I told him to call me back. Contact Tillman from now on."

"Got it." Marla ended the call and looked down at Festus as he gazed up at her.

Standish stepped over the short fence and plopped down in the other plastic chair. "My gut tells me this is more than a freak coincidence. Dead sharks, human body parts, and now a mysterious break in at your place? Someone's testing the waters—literally and figuratively."

"*And* testing me," Marla added. "Whoever broke into my rental wanted me rattled. That file wasn't the endgame; it was a warning shot."

Standish nodded. "You're right. They're betting you'll fold under the pressure."

Marla's jaw tightened. "Then they're going to be disappointed."

"Good. I'd hate to see you run scared." Standish stood again. "How about breakfast? The station will foot the bill."

Marla tucked her phone into her pocket. "I should change. These clothes are a bit rank."

"Nonsense. No one cares what anybody looks like on this island. Most of the tourists here are drunk, getting drunk, or sobering up so they can get drunk again. Come on."

Fifteen minutes later, they were sitting at the Water Taxi Restaurant on the south end of the island under a green canopy with no walls. It looked like a permanently open fifty-square-foot tent. They sat on wooden benches at the far corner nearest the beach as the waitress placed two cups of coffee on the table in front of them.

Standish held two fingers up at the waitress before sipping her coffee, and the server placed a RESERVED sign on the two tables closest to them.

Marla glanced at the signs, then back to Standish. "Having a party later?"

"No. They're good to me. When I have official business, they block the tables next to me so no one can eavesdrop." Standish sipped her coffee again before asking, "Remind me, what does OCDETF stand for?"

"Organized Crime Drug Enforcement Task Force."

"Guess I forgot that acronym."

"FBI, DEA, US Marshals, US Attorneys, and ATFE are all big dogs playing together on one field. If they come here, then you have problems in your sandlot."

"I like to keep our sand clean."

"So...give me your thoughts," Marla said.

Standish's expression darkened. "I think this place is going to be a ghost town if the media jumps all over two dead sharks with human remains in the stomachs and a rash of dead students from a drug overdose from an unknown substance. Not safe in or out of the water. It might just be my paranoia, but it seems if you want to shut down the island before summer break hits, do precisely what happened over the last few days."

Marla's mind struggled to piece together fragments of a vast puzzle. "This isn't about shutting down for spring break anymore. It's bigger than that."

"Do some of that DEA magic and find where the drug source is by this afternoon."

Marla smiled. "I can try, but I doubt I'll have an answer by the end of the day."

Another employee placed two plates of food on the table.

"Hope you don't mind," Standish said. "I always have the same dish here. I promise you'll love it. They sell out by ten every morning."

"Looks good. What kind of fish is it?"

"Red snapper from the lagoon. Great taste. They buy it off the boats at sunrise, prepare it in the kitchen, and grill it to perfection. And the hash browns are heaven, especially with the toasted potato bread soaked in garlic butter."

Marla took a bite. "Wow!" After swallowing, she asked, "Are you part owner? You seem to know everything there is about this place."

"I should be. I've given them enough of my money over the years."

Marla looked out at the ocean with a sense of urgency driving her forward. Beneath the surface, secrets swirled, and she was determined to uncover every one of them—no matter the cost.

Chapter 5

The Intracoastal Waterway was the combination of nature and man, stretching from Massachusetts down the Atlantic coast through Florida and ending in Brownsville, Texas. The US Army Corps of Engineers played a crucial role in maintaining and improving its infrastructure on the natural landscape. Along the southern Texas coast, a giant man-made scar cut through the Laguna Madre, serving as a reminder of human endeavors. Workers made the artificial islands from mounds of dredged mud, and left them to harden over time, as evidenced by a straight line of them inside the lagoon. These spoil islands, as they are called, were home to many on the fringes of society who had built makeshift houses and trailers on top of them.

On one spoil island, almost a hundred yards wide, a ten-foot-tall Mexican fan palm tree sat beside a weathered house trailer, its white paint peeling and discolored from the blistering sun. Puffs of seagrass and small dunes covered the ground. A broken satellite dish teetered against the porch railing, and a tattered Texas flag hung limp in the still air.

Inside, the trailer smelled of sea salt, cooked fish, and garbage. A streak of sunlight pierced through the dark curtains in the living room across Jax Whitmore's face, stirring him from his sleep on the sofa. His head throbbed. Scratching his two-week-old beard, he swept the hair out from his eyes before turning to his other side. An infant cried for attention. Jax covered his ears and yelled, "Damn it! Somebody get the baby!" He pulled the pillow out from under his head and covered his face. It didn't help—the baby kept crying. When he sat up, his head spun. "Somebody grab the baby!" He stood and lost his balance when he pulled up on his pajama shorts, then plopped back down on the couch. Standing again, the carpet felt sticky and stained under his bare feet.

He trounced into the bedroom. An oscillating fan groaned on the dresser, barely moving the stifling air. Raylene, his girlfriend, lay sprawled on the bed, without a stitch of clothes, one leg dangling off the edge, and her face hidden beneath a pillow. The baby flailed in a crib that was too small for her growing frame. Jax reached inside the infant bed, scooped up the child, and laid her on his shoulder. "Yeah, yeah, let's go and get you a bottle."

Stepping between empty beer cans and trash on the floor, he made it to the kitchen and pushed his semi-automatic pistol to the edge of the counter. He filled a saucepan with water and set it on the stove before opening the fridge and pulling out a bottle of formula.

"Your worthless mother won't do shit around here."

He poured corn flakes, a spoonful of hot salsa, and milk into a bowl. Just as he took his first bite, someone pounded twice on the flimsy front door.

Still holding the baby in one arm, Jax snatched the pistol off the countertop with the other and gripped it firmly in his hand. He yelled with a mouthful of cereal, "Who is it?"

The pounding continued.

"I said, who is it?" Jax stepped to the doorway and turned to have the child away from the door as if that might give more protection from flying bullets. He used the barrel to push aside the short curtain that covered a small square window and peeked outside. Junior Wells stood with his hands in his pockets. Jax pitched the gun onto the couch.

When the door opened, Junior held both hands outstretched before him. "Did you forget? You were supposed to be on my boat to go fishing. I need money." He gestured toward the sun. "It's too late for redfish, now. You made me lose out."

"I didn't make you do nothing." Jax turned to show the infant in his arm. "Can't you see I'm busy here?" After moving from the doorway, Jax plopped down on the sun-bleached red, yellow, and orange plaid couch outside the trailer. Two flat bottom aluminum boats sat floating on two feet of water and tethered to a post at the waterline of his spoil island. When the baby started crying again, Jax shifted it to his other arm. "That bitch inside does nothing. Raylene can't cook, doesn't wash clothes, won't take care of the baby half the time."

Junior fidgeted. "Yeah, man, but—"

"You take her."

"I don't want no baby."

"No, dipshit. Raylene. You take her."

"No way, man. I don't want her...I mean, I do, but not all the time."

"I've seen you eye her ass when she's dancing around inside. You want that, don't you? Take her. I don't care."

"What I want is to go fishing early in the morning so we can catch fish and sell it to my cousin at the restaurant."

"Take the bitch, and I'll go with you tomorrow morning." The baby cried louder. Jax stood, reached into his pajama pocket, and pulled out a hundred dollar bill. "Take her, and you can have this."

"Where'd you get a hundred dollars? I can't buy a pack of cigs, and you got a hundred? Where'd you get it?"

"Don't worry about where." Jax waved the bill like dangling bait. "You want it? Take both."

"No, man. I know what she'd do...steal it from me and then what? She'd come running back to you and leave the baby with me."

Jax stuck the money back into his pocket, stomped past the entryway, stormed inside the bedroom, and slammed the door. He yelled at the mother to get out of bed while the baby continued to cry.

Junior entered the house and heard water boiling on the stove. He turned the burner off and rummaged through drawers until he found one with several tens and twenties. He pocketed the bills and closed the drawer.

Jax came out of the bedroom dressed and holding an empty plastic sack. "Come on. Let's get out of here." He shot through the doorway.

Junior followed. "Where you going?"

Jax untied his rope from the post and flung the end into his boat. "Get in. It's time for me to retrieve collections for Leo."

Junior climbed in after Jax sat at the back and started the small outboard motor. "Is that where you got the hundred?"

"Idiot." The motor revved as the boat moved down the waterway. "I don't steal from Leo."

Junior squirmed around and looked at Jax. "So, where'd you get the hundred?"

"None of your business. Shut up and sit still."

Their first stop was a decrepit dock where a man handed over cash without a word. Next, a scrawny teenager appeared from a fishing shack, his eyes darting as he passed Jax a wad of bills. The sack weighed considerably more by the time they reached Pier

19. Jax slowed the boat and grabbed the handle of his fishing net. He swooped it into the water and retrieved a fish.

"Here." He flipped the net over and dropped it between Junior's feet. "Take this to your cousin." Five minutes later, Jax edged the bow of his boat alongside the post at his spoil island and jumped out with a full sack of cash.

Junior's curiosity boiled over. He jumped out and tied the rope to the post. "Hey, man. I need money. You owe me. Give me a little of that."

Jax stopped and turned, holding the sack outstretched. "You want money? Take it. Dig your hand deep inside and take whatever gets your goat."

Junior grabbed a handful.

"When Leo finds out he is short, I'm telling him you stole it from me, knowing it was his money. You want that?"

Junior released his hold of the cash. "Give me that hundred in your pocket or I'm telling my cousin you made me miss catching redfish."

"Yeah? So what?"

"So, Leo eats breakfast at my cousin's place every morning, and when I tell him you made me miss fishing today, and Leo didn't get his fresh redfish, he's going to kick your ass. Maybe he'll give me your route after he kills you."

Jax glared at Junior, then pulled the hundred dollar bill from his pocket and flung it in the air. "Fine. Take it."

Junior swooped it up off the ground. "And you better be ready for fishing tomorrow."

The front door opened when Jax stepped on the old, creaky wooden step. Raylene stood, hair uncombed, wearing a short kimono, open, holding the baby—both naked. Jax held the sack in one hand, pulled her close, and kissed her passionately before using his foot to kick the door shut behind him.

Junior stuffed the bill in his pocket and grunted, "If I gave her this hundred, maybe she'd do me too."

Chapter 6

Leo shuffled past the sturdy double front doors of his intentionally basic-looking, three-bedroom home, a sack of groceries balanced under one arm. Nestled in a rural neighborhood twenty miles west of the island and the lagoon, houses sat acres apart. The door creaked as he pushed it shut, a reminder he had yet to oil the hinges. He twisted the deadbolt into place, his sharp eyes catching a faint scratch on the doorframe near the lock. Not there this morning. He entered the kitchen, where soft under-cabinet lighting illuminated the polished granite island countertop. After unloading the grocery bag of bottled salsa, a small head of garlic, and a carton of eggs, he reached for the water glass partially filled beside the sink.

A voice came from behind him, low and calm. "You need better locks."

Leo's fingers paused on the cool glass. "Jax," he murmured, setting the tumbler down before turning around. "Been expecting you."

The oversized windows behind Jax revealed a multi-acre manicured backyard bordered by short cedar trees shrouded in shadows. His silhouette contrasted with the clean lines of Leo's pristine home. In one hand, he held a large sack stuffed with cash, and in the other, a pistol with a long suppressor attached. His sandals scraped on the tile as he adjusted his stance. Dressed in typical beach bum attire: tattered swim trunks, a sun-faded

T-shirt with PADRE across the chest and a redfish underneath, he wore a permanent, lazy half-smile that betrayed nothing but amusement.

"What are you doing in my house? Where's Jorge?"

Jax's eyes flicked toward the back door. "Out there, in the backyard," he said, loosely swinging the tip of his pistol in the direction.

Leo gave a piercing look. "Do I need a new guard for the house?"

Jax's expression altered a little as he stepped into the room, crossing the space slowly and deliberately, like a predator entering another's territory. "Might need two." He reached the high-backed chair and laid the pistol down casually on the leather seat, a silent reminder. "Jorge tried to keep me out," Jax said. "You remember last time, don't you? Told him not to play doorman with me again."

Leo's gaze shifted to the high-backed chair with the gun on the seat. A tense silence settled between them, thick as smoke, until Leo broke it. "That for me?"

"Yeah," Jax replied, raising the sack before tossing it across the room. Leo caught it with both hands and lowered it to the counter, unrolling the top to inspect the contents. Wads of cash stared back at him. "Looks lighter than usual."

"I already took my cut."

Jax rummaged inside a lower cabinet and pulled out what he was looking for. "Found a bottle of Kentucky," he said, holding it up with a sly smile. "Why don't we toast to your success?"

Leo raised an eyebrow as Jax pulled the cork with a pop, the scent of aged whiskey filling the air. He poured a generous measure into two short glasses. But just as he slid one glass forward on the countertop, Leo's hand slipped into a nearby drawer, pulling out a pistol, barrel raised just enough to make his intentions clear.

"How about I shoot you?" Leo asked, voice cool. "Then I don't have to worry about anyone breaking into my house again."

"You won't." Jax gulped all the liquid from his glass.

"Hey!" Leo waved the pistol barrel at the bourbon bottle. "Easy with the good stuff. That's reason right there to shoot you."

Jax shrugged, which seemed almost dismissive. "You're not the type."

Leo narrowed his eyes. "Not the type? I don't like people trespassing in my home."

"We've been friends for ten years," Jax replied evenly, his voice as smooth as the bourbon.

"Acquaintances. Friends would be pushing it."

"You're not going to shoot. Not here, anyway. Not with your expensive furniture at risk." Jax gestured to the pristine leather chair and the plush, ten-thousand-dollar couch. "Blood on these? You handpicked them from Argentina—special tanned cowhide, right? I remember when you bought them. And that woman? Whoa, she was..."

The corner of Leo's mouth twitched, betraying a moment of hesitation. He grunted and slid his pistol back into the drawer.

Jax took the liquor bottle from the counter, pouring a splash into his glass. "I do like the pricey stuff," he remarked with a smirk. "That's why I come here. At my place, we'd be drinking the cheap crap."

Leo lifted his glass, taking a small sip, savoring the burn as it slid down his throat. "Did you splatter blood on my outdoor furniture?"

"Relax." Jax took his own sip, watching Leo over the rim of the glass. "Jorge was considerate enough to stand in the middle of the yard." He paused, a slight smile playing on his lips. "Quick. Clean. Well, for me."

Leo smirked, tapping his fingers against the glass. "Wasn't worried." His face hardened, but he kept his tone neutral. "And what about the DEA Agent Marla Adams?"

Jax couldn't decide if he found it amusing or annoying. "You still worried about her?" He lifted his glass in a mock toast. "Don't worry. She's no threat."

Leo studied Jax, who had now focused on the whiskey swirling in the glass. "Why shouldn't I be worried?"

Jax drew a deep breath before answering. "You want her gone?" More of a statement than a question. "She's gone. To-morrow."

Leo rolled the sack tight against the cash inside before answering. "Not yet."

Jax lifted his glass once more. "To sharks and bullets, may they never come toward you."

Leo held his gaze, his own glass hovering in mid-air. The unspoken threat hung between them, thick as the silence that followed. He raised his glass and took a long, deliberate sip as his eyes never left Jax's. Each of them knew this was more than a simple toast—a message, a promise, and perhaps a warning.

Chapter 7

The following day, the sun burst bright and fresh, light gleaming on the tops of waves. The start of Sunday brought disappointment for departing tourists, as a fresh wave of visitors was expected in the afternoon.

Behind the short, turquoise-colored patio fence of the beach house, Marla and Standish settled in the plastic chairs. Standish donned standard beach wear and wrap-around sunglasses, while Marla wore her shorts and Jimmy Buffett T-shirt. Festus lay between them with his head on his front paws. The two sharks continued decomposing at low tide while crabs and seagulls picked on the insides. A computer lay in Marla's lap, and the screen showed the product information sheet on fenethylline. She read the formula weight, melting point, molecular formula, and the brown, white, or gray colors of the crystalline solid. It would all be interesting to a scientist, but she focused on the shipping details. "Here we go. You can ship it under ice."

"Like a Styrofoam beer cooler and a ten-pound bag of ice?" Standish asked.

"Or a ten-by-fifty-foot metal container and a thousand pounds of ice." Marla tapped the keys on the laptop. "How did this drug get to South Padre?"

"Yeah. Why here?" Standish propped one heel atop the fence. "And you said New Jersey is the only other hot spot in the US, almost two-thousand miles away."

"The largest eastern port is in New Jersey," Marla said. "China can't be the source. They ship to Los Angeles, unless they go through the Panama Canal. Over the past twenty years, Syria had been the primary producer of millions of these tablets, which generated billions of dollars in profits in the Middle East and Eastern Europe." Marla closed the laptop. "But after Syria's President Bashar al-Assad's regime had collapsed in 2024, drug production had fallen significantly."

"You still think it's coming in from the east coast?" Standish asked. "Or did it fall off a cargo ship and float into our gulf?"

Marla chuckled. "Great imagination."

"Okay. If someone dumped it near the shoreline, I should check on any drug raids by the Coast Guard over the last two weeks."

"I already did," Marla said. "None with fenethylline. The only answer is that someone brought it here."

A pair of four-wheelers raced along the shore, sand shooting into the air from beneath their tires as the vehicles veered left and right. They spun around the sharks before stopping at the beach house.

The engines idled as two men stepped off their vehicles. Both wore board shorts, flip-flops, and no shirts. College-aged beach bums bulked up with paper-thin layers of fat under their sculpted abdomens. One was curly blond, and the other sported brown hair past his ears and parted down the middle. Both looked like they had missed their barber appointments the last few months.

The blond smiled like he was being friendly. "Nice truck...for a ranch, but not so much on a beach."

"Good to know." Marla didn't move in the chair. "What can I do for you?"

He pointed at her. "You should leave before bad things happen."

Festus stood. A throaty growl rumbled from inside his throat as he stared at the man.

Marla continued to sit. "Look behind you. Bad things already did."

Standish scooted back in the chair, ready to stand and beat their ass when Marla laid her hand on her friend's forearm. "Easy," she said in a low voice. "Let's see how this plays out."

Standish was itching to jump the fence. "What do you want, blondie?"

"I want you to shut up, old lady. I wasn't talking to you."

Marla felt Standish's arms tighten.

The guy slipped out a hunting knife from behind him and aimed it at Marla. "You, on the other hand, need to leave town. You don't want us to come back here."

Festus barked incessantly until Marla placed her hand at the nape of the dog's neck. "What would happen if I stayed?"

The guy gestured the blade toward the beach house and then back at Marla. "We'd finish the job."

Marla raised her eyebrows. "Oh, you mean that? So, it was the two of you who sent the kid to check out my place. Since he took my folder, you know I'm DEA." Marla moved her right hand under the laptop. She wasn't ready to have Standish detain them just yet. "By the way, that folder was a copy—a copy of a copy, and when I find it in your dingy little hut, I'll arrest you for stealing federal property." She wanted to say it but didn't. *I want my cap back, too.*

The blond stepped toward them and leaned his thighs against the two-foot-tall fence. "How about I kick your ass right now?"

Festus barked more.

"Heel," Marla said.

His ears pulled back, and his tail hung low. The border collie growled with teeth showing. Marla had never seen him attack a human. Trained to round up animals, but never aggressive, until now.

"Maybe I should get rid of that four-legged yapper first?"

Marla pulled her Glock from under her laptop. "Gun trumps knife." She aimed at the four-wheeler's motor. "How about I kill your machine?"

"You're crazy!"

Marla hadn't moved from her seated position. "I'm sitting on my porch, and two strangers threaten me. I'm thinking you might try to do something dishonest."

Standish rose out of her chair and stood in a boxer's stance, muscles in her forearms and biceps taut.

The two looked confused as they eyed the police badge on her waistband. The brunette muttered, "No cops were supposed to be here."

"I'm Sergeant Standish, and I don't know you two boys. You're not local stock." She stepped over the fence, stood face-to-face with the blond, latched onto his wrist, and pulled the knife out of his hand. "What's your name?"

Blondie broke away from Standish's grip. "You think you can take both of us?"

The brown-haired bum spoke. "Wouldn't look good on the news, a cop and DEA beating on two happy-go-lucky guys on the beach."

"I thought I made it clear." Standish turned toward the kid. "You're not Padre residents. Get out of town." She grabbed a handful of hair and head-butted the guy's nose.

He staggered backward while his hand covered his bloodied face. "You don't know who you're dealing with."

"Such a tired cliché." Marla gestured at the bloody nose. "She's pretty good at hand-to-hand combat."

Blondie stared at his own knife pointing at him. "Watch your back."

"Time for you to walk back to your dingy little hole-in-the-wall," Standish said. "If you're in town tomorrow, I'll find you."

The brown-haired boy swept blood off his face before climbing onto his ATV. Blondie jumped on his.

Without hesitation, Standish stabbed the front tire of both four-wheelers. The tires hissed and flattened in the sand. "Time to walk home, boys." She waved the blade in the air. "Now git!" As the two rushed barefoot back toward town, Standish asked, "What was that about?"

"Not sure," Marla stuck her pistol back under her laptop, "but we have ruffled somebody's feathers. And thanks for not arresting them. Not yet."

"You know I wanted to beat their ass until they'd look worse than those dead sharks."

Moments later, Officer Roberts' police vehicle stopped a few feet from the front of the porch with emergency lights illuminating the scene. He jumped out and left the door open while staring at the two ATVs. "We got a call about someone selling drugs at this house. What's going on?"

Marla wiggled to the back of her chair. "Nothing much. Meeting new friends. Who called in about a drug deal?"

"Don't worry about it." Roberts noticed the ATVs flattened tires. "Destruction of property? Did you do this? I should call your boss and tell them to get you out of our town."

"I'm the one who stabbed the tires," Standish said. "In self-defense."

Roberts snapped back. "Self-defense against an ATV?"

"Against the drivers," Marla said.

"Who were they?" Roberts quipped back at her.

"Hey, Ricky?" Standish waved her hand at him. "Pay attention. I did it for evidence. Call forensics for fingerprints and DNA, then call the tow truck and take these two things to the impound. They are officially police evidence forever and a day. Investigate the tourist traps to find out who owns them...names and addresses. If rented, I want the credit card info, everything."

He trudged to his truck, mumbling loud enough for Standish to hear, "Not my place to do scut work."

Marla's phone rang. "Adams."

"Ms. Adams? This is Dr. Hernandez, the NOAA veterinary medical officer you have spoken to."

"Yes, sir. How can I help you?"

"I have something unusual to add to the necropsy."

"Okay. What?"

"We confirmed the sodium levels on both animals. Quite unusual."

"What exactly does that mean?"

"The second shark had excessive sodium in its blood, almost the same amount as the first one."

"The first shark? Thought it just died from age or something."

"I forgot you were not here during the necropsy of the first one. Yes, they both had excessive salt levels in their bloodstream."

"Help me out. What does that mean?"

"You and I would die fairly quickly if we were in the ocean. Do you know what from?"

"Sun exposure, dehydration?" Marla asked. "Always been told we can't drink ocean water."

"Right. Sharks have been in the ocean all their lives. Water doesn't flow in or out of the shark's skin. Well, not much. Humans, by comparison, will dehydrate quickly, shriveling us up like a raisin. The sodium content, table salt, would be very high in a human, but not a fish."

"Yes, understand. Fish adapted."

"Right, both sharks had similar elevated sodium levels in their blood. It had to be a sudden rise. A quick exposure, and the fish couldn't rid themselves of it. They suffered a medical collapse."

"Not following, sir."

"I think both died from a cardiac irregular rhythm secondary to hypernatremia."

She thought of Dr. Berghoff during an autopsy in San Antonio trying to explain in medical terminology how a victim died. "You doctors talk a strange language."

"Sorry. They had a heart attack from too much salt in their blood, just like you and I would."

"They live in the ocean. How can that be?"

Dr. Hernandez replied, "Good question."

Chapter 8

Roberts returned from his vehicle. "I called the station, and they'll pick up the ATVs within the hour. Should know something by tomorrow."

Marla put her phone back in her pocket. "The vet told me the sharks died of a heart attack from excessive sodium in the blood."

"I believe you could say almost everything dies from a heart attack," Standish said.

"Unless you die from a bullet or a blade," Roberts said.

Standish simulated a knife coming toward her. "I think I'd die of a heart attack if I saw a knife coming at me." She laughed at herself. "Which came first, the chicken or the egg? A knife causing a heart attack or..." she smiled, "a knife causing a heart attack."

Marla chuckled. "That's the same thing."

"Yeah. Couldn't think of anything else."

Marla poured dog food from the bag into the bowl. Festus scarfed it down in seconds. "All right. Have fun, but don't eat any fish. Understand?" The dog barked once. "Okay, go." Festus raced down the beach to the unknown.

"Do you suppose he understood you?" Standish asked.

"Oh, sure. Festus knows what I'm saying."

"Excuse me, but can we get back to police work?" Roberts asked. "The vet said both sharks had a lot of salt in their blood.

Where could fish get that much salt? What about the Laguna Madre water? It's saltier than the ocean."

Standish chuckled. "The lagoon? Most of it's not even three feet deep. I doubt a shark can swim there."

"What about along the coastline?" Marla asked. "Or the oil platforms? How about any of the ships dumping ballast in the Gulf?"

"Not sure if it makes any difference," Standish pointed north, "but up the beach, past the adventure park, is a small desalination plant."

"Forgot about that place," Roberts said. "It's just outside of the city limits, but that's pretty small. Shouldn't worry about it."

Marla asked, "How small?"

"Small enough not to require federal licensing," Standish said.

"Don't desalination plants take the salt *out* of the water?" Roberts asked. "That's supposed to be a good thing, right?"

"What do they do with the salt?" Marla laid the dog food bag on the floor.

Standish shrugged. "I guess they sell it to commercial companies."

"Who owns it?" Marla asked.

"Nico Palermo," Roberts said. "I know someone that works there, Jax Whitmore. We played football in high school together. He was a defensive lineman, and I was a cornerback."

"A lineman?" Marla asked. "Is he big?"

"Pretty much. I catch him from time to time in a store or fishing."

Marla asked Standish, "Was he one of the two on the ATVs?"

"No, it wasn't Jax. I've never seen those guys." Standish nodded at Roberts. "Doesn't he live on one of the spoil islands?"

"Yeah, but not sure which one."

Standish waved her hand in the air. "All right. Subject change. I have a friend at the Port of Mobile in Alabama who knows about saline contents worldwide. All I know is you can float in the Dead Sea because of so much salt in the water."

Marla laughed. "I don't believe any ships are coming out from there. You take that, and I'll investigate the drug problem."

"It's still my town, so how will you manage that in your white shirt and black pants?"

"I can look pretty grungy if need be. No one knows me here...especially the street dealers." She held her phone up. "I'll catch up to you at the station in a bit. Have some calls to make."

"Ricky, I'm staying here," Standish said. "You supervise the transfer of the ATVs to the station holding area."

"Supervise? Stupid word." He trudged through the sand back to his truck.

Marla stepped into the house with Standish as a police flatbed truck loaded with the ATVs followed Roberts back to town.

A few months ago, there was a television special about research centers tagging whales and sharks and tracking their activity online. Tiger sharks hunted near the coastline; many stayed in the Gulf, the Bahamas, and Caribbean waters. Marla had to ask Dr. Hernandez for another favor. She pushed redial on her phone.

"Doctor, this is Special Agent Adams again. You mentioned tags on the sharks. I'm guessing these are NOAA numbers used to track them."

Hernandez sat at his desk in Galveston. "Yes, of course. Tags were placed on these two sharks. One about nine months ago, and it has been at least a year for the other."

The heat and humidity were worse inside than out. Marla came back outside and sat on the sand. "Is there a website to see where these fish swam the last few days of their life?"

One of Hernandez's assistants placed a paper within the doctor's reach to sign. After signing it, the assistant took it back but stayed silent inside the veterinarian's office. "There is a public tracker available on our website, but not exactly to the point you want. I could send you to our restricted site, where you can obtain precise longitude and latitude for the last nine months."

"That would be great, but I just need the last two weeks."

Hernandez noticed the assistant still in the room and covered the phone with his hand. "Need something else?"

The assistant shook his head and left.

"Okay, sorry. I'll send the site and the password to you."

◆

A few hours later, clad in her T-shirt and shorts from home that weren't grungy enough for a homeless person, Marla entered a resale shop one block off Padre Boulevard. A man with a thick gray beard and a potbelly, wearing a decades-old army green shirt, pants, and a Vietnam veteran's cap, offered a two-fingered salute. "Come in. Look around. We have lots of stuff."

"Thanks," Marla said. "Where's your clearance rack?"

He laughed. "Everything in here is on clearance. Pick something out and pay what you can. Women's stuff mostly on that side and men's over there."

Several minutes later, Marla laid a washed-out pair of shorts, a faded Luckenbach, Texas T-shirt, a light jacket, red canvas shoes, a knitted gray beanie, and a long dark brown wig. "How much?"

He counted six items. "How about four a piece? That's, ah, let me write it down."

"Twenty-four bucks," Marla said.

He put his pencil down. "Sounds right."

Marla learned how to persuade someone to willingly give information they might never tell a stranger—give them more money than they asked for. She spread the garment out. "This T-shirt has got to be worth ten, and these shoes only have one hole in the toe." She took two twenties out of her pocket and placed it upon the counter. "Don't sell yourself too cheap."

He smiled and stuffed the clothes in a paper sack. "Thanks. I won't."

Marla looked around before leaning toward the man. "You know of any place I can...you know, get some stuff?"

The man's smile disappeared. "Not sure what you're saying."

"I need some coke. I haven't had any in a couple of days, and it's making me jittery."

"Look okay to me. Why are you asking me this? You a cop?"

Marla leaned back. "No. Hell, no." She laid another twenty on the counter. "Do cops give money away?"

"None that I know." He swept the bills off the counter. "You don't look like no addict."

"What does an addict look like? I know high-brows with lots of cash, college students, mamas, and people like you."

"Never said I did that stuff."

Marla held her hands up, chest high. "Sorry, just need a hit."

The man stared at her, then blinked. "I ain't saying you can get anything. I ain't helping you buy drugs, but...down at the old Pier 19 where the place burned down. Show up after midnight. I ain't saying nobody will be there, and I ain't selling you drugs."

Marla patted the countertop before grabbing the sack. "Yeah, thanks."

"And, if you see a bald guy, tell him Bucky said hello. Maybe he won't kill you, and I ain't telling you that's where to buy drugs, understand?"

◆

Marla checked her watch at 11:25 PM while sitting in the plastic chair on her patio. The waves rolled back and forth over the beach. Slow-moving red lights blinked high in the darkness while Festus ran the fifty-yard dash a few hundred times, stopping every once in a while to bark at a beached crab or jellyfish. Marla grasped the bag of dog food beside the chair. Festus' head turned around, and he shot for the patio at the sound of the dry kernels clanking on a plate. She scratched the dog behind his ears as he devoured the food. "Time to go."

Back inside, Marla donned her new outfit and pulled the sheets off the bed. She flattened them on the floor, added her torn pillows at the center, and knotted the sheet corners together. She picked it up and held it against her like a homeless person carrying all their belongings. "You stay close by, and I'll come back in about an hour." She slipped her extra handcuff key inside her shoe, then adjusted the beanie over the long-haired wig. "And don't let any more sharks get on the beach."

Festus raised his head and barked once before returning to eat.

Chapter 9

On a barren half-acre spoil island, Jax sat cross-legged on the roof of a battered single-wide trailer, its tin patched and weighted down with old tires. He took one last drag of his cigarette before flicking the butt over the edge, then grabbed the ten-pound hand weight beside him and started bicep curls. His phone lay next to him, and with his free hand, he touched a favorite. It rang.

Leo sat in a high-back leather chair and sipped his newest Garrison Brothers Small Batch Bourbon purchase. He knew Jax would call. Instead of the standard hello, Leo blurted out, "This DEA agent is too smart."

Jax arched his back, ready to hang up with any more crap from Leo. "What do you mean?"

Leo placed the glass on the table. "She called the vet and asked about the tags on the fish."

"Did she say that in her place?"

"Yeah, the kid who ransacked her rental, he did a good job taking the DEA file and placing a bug near the table." The file and Marla's cap sat on the small table next to Leo's chair. "By the way, thought you sent someone to run her off."

Jax lit another cigarette. "They will."

"Get her away from here before she finds anything else." Leo heard a small engine in the background. "Are you at your rathole?"

Jax pitched a Lone Star beer bottle cap in the air like a mini-Frisbee as he watched a small fishing boat stop at his wooden pier. "Yeah. Viggo's here."

"Good. Ask him about my four-wheelers—"

"Got to go." Jax laid the phone beside his knee and yelled, "Grab a beer out of the cooler and climb on up."

Viggo climbed the wooden ladder and sat next to Jax. "What's up?" He took a swig of his beer.

With one hand, Jax took another swig and continued his bicep curls with the other.

Viggo smirked as he bent his elbow with an imaginary hand weight. "How many ya dun?"

"Dunno, maybe five hundred. Gotta stay fit."

"Five hundred, my ass. A workout with the beer and cigs? Probably closer to five."

Jax laid the weight beside him and took another swig. "You like it in Harlingen?"

"Didn't choose to be there. Just kinda happened. No decent money there. Can't make enough for my ol' lady and me ta get out. Don't you wanna leave this dump? I wanna find a nice house near Houston, have a decent job, and fuck my ol' lady twice a week, but that ain't happening anytime soon, is it?"

Jax scoffed. "I'd have ta cut out five days a week to do that." He downed his beer and pitched the bottle over the side. "That DEA agent is still here. Why?"

"Yeah. She's tough. She had a cop at her place, and they messed up our ATVs."

Jax lit a cigarette. "Tell me what happened."

"John and I stopped at her place, just like you told us to, but she was with another woman, lookin' sort of mean and muscular. I didn't know who she was until she said she was a cop." Viggo took another drink of his beer. "Anyway, the cop stabbed our front tires, so we left the vehicles and walked away."

"The cop recognized you?"

"No. The bitch said we weren't local and wanted our names."

"You tell her?"

"Hell, no. I ain't that stupid." Viggo finished his beer and tossed it close to where Jax threw his. "So, you called me." Taking a cigarette from Jax's pack sitting between them, he lit it and blew smoke above his head. "What's up?"

"When you had that kid break into her place, did he have time to do everything?" Jax asked.

"Yeah, yeah. He took the DEA papers and placed two bugs in the place, one in the kitchen and one under the table." Viggo stood. "You want another beer?"

"Yeah."

Viggo climbed down the ladder and grabbed two more Lone Stars from the cooler.

Jax yelled out from the trailer roof. "Have another job for you."

Viggo climbed back up while holding both bottles between his fingers. He twisted the caps off and handed a bottle to Jax before sitting down. "Go on. Tell me."

"The bug in the room picks up her voice when on the phone, but can't hear the other person on the line. Now that she has seen you, it'll be trickier, but tomorrow, I want you to get near her phone and hack it."

"How am I going to be close enough for that? She knows what I look like."

"Shave your head. She remembers a guy with a lot of blond hair."

Viggo chugged most of his beer and wiped the back of his hand over his lips. "I am not shaving my head. My hair stays. I got that fake beard from last year's Halloween party somewhere in my closet. That and sunglasses and a cap, but no haircut. Give me two hundred, and I'll do it."

"Fine. Your funeral. She eats all her meals at restaurants. Find her tomorrow morning and do it there."

Chapter 10

At dusk, Marla drove to the south end of town, entered the KOA campgrounds, and parked a few hundred feet from Pier 19 before reaching inside her glove box for a baggie full of marijuana. It had been measured and checked out from the DEA supply room. She held her pistol and holster, deciding whether or not to carry it. If the dealer frisked her, it would all be over before anything started. She untied the bedsheets and placed the pistol on top of the pillows before retying it again. It wouldn't be fast, but she'd be glad to have it if needed. After turning on the phone recorder and feeling the agency's necklace once more, her fingers adjusted the beanie a little lower on the wig before leaving the truck.

About twenty feet from the burned rubble, two men stepped out, one bald. Marla stopped while embracing the bedding.

"Get out of here!" the bald guy yelled.

"I'm just looking for a place to sleep." Marla pulled the beanie down to her eyebrows, keeping her face covered as best as possible. "Stay somewhere for the night."

"Can't stay here. This is my place." His switchblade snapped open. "Go back to where you came from."

Marla turned to look behind her before looking back at the bald guy again. "I've been walking all day. Can I sit for a little while?"

He rushed toward her. "I'm gonna cut you, and you're gonna die."

She held the bedding in her grasp, making sure the microphone in the necklace remained uncovered. "Bucky told me I could come here and crash."

The bald guy stopped. "You know Bucky?"

"Yeah. Okay, if I smoke a joint before I go back?"

He nodded toward her. "What ya got?"

She dropped the bedding before patting her pocket. "Got some good stuff. You got any coke? Or anything else?"

He took a step toward Marla and said, "You think I sell? You think I'm dealing?"

Marla removed the baggie from her pocket. "I want something stronger. I'll trade you."

"That ain't enough for a trade. You got money?"

"All I got is the baggie and my stuff, but I can get money tomorrow."

The second guy stepped in front of Marla and snatched the baggie. He opened it and then sniffed the inside. He nodded. "It's good." He smelled again. "Fresh. Let her have a small one."

The bald guy removed a clear packet from a pocket with white material inside. The second guy took it and handed it to Marla. "Bring money tomorrow. Now, get your ass out of here."

◆

At 6:40 AM, sunlight crept up the wall inside the beach house. Marla woke sprawled behind the box springs with the mattress still leaning against the window of the house. The A/C motor continued to roar, fighting the humidity and heat. Festus lay on the box springs and raised his head toward her. Marla stood and patted him on the leg. "I do believe we have this backward. I am supposed to be in the bed and you on the floor."

Festus lay on his side, ready for a rub behind his ear.

Marla changed from wearing her resale T-shirt and shorts to her long-sleeved shirt and pants before clipping her holster to her belt. After slipping on the windbreaker, she poured the last of the dog food on his plate, and Festus gobbled it down. "Come on. We need to drop this stuff off."

At the Brownsville DEA office, Marla prepared two agent reports, one for the contraband she traded with Baldy and the second for money, four hundred dollars. Hopefully, the snag from last night or tonight might have fenethylline. Could she be lucky enough for the next packet from Baldy or anybody else she finds to have what she was after? Probably not.

As she turned onto Padre Boulevard from the Queen Isabella Bridge, half a mile away stood the burned rubble of Pier 19. She would never be a good undercover agent. As soon as she bought or traded something for drugs, she wanted to jump on the dealer, handcuff him, send him to jail, and let the lawyers fight it out. She had to fight every urge not to do that to Baldy.

Marla picked up Festus before returning to the Ocean View restaurant. After zipping the windbreaker halfway to conceal her gun, she sat at a table for two and drank her coffee. Festus perched on the chair opposite her. She was easy to pick out. Every other person wore sunburns, flip-flops, T-shirts, and shorts. A man wearing a ball cap, sunglasses, and a six-inch long black beard stopped near her. He stared out at the water while holding his phone.

"The curtains aren't the same color as the carpet," Marla said.

"What?"

"Blond hair and black beard. Wherever you bought that fake beard, you should return it and get your money back. You can leave on your own or I can help you out the front door."

Viggo turned around and faced Marla. "I'm free to stand where I want." He slid the chair out across from her and sat down. "Or sit where I like."

Marla sipped her coffee. "You like playing with fire?"

He faked a glance left and right. "No fire. All I see is sand and water."

Marla dabbed her lips with the napkin. "What do you want?"

The waitress placed a plate with two warm hamburger patties and a second with an omelet and bacon on the table before turning to Viggo. "Do you want something to drink?"

"No. I'm leaving in a minute."

Marla laid the plate with the meat on the floor and Festus chowed down. She flipped her napkin up and dropped it upon her lap. "Tell you what, stay, and let's talk. I'm buying." She waved a finger at Festus, and he hopped from the chair and sat next to her.

The waitress's eyebrows lifted. "Coffee? OJ?"

"You got Lone Star?"

The waitress glanced at her watch. It was after seven in the morning. "Have ta eat something with a beer this early."

He pointed at Marla's plate. "Okay, that."

After they were alone, Marla said, "This is the second time you've seen me."

Viggo turned his head away. "Me? No."

"Want your knife back?"

"I ain't got no knife."

"That's true. The police have it." She tugged the tip of the beard. "Take that stupid thing off and tell me why you are here."

Viggo removed his cap, put it on the table upside down, and dropped the sunglasses inside it. He winced while peeling the beard off before dropping it over the glasses. "I think you're cute."

"And I think you're lying." She grabbed the dinner knife, stuck it inside the cap, and pulled it toward her. "What's your name?"

"Not tellin'."

"Okay." Marla laid her napkin over the cap and contents. "What do you want?"

It had been long enough for Viggo's phone to hack into Marla's.

The waitress set the beer on the table. "Your food will be out in a minute."

"Tell me your name and what you want from me," Marla said.

Viggo downed the beer all at once before placing the bottle back down. "Nothing." He let out a long burp.

"I'm sure your mother's proud."

"Like I said. It's a free country. I can stand anywhere I want." He rose to his feet, eased past the waitress with his order in her hand, and left.

"Want me to box this up for you, sweetie?"

The waitress reached for the empty beer bottle, but Marla stopped her. "If you don't mind, I'll take that, too." When she finished her omelet, Marla wrapped the bottle in the napkin and made a call from her phone.

"Standish here."

"We got a lucky break from the two men that stopped outside my beach house yesterday. I have fingerprints on a beer bottle from the blond. He also left his cap, sunglasses, and fake beard with me. Lots of DNA."

"That's pretty generous of him. Are you bringing it over now?"

"Later. Have a few things to do."

Leo listened to the phone conversation, then called Jax and told him the DEA agent pinned Viggo. Jax had to decide what to do with his drinking buddy.

After leaving the restaurant, Marla decided she needed different old clothes for tonight—different from the ones Baldy saw last night. It wouldn't be wise to stop at the same store again; luckily, there was a Goodwill nearby. Walking while wearing her DEA outfit wasn't a smart idea, and the beach house was too far to return just to change her garb. Tourists changed all the time in public, so she opened her truck's front and back doors, stood between them, removed her shirt and pants, and replaced them with last night's clothes.

After arriving at the Goodwill store, she gestured toward Festus before pressing her finger to her lips. "On the floorboard...and be quiet." She moved the gun and holster to the small of her back before exiting the truck.

A few minutes later, Marla came outside holding a plastic sack with her earlier clothes while wearing a large South Padre sweatshirt and flowered shorts. Festus jumped up from the floorboard into the passenger seat when the door opened, and she pitched the sack where the dog had patiently waited. "No problems?" She placed the long wig and beanie from yesterday on her head. "What do you think? Good enough?" Festus barked once. After opening the console and slipping several twenties from the envelope holding the DEA cash, she said, "Time we walk the streets." She pulled the large sweatshirt down over her holster and stuck different numbers of bills in different pockets. Each drug deal cost different, and dealers didn't give change.

Festus walked next to Marla on the main streets. This was where tourists hung out, not drug dealers. A green, yellow, and black painted building with large letters printed across the front read, CBD HERE. A large Jamaican flag flew above the structure on a tall flagpole. While Marla crossed the intersection, a thirty-year-old car exited from an alley behind the store. Marla waited a moment for any others before turning into the back-street.

"This is a possibility." She peeked around a well-worn wooden fence to see a thin, black male wearing a reggae rasta style knit hat over dreadlocks, a sleeveless ribbed T-shirt, and baggy shorts with the crotch hanging halfway down his thighs. She glanced at Festus. "Looks promising." After messing the wig hair up a bit, she felt the holster against the small of her back and turned on the recorder in her phone before traipsing down the alley. "I am so glad I finally found you."

The guy turned toward her and grimaced at her smile. "What you want, bitch?" he asked with a strong Jamaican accent.

"What? You don't remember me from last week?"

"Don't remember last week." Three chickens pranced out from behind the guy's back fence gate to the alley. He ignored their clucking.

"You know me. I was with Bucky and the other guy."

"How you know Bucky?"

"I help him at the store."

"So? Got nuthin' for you. Get lost."

"You got to remember us at your party. What color was the house, gray or something?" She needed more. There was always a jacked-up guy hanging with a dealer, so she used that thought. "You and that big guy were there, the buffed-up one."

"Jaymyr?"

"Right." Marla stepped closer. "Jaymyr works out all the time. He pumps iron...and that girl. What's her name?"

"He left that bitch. Got him a new one."

"Yeah, well, I could tell she was seein' someone else. She got it coming, right?"

He smiled and grabbed his crotch once. "Damn right, she did."

Marla tilted her head a bit. "Can ya hit me again?"

"No."

"Come on, man. Call up Bucky and Jaymyr. They know me. I just want what you had at the party."

When he stuck his right hand in his pocket, Marla tightened. Was he reaching for drugs or a weapon? She looked at Festus and aimed a finger toward the chickens. When Festus charged the animals, the guy took his eyes off Marla. Festus rounded them up against the fence. That was when she lifted the back of the sweatshirt, clasped the gun handle, and eased it slightly out of the holster.

When he turned his attention back to Marla, she concentrated on his hand, waiting for a glint of chrome or metal. Her finger eased on the trigger. Between two fingers, he removed a small, self-sealed packet the same size as Baldy's packets: "Fif-teh," he said.

Marla eased the gun back into the holster and pulled the sweatshirt back down. She wondered why all people who sold illegal drugs used the same small, clear, self-sealing packets. It seemed as though the one-by-two-inch packet was the standard for drugs. Who came up with that? Did the company who made them expect the packets to only be utilized for holding tiny electronic parts, screws, or extra buttons attached to a new shirt, not realizing drug dealers used millions?

"You deaf? I said fif-teh."

Marla caught herself daydreaming in the middle of a drug buy. Stupid. She thought for a second about asking him where he bought the packets, but decided to screw with his head instead. "Fifty? It was forty last week."

"Fawty-five."

"Forty. I know a girl you might like."

"Wah kinda gyal dat?"

She withdrew two twenties from her left front pocket and folded them between her fingers. "Forty is all I got. I'll send the girl."

Chapter 11

After dropping the drug purchase into an evidence bag and sealing it, Marla entered the shooting range wearing her beach attire, without the beanie or wig. The parking lot was empty. After showing her badge and purchasing a couple of boxes of ammo, she headed for her assigned stall. Midmorning, tourists and locals were absent, but within half an hour, several of the stalls filled with police officers.

After emptying the first box, shooting between ten and twenty-five feet, she had to change paper targets. Roberts stopped at the stall next to her as she changed the target. He ignored her actions.

"Morning," Marla said.

He leaned over to see who it was. "Why aren't you out hunting down that drug?"

"I came to get a little practice."

"Hmm." As soon as his target slid out to ten feet, Roberts drew and fired until the magazine emptied. A nice cluster of bullet holes filled the chest. He opened his box of ammo and reloaded his magazine. "You probably need it. DEA agents don't shoot much in their raids, do they?"

Marla wasn't sure if he was trying to impress her, but just in case, she sent the target out beside him and emptied her magazine in the chest with a much tighter cluster. Before losing part of her finger in a gun battle, the cluster would have been even tighter. "Practice, practice, practice."

He snapped the magazine back into the pistol, drew, using both hands, and fired twice before holstering the weapon. He did it again. Both times, the first shot was wide.

Marla laid her pistol on the shelf and leaned past the divider between their stalls. "Bring your fingers a little higher around the handle."

"I'm fine. I don't need your help."

"Sure, but I've had a lot more practice *and* I have won a few competitions."

He fired two more rounds at the target, hitting almost the same spots as before. "What do you mean, competitions?"

"Fast draw, shotgun, rifle."

"Have you won a fast draw competition?"

"A few. May I show you a better hand placement? And your arm positioning needs tweaking. Not much, just a little."

"Show me your fast draw."

"Well, not the same with a holster on a belt and a 9mm semi-automatic as my competition holster and revolver."

"So, you can't show me."

Marla holstered her pistol and drew as fast as she could from the holster attached to the belt. She drew three times, leaving three holes millimeters apart.

"You don't seem that fast."

Marla never backed down from a challenge. She glanced around, making sure Standish wasn't nearby, then leaned in toward Ricky. "We're not supposed to fast draw, but we could sneak in a little. Just you and me."

He raised a brow. "How?"

"Simple. Someone calls it, and we draw."

"I'm not dragging someone over here to referee."

Marla smirked. "I'll let you do the call-out. I trust you won't cheat."

Four rounds in, he softened into curiosity as Marla's speed and accuracy surpassed his. Within ten minutes of coaching, his shots landed cleaner, quicker. His confidence grew with each pull of the trigger.

She gathered her things and left, hoping for a better relationship.

◆

After leaving the range, Roberts headed for the grocery store. Inside, he turned the corner in the store with a warm breakfast burrito in one hand and a steaming coffee in the other. He grazed someone heading the opposite way.

"Watch it, asshole," a familiar voice said.

Roberts froze for a second, his coffee tilting precariously before he caught sight of Jax Whitmore. Jax's grin widened as he steadied the six-pack of beer in his hand.

"Jax," Roberts said, his voice neutral. "Didn't think I'd run into you here this early in the morning...anytime, any morning."

"Small town here, little Ricky-Dickey," Jax replied. "Bound to happen." He nodded at the burrito in Roberts' hand. "Breakfast of champions?"

"Something like that," Roberts said, stepping aside. "You?"

"Just grabbing supplies," Jax said, lifting the six-pack of Lone Star. "Nico's got me working extra. Figured I'd treat myself later."

Roberts' expression didn't change, but he felt a subtle weight settle between them. "Still working for Nico, huh?"

Jax's tone was casual. "Not all of us get a steady government paycheck."

"Anybody else keeping you busy?"

Jax leaned his shoulder against the shelf. "You talking about Leo? He's got his hands in a lot of things. You know how it is. Keeps people in line, keeps the money flowing."

"Yeah, I know how it is."

For a moment, neither spoke. The hum of the store's overhead lights seemed louder in the silence.

"Leo ever talk about me?" Roberts tilted his head a tad.

Jax chuckled. "Not in a bad way, if that's what you're worried about."

"Funny. Didn't know Leo handed out compliments."

Jax's grin turned sharper. "If that's what you want to call it. Buy my beer, and I'll put in a good word for you."

"I'm a cop. I'm not buying beer this early in the morning."

"Fine, Mister Big Time Police Officer Ricky Roberts. I'll just tell Leo all about today."

Roberts set his coffee on the floor, dug into his pocket, and pulled out a ten-dollar bill. "Here. Go buy your beer."

Jax shook his head. "Nah. You buy it, or I leave empty-handed."

Without looking at the cashier, Roberts placed the six-pack on the counter and slid the money next to it.

"Are you okay?" the middle-aged woman asked. "Never seen you buy beer at such an early hour."

"Yeah. Just uh...I'm buying it for my friend over there." He held his coffee up for the woman to see. "This is mine." He looked around for Jax. "The guy's somewhere over there."

"Sure. Okay."

When Roberts exited the store, Jax leaned against the outside wall before standing straight. He grasped the sack with the beer. "You know, if you ever get tired of that badge, Leo's always looking for guys who are familiar with how to keep things quiet around town. I'll tell him you bought him a beer."

"Leo doesn't drink that horse piss."

"Jax snarled. "Don't get on my bad side."

Fingers tightened around his coffee cup. "I'll keep that in mind, *Jax*."

He gave a low laugh and clapped Ricky on the shoulder twice. "You do that."

Jax's words lingered like smoke pervading his space, impossible to ignore. The burrito and coffee had gone cold, so Roberts tossed both in the trash.

Chapter 12

After Marla checked on Festus and left him at the beach house, she stopped at the police station. Opening the glass front door, the cool, dry air hit her face. The officer behind the counter did a double take at Marla, wearing a sweatshirt and shorts and holding two paper sacks. He buzzed the latch on the wooden door, and she entered. Standish came out of her office with a smile. "I see you've gotten into the jive of the town. Is that the bottle with the fingerprint? Let's check it out."

The paper takeout sacks had a restaurant logo on the sides. Marla lifted one in the air. "Should be easy. There are nice clean prints on the base of the bottle."

Ricky rose from his workspace with a scowl on his face. "Don't give that to anyone but me." He snapped the sack out of her hand. "I am the forensics officer in charge. This goes to me." He placed it on his desk. "And don't leave until I say you can."

"Excuse me?" Marla wondered what happened to the potential good relationship after the shooting range.

He pulled out forms from his desk drawer and filled in the information. "Evidence is worthless unless there is an accurate chain of custody."

"This is not evidence," Marla said. "No crime yet. I'm asking whose fingerprints these belong to."

He stopped writing. "Is this for personal information? We don't do that. There are several private companies in Brownsville and Harlingen for that." He lifted the sack by the handles and held it facing her. "Call them."

Marla relaxed her shoulders and placed the other sack on his desk. "How about breakfast? The restaurant gave me an extra omelet and bacon. Mine was good."

He opened the sack and looked inside, revealing a pair of sunglasses and a fake beard in an upside-down cap sitting on top of a cardboard box and two containers of hot sauce. "What is this?"

Marla looked in. "Oh, sorry." She grabbed the cap and put it on the desk. "There's the guy's DNA in this stuff. Listen, Ricky. May I still call you Ricky?"

He opened the box and smelled the bacon before answering. "Sure."

"Might need to warm that in the microwave. Listen, I think we got off on the wrong foot. Let's start over. This is not for personal use. This is from one of the two guys on the ATVs who came to my beach house and tried to harass your sergeant and me."

With a slight sideways glance toward Standish, he waited for confirmation of his unspoken question. When Standish raised her eyebrows, he looked at Marla again. "Go on."

"I have a sack with one of the men's fingerprints on a bottle and want you to run it through the system...please. If nothing comes up, fine. It goes in the trash. If positive, you have a cap and a fake beard to analyze DNA samples."

Ricky touched the omelet with his finger. She was right. The food was cold. "It might take most of the day to obtain the results."

Marla pulled a DEA business card from her shorts pocket and handed it to him. "Call me when you do."

He flipped the card toward the end of his desk. "I'll give the info to the Sarge."

"Whatever you want to do." Marla turned toward Standish. "Let's go check on the desal plant."

Standish patted Ricky on the back. "Officer Roberts? I'll be out for a while. Contact me if you need anything. And enjoy the free omelet."

As they headed for the outside, Standish said, "I did a little research on the place. In 1984, a state representative for this area somehow passed a bill to allow the construction of the first seawater desalination plant and a gulf side pier in Padre. Protected-area development protests failed to stop the governor's signature."

"Any problems since?"

"No, none," Standish said. "Life in the sanctuary is good."

"Is the pier well kept? Do you know if it is still used?"

"I've heard forty-foot boats dock there."

"Like charter fishing trips?"

"Not sure about that part. I could check if it's available or if everything is private."

Marla headed for her Dodge Ram. "Let's take mine. No police markings on it."

Standish climbed into the passenger seat. "Nice truck. Big. Is this new?"

"After my husband died, I traded in both our pickups for a new one."

Standish rubbed her hand over an image of a heart painted on the dashboard. "Not a standard accessory?"

"No. That's from a brand he made me for my wedding day. After I bought the truck, I had that put on."

"Why this? The symbol of the female in the center."

"I added that. All my ranch hands are female."

The diesel engine cranked on, and Marla backed out of the parking spot.

"Head up Padre Boulevard about ten miles, and when you get to the end of the road, keep going."

"End of the road?" Marla asked.

"Asphalt stops and turns to sand."

"How far past?"

"Two or three miles on the sandy beach."

"No paved road to the plant? How do the employees get there?"

"Guessing, Four-wheelers, mostly," Standish said.

"Like the two that came to the house?"

"Like the two," she chuckled at Marla, "I stabbed."

"Anybody come to claim the ATVs at the impound?"

"No. That would be an admittance of guilt. We'll sell them next year at our annual auction."

"Got to stop by the beach house and pick up my dog."

Fifteen minutes later, Festus occupied the back seat staring out the side window as Marla passed the END OF THE ROAD sign and dropped onto the beach. She slowed and put the truck into four-wheel low. "You weren't kidding about the pavement. Nothing but scrub on the left and ocean on the right." They drove past sand dunes before stopping several hundred yards from a twenty-thousand-square-foot gray building. "Looks like a military fortress with a twelve-foot-tall chain link fence surrounding it." Marla used her binoculars. "Why are there men standing inside with assault rifles?"

"It's Texas. That's what they can do, so they do."

Marla noticed the long pier on the Gulf side. "It is strange to see that."

"You can thank the Texas government for it."

Marla parked the pickup behind a sand dune and cut the engine. "I've got something in the back that might help us see what's going on around the building. Festus, stay." She stepped out, raised the bed cover, and pulled out a large rectangular box.

"You carry a drone with you?" Standish asked.

"Seems like everyone has one nowadays, so I bought it." When Marla pushed the power button, the four blades spun, rising high in the air. "Let's see what they have."

They sat on the tailgate and watched her phone as Marla maneuvered the drone above the plant. Behind the larger structure were long, rectangular drying bins on the ground. All the people walking around the area wore green T-shirts, camo pants, military boots...and carried rifles.

"Interesting. All the desal plant employees carry weapons," Standish said.

"And why is everyone wearing those blue disposable masks? The Covid pandemic ended a long time ago." Marla zoomed in on the phone screen. "Is that sea salt in those bins?"

"Not sure. This is the first time I have seen the back of the plant."

"Uh, oh. Someone came out of the building and looked up. I think he sees it."

"That's Jax Whitmore," Standish said. "At least I think it is, with the mask covering half his face."

"They're pointing their guns at the drone. Time to leave." Marla backed it away. "I'm turning it toward the lagoon, drop low, then circle back."

Jax watched it dart away. "Go get that thing!" He unlocked the back gate and slapped men on their shoulders. "Go, go, go. Bring that back to me."

They charged out toward the lagoon, but the drone had already swooped down and circled to the Gulf side. It landed beside Marla, and she laid it on the bed. "Let's get out of here."

She glanced in her rearview mirror at the men running through the grassy dunes and pointing at her truck. "They've seen us. My guess is they think we know something, just not sure how much."

"Can that thing see at night?" Standish asked.

"Surprising you ask that. I picked the one that does."

"Good. There's a paved road about a mile ahead. When we get on it, turn and drive until you reach Wharf Street."

"What's there?"

"My boat."

Ten minutes later, Standish pointed to an intersection with a large resort on the Gulf side and residential housing on the lagoon side. "Turn here. Go down to the end, and it will curve around to a small row of boats."

Marla gazed at the large, two-story homes. "These look like they are four thousand square feet or more. You live here?"

"I wish. The city council would have to quadruple my salary for anything out here. I have a friend. I saved his little boy's life years ago, and now he lets me lease a spot for mostly nothing. Exactly what I can afford."

"And what is the plan with your boat?"

"Are you sure the drone is set up for night vision?"

"The box says it does."

"Okay, we come back after dusk and head for the plant. They won't expect us at night from the lagoon side. From there, you launch your drone from the boat and see what happens."

Marla nodded. "You know how to get there and back in the dark?"

"Pretty sure. I've fished many times in this area, just never behind that building."

Marla brought the truck to a stop near the row. "Which boat?"

"Third from the end—the aluminum flat bottom. The cheapest one here."

Chapter 13

Marla dropped Standish at the station, then turned off Padre Boulevard and drove to the beach house. After stopping, she opened her truck door, and Festus shot out as if he had been trapped for hours. He ran in a wide circle at full speed on the shore. Marla tried to ignore the decaying carcasses, but the odor and the twenty-something squawking seagulls picking at them made it impossible. Tire tracks in the sand cut across the front of the house, with footprint divots near the porch. She unlocked the door and heard the A/C roar as it circulated semi-cool air. There was nothing out of place. Marla whistled, and the dog charged through the entryway and plopped on the box springs. "Oh, no you don't. Don't get used to life on a bed, because you are outside when we return home, mister." After snapping her fingers and pointing to the floor, he hopped off.

After locking the front door, she took a seat at the small table with the packet of drugs bought behind the CBD store in an evidence bag. She would take that and tonight's buy from Pier 19 to the Brownsville DEA office tomorrow morning. After shoving the single wooden chair under the door handle, she told Festus, "I am taking a well-deserved shower, and you will stand guard. Bark if anyone comes near. Got it?" He sat and stared at the door. "Good." Marla picked up a fresh set of clothes from her luggage and the pistol before partially closing the bathroom door behind her.

Marla exited the bathroom a moment later, never turning on the shower, and wearing the Goodwill-purchased sweatshirt and shorts. "You see, Festus. I suppose homeless people don't bathe too often. At least, not daily.

Wouldn't be good to buy drugs while smelling like flowers and whatever else is in the soap." She dropped her other clothes in her open suitcase. "It's time to head to the station and meet up with Standish again." That's when her phone rang.

While listening to Marla's phone call, Leo sat at his desk and poured himself more whiskey.

"We got trouble, Marla," Standish said. "A couple of dozen more fish are dead on the beach. Not sharks, but still dead fish."

"Where?"

"Not a good place. Right in the middle of where the tourists play."

Marla remembered what the veterinarian said. One shark died days before it beached, dropping to the ocean floor before rising and floating to the surface. "Do they look like they've been dead several days?"

"No, not like the sharks. These are five and ten pounders. Once the fish die, the current pushes them, and they either wash ashore or in a hungry fish's mouth. So, dead a day or so."

"Where are they now?"

"Since the sharks beached, NOAA is taking everything that dies. My guess is all the fish are stuck in an ice chest and on their way to the Galveston office. By the way, I have new info."

"Me too. I'll meet you at the station."

After passing the bustling Goodwill store with a packed parking lot, Marla turned onto a side street and drove past the empty Vietnam vet resale shop where she bought her first clothes. No vehicles meant no one was inside, which meant no sales and no income. She wondered what or who paid Bucky's living expenses. No doubt, Baldy inhabiting a burned-down building at the end of a pier made more than him.

When Marla turned into the station lot, several police vehicles were parked, all sparkling clean, except one with sand spray around the wheel wells. She exited her truck, knelt beside the back tire of the dirty vehicle, and brushed the tread and the sidewall. The moist sand clung to her fingertips. Whoever had been driving traveled close to the water's edge. Maybe her place. Festus stuck his head between Marla's arms, like saying, "Hey, look at me." She smiled and rubbed his face and ears. "Okay, let's go inside."

Before opening the doorway, Marla noticed a single footprint with sand on the doormat. She opened the door open and entered the vacant lobby, the officer behind the desk not startled by her beach attire anymore. He nodded once before buzzing the wooden door. The scene mirrored her last visit with Standish standing near her office, gesturing for her to come over. As Marla approached, her eyes darted at the shoes of everyone nearby—no sand.

A set of eyes staring caught her attention. "Ricky," she called out, but he didn't reply. Her gaze shifted to his feet under the desk, but they were too far in for her to see. In his wastebasket sat the empty omelet box from earlier.

The two entered Standish's office, and Marla shut the door behind her. After they sat across from each other at the desk, Marla asked, "What else about the fish?"

"A hotel manager called here with a complaint about several fish being beached." Standish chuckled. "Somehow, he thinks the police department is expected to keep the beaches clear for them. He didn't like my suggestion of picking them up and taking them to their kitchen. It could remain a secret with a little extra garlic and lemon."

"Glad he didn't. Did you go down to the beach?" Marla asked.

"No. I sent Ricky down there."

"By himself?"

"That a problem?"

Marla shook her head. *That explains the sand on the vehicle outside, but not at my place.* "No. Go on."

Standish opened a drawer and placed two Manila folders on the desktop. She opened the first and handed a sheet of paper to Marla. "Ricky completed his investigation of the ATVs this morning. If you drag him away from his self-pity, he can be a good cop. They were stolen in Brownsville, thirty miles from here."

"When?"

Standish turned another paper around and handed it to Marla. "Yesterday morning, before the beach bums approached us at your rental, the owner contacted the police and filled out all the forms with them and the insurance company. Everything seems on the up-and-up." She opened the second folder. "I started checking the charter boats in the region."

"How many are there?"

"Couple of dozen. All of them small time, family-owned, stuff like that." Standish handed several pages to Marla. "Some have been here for decades."

Marla flipped through the pages, which featured photos of happy captains or boaters holding fish beside them. "Do you know many of the owners?"

"I am familiar with the majority. I'll make the rounds today and tomorrow and ask about the ATVs."

"Like what?" Marla closed the folder.

"Not sure yet. You know, ask a question and let them tell you more than you want." Standish opened her drawer and slid the folders inside before closing it again. "What about you?"

"Do you know the veteran running the resale shop?" Marla asked.

"Sure. He's been there for several years."

"I bought a few clothes to go undercover. When checking out, I asked where I could get drugs."

"Just like that? A customer asking for drugs?"

"Well, if you know how to ask, I guess so. Anyway, he sent me to the pier where the building had burned down."

"Pier 19? The city council had been trying to get the owners to clean up the mess, but no luck so far."

"I bought an eight-ball of white powder last night. If it's positive, it might be time to bring him in for questioning. All that could lead to someone, something bigger. Do you know who owns the CBD shop with the Jamaican flag waving above the store?"

"Yeah. I've been ordered to leave them alone."

"Why? I bought a packet of white powder from a skinny guy with a Jamaican accent. If it's drugs, he's going down."

"You need to back away for a while. A city councilman owns the shop. He's very popular in town, throws big parties, and brings in big name Jamaican bands. That's a lot of money brought into this town."

"The chief told you to back away? Is he in on it?"

"No. Not to my knowledge. Let's say it is someone influential. I like my job and ain't got no interest in moving away."

Marla straightened in the chair and wondered if Standish was a dirty cop. "Who?"

"Let's just not go any further for now. White powder is probably coke or meth and not what you are here for, right? You're after fenethylline."

A knock on the door stopped the conversation. Ricky stuck his head inside the office. "The sheriff's department called about a man and a woman dead in a ten-foot flat-bottom boat beached near the Laguna Atascosa National Wildlife Refuge." He threw an impertinent glance toward Marla. "That's the west bank of the lagoon."

"That's not part of South Padre," Standish said. "It's in or near the refuge."

Ricky shifted his attention back to Standish. "Near. Not federal jurisdiction. The deputy knows we have had several ODs and thinks this may be connected. Besides, you know the area better than anyone." He turned to walk away, then spun back. "Almost forgot. The boat is unregistered."

Standish pushed back from her desk and stood. "The boating industry just became more interesting. Let's go see what happened."

✦

Marla sat in the passenger seat of Standish's Police Broncho. After crossing the water on the Queen Isabella Causeway, they continued a short distance on Highway 100 before turning and heading north along the lagoon's western shore. "You said you've spent most of your life here, right?" Marla asked.

"Yep. Since I was nine. The southern part of the lagoon is fifty miles long, and from the time I was thirteen through graduating high school, a bunch of buddies and I walked all the way around it a dozen times. We'd backpack after classes on Friday and get back home Sunday for dinner."

"When was the last time you did that?"

"A few years ago, after a high school reunion, we got a wild hair and did it again." Standish passed several unpaved roads as she watched the GPS map on her phone. "Okay, here we are." She turned off the asphalt road to a dirt road one and a half cars wide. "Just a little more." When the bushes and trees ended alongside the trail, the land was flat, and a line of water appeared. "We won't be able to drive up to the waterline, too boggy. We'll stop where the other vehicles are and walk the rest of the way."

Two deputy vehicles had parked with their emergency lights still flashing. The back ends of a pair of funeral homes' hearses were open, and the gurneys were missing. Standish positioned her vehicle next to them. "Ready?"

When Marla stepped out, her shoes sank into the softness of the soil. Two attendants waited while a deputy snapped pictures with a digital camera of a fourteen-foot-long, flat-bottom boat with an outboard motor wedged between high grass and mud. The other deputy photographed the muddy waterline and plant life around the craft. A backpack with a logo patch for the sheriff's department lay unzipped on the ground fifteen feet away.

"Bill? Carlos?" Standish called out. "Whatcha guys got?"

Bill stepped away while Carlos continued taking photos. "Two individuals in their twenties, fully clothed, with short-sleeved shirts, pants, and shoes. The guy is flat on his back, and the woman is on her side. There's a small amount of water in the boat. I found an open, clear plastic packet near her feet with a mess of white slush inside. Did a field test for amphetamines, and it turned positive."

"How long have you been here?" Standish asked.

"Several hours. The JP has come and gone, pronounced them, so we're ready to move the bodies out of the boat."

"Any ideas from the JP?"

"You know those guys. They mumble it maybe this or that...need an autopsy, blood for tox, and all the other tricks in their bag before their final determination."

Marla held her badge up to him. "DEA Special Agent Adams. I'm investigating fenethylline overdoses in Padre."

"The stuff made in Syria, right?"

"It is...was...we think it's being made somewhere else," Marla said. "What size is the packet?"

"Standard druggie size."

Of course, like all the others. "One packet? Any other paraphernalia?"

"So far, we found a syringe, disposable lighter, soaked cotton balls, and a bent spoon, but we haven't checked their pockets. There are puncture holes in both of their left arms. It looks like they injected rather than an oral route."

"I bought a packet of white tablets last night," Marla said. "May I see your packet? It could be the same thing."

"You're undercover?"

"Soft undercover." Marla gestured toward her clothes. "Just wearing old clothes and pretending to be homeless."

Bill nodded, then reached inside the backpack and removed an evidence bag. "Not going to help much with no tablets."

Marla extended her hand. "May I?"

"You already know, but just a reminder, look but don't open the bag."

After studying the plastic evidence bag as best as possible, Marla asked, "Where will you take this?"

"Anything we find is sent to the sheriff's office to be processed before going to the crime lab."

"I see." Marla returned the evidence bag to him, knowing it was a lost cause to push further. "And when will you send it?"

"I think tomorrow or the next day."

"Thanks. I'll contact my office and check if they can speed up the drug analysis." Marla gestured toward the two bodies in the boat. "Mind if I take a few pictures with my phone?"

Bill gestured behind him. "Go ahead."

Standish changed the subject. "An officer at my station said the boat is unregistered. Are we clear to look?"

Bill pointed at the boat. "Yeah. No numbers on it, but we found a wadded-up cash receipt from a tackle store near the bridge."

"That's ten—twelve miles from here." Standish maneuvered through the mud and gazed at the couple. "Well, well. We meet again, Blondie."

Marla nodded once. "That's him, and he came to my table at a restaurant with a fake beard."

"The free omelet?"

Marla chuckled. "Yeah." She took several photos with her phone. "Not sure what that was all about, but he came over and hung around the table for a few minutes, then left."

"Did you get a name?"

"Wouldn't give it to me, and didn't want to make a scene, so I let it go. We may never know if the fingerprints on the bottle are negative."

Standish glanced around the area. "Why here? "Looks like someone pushed the boat up

on the shoreline."

"What do you mean?"

"It's half in the water, and someone had to push or pull it to get that much of the boat out of the water."

"Yeah, okay."

"Did they OD on heroin or coke, or smack, or your drug?"

Marla raised her eyebrows as she quipped back at Standish, "I don't have a drug."

"You know what I mean. The drug you're investigating."

"It'd be nice if it came out positive. Okay, another thought. Accidental or intentional?"

"You thinkin' the same thing I am? Murder?"

"Could be. You're the local expert. Think it through," Marla said. "Tell me why the boat is here."

Standish gazed south, then north. "Last night, the wind blew from the northeast, meaning this boat headed from the bridge into the wind to reach here. Like I said, that's a lot of miles. And why here? If it was a drug deal north of here, in or near Port Mansfield or Arroyo City, why start way south near the bridge? And if you don't know the area, you can bog the propeller in the muck and easily get stuck."

Marla saw Standish's brain working. "You got it. Keep going."

"It's possible another motorized boat towed this thing here after the two died and pushed it on the shore. The tide's already erased the footprints."

Marla looked up and down the shoreline. "If we get lucky, we'll find the fingerprints of the drug dealer on the boat."

Standish shook her head. "Possible, but there could be hundreds of prints on the aluminum hull."

Marla nodded. "What about on the plastic bag?"

"You mean the one next to the victims? Nice thinking." Standish gestured toward the water. "Bill, let me see your camera." She aimed northeast, zoomed in a few hundred yards out, found a line of spoil islands and floating houses with wooden docks, and took several pictures. "There. Someone tried to mislead us into believing the boat came from the south. It didn't happen like that. I'll bet one of those dwellings is where the deal went down, and after they shot up and died, someone dragged it here."

A funeral home attendant called out, "Hey, deputy? I found another packet next to the male body, and this one is sealed with white tablets inside."

◆

Jax Whitmore knelt in his trailer, looking through his binoculars at several emergency vehicles, a beached aluminum boat, and a deputy holding a packet of tablets. He spun around and leaned against the wall. "I didn't think it would kill 'em that quick."

Chapter 14

Marla's headlights cut through the night, illuminating the boats docked at the cove. The canvas covers over the expensive small fishing boats stood out against Standish's lone aluminum flat-bottom boat. The lagoon fell into darkness when she turned off the lights. Clouds rumbled above their heads.

"You sure you want to do this?" Standish asked. "We can do this tomorrow night. This storm looks wicked." Lightning streaked the sky above the ocean. Thunder clapped. "These might be anywhere from just the wind lasting a few minutes to a downpour all evening. Like I said, tomorrow should be better."

"No," Marla said. "We need to know what is going on tonight."

"All right." Standish opened her door and rushed to the boat. Marla grabbed the straps of a gym bag holding the drone and controller from the back seat and left Festus in the truck. Standish climbed in and cranked the engine. "All aboard."

Glad she had changed back into her button-down shirt, black pants, and windbreaker, Marla placed the bag inside and hopped aboard as well. The smell of fish and flora filled the air as Standish pushed off and steered up the lagoon toward the desalination plant at an even pace. "We go nice and slow and keep the engine prop from digging into the bottom."

"How shallow is this?"

"One to three feet, but gotta be careful. The grass'll trap you like quicksand." Standish pulled a flashlight out of a small tackle box and shined it on the water in front. "With the flat bottom, we could run the boat onto the sand and grass, get off, and walk up near the back gate." A fishtail slapped the hull's side. "After we land, launch your drone and take pics from a hundred feet above."

"With the clouds covering the moon, hopefully, they won't see anything," Marla said.

The wind kicked past thirty miles per hour and pushed the boat farther from the shore. Four hundred yards away, bright floodlights lit the fence line every few yards. Standish sped the engine up and turned toward the plant.

"My drone can't fly in this much wind."

"Let's get on land and walk closer." Standish cut the engine as the bow of the boat scraped over the sand and stopped.

Marla jumped out while holding the bag handles. Standish pulled the boat farther up the shore and aimed the flashlight beam on the ground.

They trudged through the grasses and wet sand until they were nearly a hundred feet from the corner of the fence.

Marla knelt on one knee. "We wait for the wind to die."

"Could be hours...all night."

"We're committed, and patience will give us better intel. I'm willing to sit here all night if necessary." She wriggled her foot in the sand. "Waiting, observing, doing nothing. That's how we'll get the best results."

When the wind died, Marla touched her watch, and the face illuminated 2:14 AM. Lucky for them, it never rained. She removed the contents from the bag, started the drone, and it rose straight up into the air. The entire area inside the fence was lit up on the phone screen with people active. "We don't need the night vision."

"Look at the back corner." Standish pointed out. "Why is a five-foot-tall pile of sand there?"

"Good question."

"There." Standish pointed to the right side. "Someone's coming out."

A man wearing a disposable mask pushed a tilt truck out of the building and dumped a wet load of slurry in a drying bin. Others with masks smoothed it with rakes.

"Drying bins at night?" Marla asked. "Don't see why."

Standish chuckled. "Oh, there ya go."

Someone else rolled out a big industrial-size heater. In a few seconds, the coils turned an orangy-red.

"Betcha that'll dry it," Standish said.

"More men coming out," Marla said. "They all look His-panic."

Others carried drying bins from the inside of the building to the outside, placed them on the concrete, and shoveled the material into fifty-pound polypropylene bags before lining them up against each other unsealed.

"Pretty smooth operation," Standish said. "Looks like they have done this many times."

Marla asked, "The big guy that just walked out...is that Jax Whitmore?"

Standish nodded when Jax pulled his mask down and yelled at the men, then replaced it over his mouth. "That's him."

"Ricky's right. He's big."

Standish squinted at the phone screen image. "Can't read what it says on the bags beside him. Can you get a little closer?"

As Marla eased in, men stacked the open bags with a logo on a flatbed cart. Standish leaned back with a puzzled look on her face. "This can't be right. The logo clearly reads SPIFB, which stands for South Padre Island Food Bank."

"Drugs?" Marla asked.

Standish nodded. "I never paid much attention to the food bank trucks passing in and out of town, but you can be sure I will from now on."

◆

An hour later, Standish docked her boat, and Marla drove down Padre Boulevard near the bridge to the KOA campgrounds and Pier 19. It was late, and all the businesses had closed for the night. The traffic lights turned green as she approached each intersection from the north end to the south, with no other vehicles on the street. She cut her headlights off half a block away from the campground entrance and eased off the road. With her night vision binoculars, she scanned the area for anybody outside. There were none.

She changed back into the sweatshirt, shorts, wig, and beanie before activating the necklace's audio transmitter from the DEA. Festus sat patiently on the floorboard. In the back seat lay the tied bedsheets with the hidden pistol and torn pillows inside. With money in one pocket and more in the other, she exited her truck and felt the handcuff key rub against the bottom of her foot as she paced past all the RVs toward the rubble on the pier. Beyond the motor homes and travel trailers, no overhead lights illuminated the area, and the moon, less than half full, offered little help.

Almost as if she had passed a tripwire, men appeared on each side of her, different, smaller than the brutes from last night.

Maybe they take shifts. Marla continued to advance toward the rubble where Baldy hung out. He emerged from a pile of burned wood and presented himself like he was king of the mountain.

"You bring me money?"

Still holding her pillows, she nodded. "Yeah, sure." She knew not to rush the deal. "Said I would. What I got last night was okay."

"Bullshit. What was not okay was that weed you gave me." He eased his stance a bit before looking to each side as if people were listening.

"You got more stuff?" Marla asked.

"You said it wasn't good. Why'd you come back?"

"It was good enough for me to come back."

He held his hand out. "Give me the cash."

When Marla stepped forward, she dropped the sheet with the pillows wrapped inside on the ground, dug into her pocket, and handed two hundred to him. He quickly counted it. "This ain't enough to buy you squat. You need more."

"Yes, it is. I buy from the downtown guys, and it's enough for a night."

"Downtown? Who's sellin' to you? Someone muscling in?"

"I don't have a name. Like you, you got no name. Don't want to know your name." She picked up her bedsheet again, thinking she needed her pistol close by. "I just want something for tonight."

"Where'd you get the money?"

"Where'd you get yours?"

The guy on the left stepped toward Marla. "Maybe you can give me something besides money."

Marla juggled the pillows into one hand and shoved him away. "Back off, asshole."

The guy to her right closed in. Both stood inches from Marla. "Take your clothes off and you can do me and then him before you get anything," one said.

It took them both by surprise when Marla dropped the pillows and swept the legs of the guy to her left. He fell, and she punched him in the throat. When the other guy grabbed her shoulder, she spun, latched onto his wrist, and bent his hand back until he dropped to his knees. She glared at Baldy, who never moved. "Don't mess with me."

He snapped open a switchblade. "You a cop or something?"

Of course, she wouldn't say yes. "Ex-Army. Just give me what I came for, and I'll be back another night."

He closed the blade before reaching into a different pocket for a small clear baggie. "Next time, three hundred."

Marla stepped closer and took the baggie. "Hope this is better than last night."

Baldy nodded once. "You want something better? Four hundred for that."

Did she find it? She dared not ask. Say the word fenethylline, and he might either look at her funny or shoot her dead right there in the parking lot. Pretend like she knew nothing, and she may get lucky enough to get what she wanted. "For what? Crystal? Too much."

She couldn't help but stare at his broken black teeth when he smiled.

He kept the closed blade in his right fist. "How 'bout I take what's between your legs?"

"How about I take that pig sticker from you, cut your liver out, and feed it to the fish?" Marla stepped back. "I can handle myself. I got a little more cash for the good stuff."

He continued to smile. "I like you. Could use a tough bitch."

She almost jumped out of her skin at the thought of joining him, but what if he didn't have the fenethylline? What if a competitor down the street did? She didn't want to lose the deal, so she pulled out the rest of her money. "That's all I got."

Baldy snatched the cash from her hand, spun around, and disappeared behind the burned pile of lumber and trash. It sounded like wood being dragged on the cement. Was he pulling out a hidden stash? Moments later, he returned with another packet between his fingers and then extended his arm toward her. "Where you sleeping at night?"

The packet held four white tablets. Marla reached for it, but he pulled his hand back.

"You planning on sharing it with anybody?"

She snatched the packet from his hand and stuffed it in her pocket. "Don't worry where I'm sleeping."

"I don't want a bunch of people here," Baldy said. "Too much noise brings the cops."

Marla grabbed the sheet tied around her stuff. "I won't tell anybody where I got it, and I'll be back tomorrow night."

Chapter 15

When Marla's phone alarm chimed at 5:40 in the morning, she flung the two torn pillows duct-taped together out of the bathtub onto the tiled floor. With a swift motion, she kicked the blanket off herself, then hoisted herself out. She turned on the bathroom light, grasped her pistol on the closed toilet lid, and entered the main room of the beach house. Festus was already awake and sat up on the box springs, with the mattress still propped against the window as it had been the night before. Marla rubbed her eyes before smiling at the dog. "Did you sleep well?" Festus barked once for a yes.

Marla decided sleeping in the bed was still too dangerous. A great place for vacationers to listen to the waves all night, but too open if one had to worry about someone emptying a semi-automatic rifle magazine through the window.

After letting Festus out to do his business, she grabbed the dog food sack. Hard chunks clattered on a plate. "Sorry about the selection. Eat your breakfast and stand guard." Festus charged at the food. "Bark if you hear someone." Marla checked the chair under the doorknob before rummaging through her clothes and returning to the bathroom. She closed the door, then paused before opening it again. With the shower on, she couldn't make out any sounds at the front door or the window. She released her pistol magazine from the handle—full, then snapped it back in place. Seconds later, steam rolled out from the open doorway to the ceiling.

◆

Dressed in her white shirt and black pants again, Marla drove across Queen Isabella Bridge and headed for the forty minute drive to the DEA office in Brownsville. The moon shone into her back window and onto the sealed evidence bag that sat on the console while Festus gazed out at the windshield as if he were helping her with directions. After turning into the parking lot and entering the building, she exchanged the drugs for more cash. On the return trip to the island, the sun rose from the water's surface and helicopter blades thumped in the distance. Marla looked out her side window at one copter following another.

After crossing the bridge and returning to Padre, a few vehicles occupied the boulevard, unlike the chaotic, bumper-to-bumper San Antone morning traffic she was used to. The vacationers were just getting ready for a day of lounging, swimming, and touring the island. Could this be someone's last day alive after overdosing on fenethylline? She called the police station to confirm that Standish was there before turning into the parking lot near the Bronco and two other cars.

When she entered the building and looked around the empty lobby, the officer at the desk gave her a half wave with his hand and buzzed the wooden door open. Marla smiled as she walked past Ricky, who did nothing but stare at her.

Standish and Marla entered the office and sat in their respective chairs. The sergeant took a drink of coffee from a small Styrofoam cup before putting it down. "Oh, sorry. Want some?" She stood, but Marla waved her back down.

"That's all right. I'll get it. Kitchen to the left and down the hall?"

"Yep. We use a carafe. I don't like those little pods. Anyway," Standish held up her cup, "got these or the bigger cups in there."

Marla went into the kitchen, noticing the carafe was half full. She chuckled at the coffee machine, which was the same one she had at the ranch. After pouring herself a cup, Ricky knocked twice on the surface of the refrigerator when he came in. She wondered how this conversation might go. "Good morning."

He reached for an upside-down small cup on the counter. "Morning."

Marla sipped her thick black swill and waited. There had to be a reason for him to show up. This was no coincidence.

Roberts poured the coffee into his cup and said, "I want in."

She wondered why he insisted on being involved after making it clear during their first meeting that her meddling in police matters wasn't welcome. Since then, barely a word had passed between them, yet now he aimed to be her partner. "I appreciate you wanting to step up and help, but as a DEA agent, I work alone."

"No, you don't. Standish is involved. You could use the help with this drug problem."

This wasn't going to be easy. Ricky was nothing but a pain in the ass, and the last thing she needed was to babysit a hothead. "I'll think about it." Marla left the kitchen and made her way to the office.

When she rounded the corner and entered, Standish still sat while studying several pages on her desk. "Find everything?"

Marla took a seat and sipped her coffee. "Yeah, good. I made another drug transaction last night and drove—"

Two sharp raps against the open door startled Marla. She didn't have a chance to turn around when she heard Ricky's voice.

"Hey, Sarge. Let me help. I want to learn a little more about this drug."

Standish looked up. "What drug?"

"You know, the one the DEA is here about. Fen...fene...um...fenethyl."

Standish corrected him. "It's fenethylline. And you don't even know the name of the drug. Why should you be involved?"

He folded his arms across his chest. "Because I'm second in line. I've got seniority."

Marla stayed a silent spectator as she sipped her coffee, leaned back in the chair, and listened to the conversation unfolding before her.

Standish furrowed her brow. "You're not second in line. There is the chief, who's out for a few weeks, and then there is the lieutenant's position, which at present is open, and then me. Even if the chief considered you, that'd make you fourth, but seniority doesn't mean crap around here, so you might as well be fifth, or sixth, or twelfth. Why do you suddenly care about this investigation?"

He dropped his hands to his side. "This is a good career move for me."

Standish leaned back in the chair. "Career?" She smiled. "I believe that is the first time you said anything about that. You've always claimed you were heading off to Houston or Galveston someday."

"Well, I changed my mind." He dragged an empty chair from the hallway, placed it next to Marla, and sat down. "No need for me to leave, so I've decided to stay in town."

Standish drained the last of her lukewarm coffee before setting the cup back down. "I appreciate you letting me know about your future plans with us, but Agent Adams and I are in the middle of a discussion. I will think about it—"

"She already said that to me. What's to think about? I'm volunteering for this, and you should let me help."

Standish turned on her best supervisor dialogue. "I'm encouraged by your new desire to be involved. I will note that to the chief. After he makes that decision, one way or the other, you'll hear from me. Now, please close the door behind you as you leave."

Chapter16

Twenty-year-old Harlow Palermo wore tight black pants and a white shirt, almost completely unbuttoned and tied in a knot above the navel. Midday, she sat in her living space inside the desalination plant, which was more like a luxury dormitory room. A plush comforter with a deep red and gold pattern, with numerous pillows in different shapes and sizes, covered the queen-size bed. Walls painted light blue. A vase of fresh flowers, cut daily, stood on the nightstand, giving off a faint scent of lavender and baby's breath.

Escape was impossible without windows, but Nico, her older brother, didn't see himself as cruel. To prove that, he had a window painted on one wall depicting a distant sailboat on the water behind sheer white curtains, thinking this should comfort her. He controlled his little sister's life and saw no reason for her ever to abandon him. After all, she had everything she could ever want: top-of-the-line electronics, television streaming, books, and music. Nico couldn't let her leave because the outside world was too dangerous. She could drown in the ocean, or someone run her over, rob her, or kidnap her if she went into town—or if she talked to the police.

At first, the idea of Nico signing them both up for exercise and self-defense classes made her furious. He never let her make her own choices. Why should this be any different? And he didn't even take her outside the plant. Instead, he brought in an instructor twice a week to teach karate and hanbo stick fighting. But it didn't take long for Harlow to surpass her brother. Every time she faced off against the instructor, she fought with a vengeance, gripping the wooden staff tight and striking harder and faster. Each blow landed with the force of all the anger she wished she could unleash on Nico himself.

Harlow tried to be happy inside the facility, surrounded by a fence with concertina wire on top and bright industrial lighting covering the area, but the alternative was no better. Living off the land or finding a job held no appeal.

With no other family to fall back on, she hated her childhood and her parents' free-wheeling life in southeast Georgia or wherever they were. A VW Microbus that barely ran sat in the center of their front yard, while others littered on cinder blocks. With no grass, they didn't even need a lawnmower, just a tall metal fence hiding their large backyard from curious eyes where marijuana grew to make money for food and cocaine. But when Harlow turned eighteen, the police questioned her about how she got enough cash to bail her parents out of jail a second time. But when someone set their house on fire, her mother and father took the savings hidden in the backyard, leaving Nico and Harlow to look after themselves.

In defiance to Nico and her dead parents, last night Harlow cut her shoulder-length hair, with one side below the ear and the other trimmed higher at the nape. But the act wasn't complete until she sprayed her natural light-blonde color bright green to make everything perfect.

Before exiting the back of the building, Harlow placed a black, COVID-style disposable mask on her face and wrapped a long, black shawl around her shoulders, which covered most of her body. As the sole female at the plant among fourteen males with too much testosterone, Nico, Jax, and a dozen undocumented Mexican men, she had no desire to be ogled by the workers. She didn't know the names of any of the Mexicans, and didn't want to. The panic bar on the metal back door clanked as her hand shoved it open. Stepping outside, she ignored the perfect beach weather of sunny skies, eighty-two degrees, and a calm breeze. Just past the entryway, a man, potbellied and covered with tattoos, stood holding an assault rifle. He stopped asking how her day was. She never replied to him, always staring straight ahead as if he were invisible.

A sixteen-square-foot garden at the far corner of the fence line held wild flowering plants. She told herself it was not the same thing as her parents' marijuana. A bevy of quail cooed within a five-foot-tall bird cage made of chicken wire and boards.

A quail farm delivered a box holding ten more birds with white leg bands. Harlow stopped in front of the cage, un-latched the door, placed the box inside, and removed the lid. The birds flew out and perched on wooden rods. Lucky for them, white-banded ones waited a week for their chance in the kitchen. She sprinkled seeds from the plants nearby onto the bottom of the cage. The birds fluttered, trying to dodge her grasp. She took two with blue leg bands, snapped their necks in one swift motion, and returned to the building with the main course in hand. The survivors in the cage pecked at their food, ignoring the possibility that tomorrow might be their turn.

Once inside, Harlow pitched the shawl onto a chair, pulled the mask off, and dropped the birds on the counter. She hated the mask, but kept it on while inside or outside the desali-nation plant facility, except in her bedroom and the kitchen, which used high-efficiency filters.

After turning on the faucet, the rushing water slapped against the porcelain sink. She removed the feathers and gutted the birds before rinsing them in a colander, something she had become quite adept at. Nico enjoyed his exotic and game meats, anything not raised on a farm.

Cooking was one of the few tasks Harlow had to do for Nico since he didn't trust anybody else to prepare his meals.

Clearing the countertop, she eased the quail into a hot pan. The oil sizzled as soon as the meat touched it.

Two books lay open on the counter, one a cookbook and the other on finance.

When Nico entered the kitchen, he opened the top door of the double oven and smelled the simmering garlic and parsley. "Fantastic. What is it?"

Harlow placed the cookbook on top of the finance book. "Elk meat with potatoes and mixed vegetables in Italian seasoning. Just like you like them. Drink your glass of wine." She flipped the bird in the pan with tongs. "Where's your mask?"

"Told you a hundred times, I'm not wearin' that. I don't care what happens." Nico tried not to stare at Harlow, but the black tights hugged her body like paint, accentuating a flat stomach and rounded ass. Her finger pushed a strand of green hair away from her face, only for it to fall stubbornly back into place. Nico had to remind himself she was his sister, and thinking about that was wrong. But he had done plenty of wrong things in his life. "Smells great. When do we eat?"

Harlow knew what he was doing and shot him an annoyed look. "Stop staring at me like that."

The sunlight coming through the small window above the sink caught her hair, making the green appear brighter. Nico hated the haircut, but would never give her the satisfaction of saying so. "I like your hair." He wondered what shampoo she used. What perfume? Leaning on one leg and cocking the other caused one side of her buttocks to tighten. Nico reached for the wineglass and forced himself to turn his eyes elsewhere. "Why is there only one plate? Are you not eating?"

"Didn't think you wanted me to...not after our argument earlier."

"Forget that. I've decided you can go into town, but only with someone."

"Why? I just want to walk around the downtown shops and wander the beach alone. I don't need one of your lugs following me."

"What's the big deal? He can be discreet."

"The big deal is, I want to be alone, without having to look at any of your paid assholes every second of my life."

"No. Someone with you, or you don't go."

"Like a chaperone? Is he giving me a corsage? How about he pins it right here?" She patted her open shirt. "Or maybe I could hold it and pledge allegiance." She placed her hand over her left breast. "I pledge allegiance to my asshole brother who won't let me—"

"Enough!" he pointed at the cabinet, "grab a plate and come sit with me."

"I don't eat any of your wild game meats."

"Are you turning vegetarian on me?"

She shook her head and murmured, "Such an ass." After removing the quail from the frying pan, she gestured toward the lower oven. "I have chicken cooking in there."

"And where are you going to eat?"

After spooning the elk and vegetables onto the plate and placing the two birds in the center, Harlow placed Nico's platter on the table. "I'm eating at the counter after you finish stuffing your asshole mouth."

Nico sat down. "You'll sit where I'll tell you to sit." He kicked the legs of the chair next to him. "And do what I say. Sit your ass down alongside me."

Slats, a robust man with unkempt hair and baggy clothes, was the only man there 24-7 that wasn't one of the Mexican cartel's men. He peeked into the kitchen and slid his mask onto his forehead. "Boss?" Slats leaned forward and whispered something in Nico's ear.

"See?" Harlow snapped at the two. "He comes in here and interrupts our family discussions. He was probably eavesdropping...and ogling me."

Nico nodded to Slats. "Yeah, sure. Tonight. I can have it ready." Then he whispered into Slats' ear as he glanced at his sister.

"What are you looking at? Is my brother telling you to lock me in my room again?"

Slats nodded at Nico and left.

Nico cut a slice of the elk meat and jabbed his fork in it. "Sit down."

Harlow plopped down next to him. "You better eat all that. It was a lot of trouble making it for you." She crossed her legs and leaned forward, letting him glance at her chest. *You just think you can control me.* "You're going to town tomorrow, right?"

"Yeah. So what?"

"So, you should let me go to town with you."

"I'll think about it."

After both finished eating, Harlow cleaned the kitchen, headed for her room, and shut the door. At her desk, she fiddled through social media and left harmless comments on her laptop before playing a quick game. She knew Nico could access her computer, but she wasn't worried because he never looked at his credit card bills, which listed a monthly virtual private network (VPN) charge. After a short while, she logged in and typed a message. *He's coming tomorrow.*

A reply came almost immediately. *Ready.*

Harlow contacted another person. *I will see you tomorrow.*

It took a moment for a reply. *I want you spread across my bed.*

She typed back, *Don't be wearing anything when I come upstairs.* She logged off and closed her laptop.

❖

The next morning, a harsh banging on Harlow's door startled her awake. Irritated by the noise, she flung her sheet off after another round of loud knocks. "All right. Shut up. I'm coming," she grumbled as she made her way to the door while more aggressive knocking continued. "I'm going to kill whoever it is." She snapped the lock on the deadbolt and threw open the door.

Nico stood and smiled. "Time to get up and go to town."

When Harlow stretched, a sliver of smooth skin peeked out from between her T-shirt and shorts. Avoiding a direct stare, Nico leered into the gap of her short sleeve and caught a glimpse of her breast before she dropped her arm down.

"What do you want?"

He kept his smile aimed at her. "You said you wanted to go to town, so here I am, ready to take you."

"It's too early. Nothing will be open at this time of the morning." She tried to close the door, but his foot blocked it.

"Wrong. The bait shops are open."

"When I said I wanted to go shopping in town, I didn't mean a bait shop."

"You like fish, so let's go fishing."

"I like hamburgers, but I'm not going to go out to a field and kill a cow for it. Downtown shops open at ten, and don't forget about your massage today."

"I won't, but I decided we should get out early this morning before that."

He can't miss his appointment. "I have you scheduled for a massage this morning."

Nico eased the door open further with his hand. "After last night, thought we should do more things together, like fishing and shopping."

Harlow crossed her arms in front of her. "Lagoon or gulf fishing?"

"Lagoon for the redfish."

"I'll fish for a couple of hours only if you go to the massage parlor. You need the stress relief."

"Good. We meet Jax in twenty minutes at the lagoon dock."

"Is that the best you can come up with? The guy needs a shower. Every time I've seen him, he's drunk and smells."

"Hurry up and get dressed. I have a massage scheduled for 10:30."

"I know when your massage is. Scheduling them is my job."

◆

After two hours of fishing, Jax took their catch to be cleaned while Nico and Harlow walked a half mile into town. They paused outside a business in a strip mall on Padre Boulevard, with a bright red sign above the door that read CLEAN U UP and a window display advertising hair, nail, and body treatments.

Nico chuckled. "Maybe I should send Jax in here."

Harlow disagreed. "Jax needs to walk through a car wash. And why are we here? I have you scheduled at the other place, never here."

"I changed my mind. Why do you care where I go?"

"I don't care." She looked to her side. "I'm turned around. Where is the other place?"

He opened the glass front door. "It's near the CBD shop. Come on." He patted her buttocks. "Get your cute ass inside."

A middle-aged Asian woman sat behind a desk. She stood and smiled. The scent of massage oils and incense filled the air. "Good morning, and welcome back, Mr. Palermo. I don't have you for an appointment, but I can see if Duri is available. This way, please."

"My sister is with me. Give her the same treatment."

The employee eyed the girl wearing an oversized T-shirt, shorts, and Crocs. "Yes, of course." She stopped in front of two empty manicure tables. "Please, sit. I will send over Duri and another."

Harlow conceded to have her nails done for the first time. She didn't like anyone messing with her hands and fingers, and the manicurist was unhappy about Harlow refusing the color she recommended.

Nico, being who he was, let Duri use a grapefruit scrub, exfoliating his hands and fingers until they were smooth to the touch. "I love this. I like it here better because Raylene wears gloves in the other place. Feels nicer with her using her bare hands."

"Gloves are more sanitary," Harlow said. "You don't know what those hands were touching before you."

Duri snapped back, "I wash hands every time."

"See," Nico said.

Harlow shook her head. "Gloves are cleaner. Next time we go see Raylene at the Padre Nail Salon and Massage Parlor."

After buffing the nails, Duri applied a clear polish.

Nico slid away from the table with a big smile on his face. "Next is the massage. We should get a room for two."

Harlow laughed at him. "I'm not having you next to me like we're lovers. We aren't holding hands, and you're not looking at me on the table. I want a separate room."

"Fine! No problem." Nico flipped his hand at her. "Meet me in the waiting area in an hour." He pointed at Duri. "Make sure she gets the same thing I do."

Harlow threw a fake smile at Nico. "Fine...no problem." She followed him, and as he entered the changing room, she went to another and closed the door. Seconds later, Harlow eased it open. "I'm outta here."

"No, no," Duri said. "You not leave here."

"Don't even try to stop me. And if you say anything to my brother while I'm gone," Harlow shook her head, "you will not like me angry at you." She pushed the front door open and left the building.

Harlow hurried down the street, crossing the intersection before a gnawing realization hit her—she hadn't eaten breakfast. Hunger clawed at her stomach, and she wanted to grab something before meeting her...friend. But there was a problem. No cash, no card, nothing. Nico hadn't given her a dime. At almost noon, the need to eat was impossible to ignore.

Chapter 17

Marla entered a little sandwich shop on Padre Boulevard. The smell of fresh bread filled the air. Shelves of chips and snacks lined one wall, and two small tables and chairs sat near the window. A young girl with bright green, lopsided hair and wearing a T-shirt, shorts, and Crocs argued with a woman standing on the counter's other side. As best Marla could tell, the girl wanted food but had no money.

"You know Nico. He's my brother," Harlow said. "He comes in here all the time for takeout. I eat your sandwiches at least once a week."

"Sorry, but I'm acquainted with a person named Nico, not you. Please have him come by."

"I can't ask him...he can't come right now. He's down the street at the..." Harlow won't bring herself to say where he is. "He's down there somewhere. Listen, I'm hungry, and Nico will pay you later."

Marla held a twenty in her hand. "It's on me."

Harlow turned to see a woman wearing a windbreaker, white shirt, and black pants. Normally, she'd tell anyone to butt out, but her hunger and not used to waiting for much of anything stopped her. Harlow swept her vibrant green hair behind her ear. "Thanks."

Marla sensed something. She should find out more about the girl. When you want someone to have a good first impression, mimic their actions. Marla did the same with her hair. "You're welcome."

When the cashier disappeared behind a larger counter, Harlow stuck her hands in her front pockets. "I'm not a homeless person. I just didn't bring money because my brother took me out to do things in town."

"Right, of course." Marla stuck her hands in her pockets. "What's your name?"

"Harlow. My mother named me after Jean Harlow, the movie actress from the twenties, or thirties, or somewhere around there."

"Interesting name." Marla held out her hand. "I'm Marla, Marla Adams. Nice to meet you."

Harlow shook her hand. "Yeah, me too."

The cashier returned with a sack and set it on the counter, along with the change.

"Give that to Harlow," Marla said.

"I don't need your money."

"Never a doubt. Want to leave it as a tip?"

Harlow glanced at the girl behind the counter before swiping the change off the countertop. "No." She grabbed the sack. "Thanks again. I'm leaving."

"Wait." Marla pulled a card from her shirt pocket and handed it to Harlow. "I am always available to talk...anytime."

Harlow took the card and read it: DEA Special Agent Marla Adams. "Hmm." She stepped outside and dropped it on the ground as she left. Seconds later, she returned to pick it up and stuck it in her shorts pocket.

"Care to order anything?" the cashier asked.

Marla turned her attention again to the menu on the wall. She placed her palms on the wooden counter, her fingertips touching small nicks and scratches etched into its surface.

The woman spoke, "I'm sorry to ask, but your finger...what happened?"

Marla lifted her right hand from the counter and glanced at her fifth finger nub. "Accident." She gazed at the wall and read the lunch special: a BLT sandwich with a side of chips. "I'll take today's special. And, by the way, do you know who that was?"

The cashier tore off the printed receipt and spun it around for Marla to see the amount due. "That is Nico's...um...I forgot his last name, his sister, at least that's what she says, anyhow. Nico comes in once or twice a week and is a pretty good customer. He mostly orders two of whatever the special of the day is. Never complains and pays with cash from a wad of bills in his pocket."

"Good tipper?"

"From him, yes." Her hand waved toward the tables. "We don't get many tips here. You know, we're pretty small. Only a couple of places to sit. To most everyone, it's a pickup and go place."

"What does Nico do?"

"Mmm, not totally sure. He has a business north of town."

"And the girl?"

"First time I've seen her. Let me get that order for you." The cashier disappeared into the kitchen for a short time before returning with a paper sack bearing the business logo on the side. She placed it on the counter. "Here you go."

Marla placed two twenty-dollar bills on the counter. Over-tipping almost always made friends and often gathered helpful information. "Thanks for helping out with the girl, and keep the change. I'll come back tomorrow." Marla handed her a business card. "Just in case you have questions about anything."

The cashier read the card. "Are you here about those recent overdoses?"

"Can you tell me anything about them?"

"I told Officer Roberts that I had a couple come into the shop the day before the last overdose reported on the news. I think it looked like them, but not sure. They were smashed and ordered way too much food for just the two of them."

Marla didn't remember Standish saying anything about a report from Ricky. Did he tell Standish? "May I show you a picture from my phone of two victims we recently found? It may help if it was the same couple." She motioned toward the street. "We might find an outside surveillance camera catching them walking on the sidewalk."

The cashier closed her eyes briefly before opening them again. "I've never seen a dead body before, and not sure if I want to."

Marla nodded. "Sure. Understand." Sometimes, if you just wait, people help. "I can always come back later and ask if you have changed your mind."

The cashier's lips tightened before she eased her hand out toward Marla. "Okay, I'll look, but I can't ..."

"Oh, sure, of course. I appreciate any help in trying to stop the deaths in town." Marla slipped her phone out and pulled up a picture of the two lying inside the flat-bottom boat. "Take your time."

The cashier grimaced without a sound and looked for a second before turning aside and then back toward the phone. Marla watched the cashier study the photo. The woman rubbed the back of her hand over each eye before looking away. "I, I think so. I mean...they look terrible, but I believe so."

Marla thanked the cashier, pocketed the phone, and grasped the sack of food. "Do you remember if they paid with a card? Might get a name?"

"I don't know. We're small, but I couldn't go through all the receipts that day."

"Understand. Thanks for your help." When she reached for the front door, a man barged in and asked, "Have you seen a young girl in a T-shirt and shorts?"

The cashier smiled before glancing at Marla. "Hello, *Nico*. There was one, but that describes almost every girl in town."

Marla stayed still and as invisible to the situation as possible.

Nico's fingers squeezed against his temples. "She gives me nothing but a headache." He held onto the door handle and coughed hard.

"You seem out of breath," the cashier asked. "Can I get you a glass of water?"

"Yes...no. I'm just out of shape and running after.... Which way did she go?"

The cashier pointed. "Down the left side, but I'm not sure after that."

After Nico rushed down the street, Marla stood next to the door and asked, "Do you know where Harlow could possibly have gone?"

"With only the small amount of money she took? No clue. There are trinket shops and beachwear clothing stores down the street. Even a vape and CBD shop, but no one's going to give away their stuff."

When a young couple wearing beach clothes entered the shop, Marla said, "Thank you. You've been a great help."

Upon leaving the shop, Marla looked in the direction where Harlow and Nico had gone and wondered if he had found her.

Was he physical with her? Violent? Was he pimping her? Running—hungry—no money. She had dealt with sex trafficking before, but this felt different. There were a lot of questions and not many answers...not yet. At least the girl picked up the card from the ground.

A man, thin as a rail, with clothes ragged and dirty, sat on a sidewalk bench by himself. He smiled when Marla handed him the sack of food. Repetitive thumping overhead made Marla turn her head. Two helicopters far from the Queen Isabella Causeway Bridge slowed and eased toward the ground before disappearing from sight. She thought about how easy it could be for someone to cross the border with a cockpit full of drugs.

Marla's phone rang. UNKNOWN was on the screen. "Hello?"

A girl's voice spoke. "Can I talk to you later? Not now, later."

"Har—"

"Don't say my name. I should have lied about that."

"Are you safe? I can help you. Just tell me."

"I'm fine."

She heard an acoustic guitar strumming in the background. "So, you're with someone?"

"Thanks for the sandwich." Harlow hung up.

Chapter 18

Inside the one-room apartment on the second floor of the Padre Boulevard Nail Salon and Massage Parlor, Raylene's younger brother sat on the bed naked. With his legs hanging down one side and a half-burned cigarette between his lips, he strummed his guitar. Harlow placed his phone on the dresser, locked the door, and slipped her shoes off before perching on his lap. She played with his ear while he struggled to strum the instrument.

"Thought you liked me playing," he said.

She felt the vibrations of the strings against her body as he strummed each chord. "I do, but it's time to play with something else." Her fingers pulled the cigarette from his lips and dropped it in the ashtray. She leaned in against the guitar, her tongue tasting the tobacco in his mouth as her hand slid up the inside of his thigh. He slid the instrument out from between them and laid it at the foot of the bed.

Harlow pushed him down and kissed his stomach, then his chest. "My dumbshit brother almost messed this up."

He kissed her hard on the lips. A hand slid under her T-shirt. "I'm glad you came up. Very glad."

She checked the clock on the nightstand. "I can stay for about twenty minutes."

Pulling her shirt over her head, he pitched it to the floor. "Plenty of time."

The time was too short between them. Harlow rolled out of bed, wanting more, but she took what she could get while putting clothes back on between bites of the sandwich. "If I know my brother, he is snooping around and will knock on every door. I'm tired of unimpressive men becoming unimportant in my life. Where'd I put your phone?"

The young man stayed in bed with the sheet covering him from the hips down. "I thought my moves were pretty impressive."

Harlow threw a sheepish grin at him. "Mostly." The grin left just as quick. "I'll text him to meet me at that stupid massage parlor down the street. Where's your phone?"

"You put it up there on the chest. Make sure you use the number blocker."

She held her hand up for him to be quiet before cracking open the door. Several people spoke downstairs. "It's my brother."

When she grasped the phone from the chest of drawers, he whispered, "Hey! Don't forget to block my number."

"Yeah, of course." Harlow texted Nico. *I'm here at CLEAN U UP. Where are you?* "That should throw him off for a bit."

Nico stopped talking downstairs, and the front door slammed shut.

"I have to convince him to only come here," Harlow said. "The other place won't be as easy for us." She grasped the bedsheet and pulled it off him. "You want me to come back, don't you?" After taking one more bite, she dropped the rest of the sandwich on the edge of the bed. "Here, you eat the rest."

Harlow watched Nico pacing outside CLEAN U UP. She slipped down the other side, sidestepping into a storefront and stooping behind parked cars when he glanced down the street. After Harlow snuck around a parked car, hurried across the pavement, and acted like she came from the opposite direction, she jumped on his back and laughed. "You are such a dork. I was playing hide and seek like we did as kids."

"Where were you? We don't play games anymore." He glanced both ways to see if anybody was looking. "We have to go."

Nico swung her off his back, and a shiver ran through him when Harlow latched onto his hand. He craved more—it was his sister, but he didn't care.

Nico called Jax, and they met at the dock. The three remained in the boat as the motor hummed. Harlow played the teasing little sister, making Nico's anger diminish. By the time they reached the desalination plant, she had convinced Nico that she had to go with him every time and only see Raylene. Harlow finally had something to look forward to—the boy upstairs for thirty minutes.

Chapter 19

Standish called her contact at the Port of Mobile, Alabama. They discussed various topics related to shipping and transportation, including drug smuggling, port salinity levels, and ballast discharge that kept a ship level.

They also talked about what happened on a ship a few years ago, causing dead fish to wash ashore. The ship originated from an area of high salinity off the coast of Eastern Africa and carried fertilizer destined for America, but it leaked into the ballast tanks. Upon the ship's arrival near the port of entry, it discharged the water holding the high salt content and chemicals, killing fish close by. The toxicology report of the fish confirmed that both the excessive salt and the fertilizer were sourced from one ship. Standish asked about testing the ocean waters, but her friend said both would diffuse into the sea and vanish too soon. She then asked if a ship from the East African port had recently come near South Padre. The answer was no, but several originated from a Syrian port last week.

◆

After sundown, Marla changed into her grubby resale clothes and was ready to return to the drug dealer at Pier 19. Someone in town had fenethylline, and she wanted it. Over the last few days, the two played the back-and-forth game of drug negotiations, and Marla always gave in. Each time, asking for something stronger; each time, giving her the same heroin.

After Pier 19, Marla's next stop was the alley behind the CBD shop. It was a different setup from the dealer at the pier, who looked like he sampled the product too often; the connection near the shop was alert and awake. This business had a line of people longer than Walmart on Black Friday.

Festus stayed close as Marla stepped around to the alley. She asked for something better and wondered if the two places sold the same drugs, like all the tourist spots buy the same touristy crap from the same wholesaler. Did the dealers know each other? It was a small town, but with contrasting life philosophies—Jamaican versus southern white trash.

After several buys, she learned the Jamaican's name—Arley. Each time, he took her money and handed over a plastic baggie. His voice carried a thick patois.

"I know what yuh want... di strong stuff. Di same ting dat kill dem tourists. But why yuh want it, eh?"

Marla didn't answer right away. She just held up more cash. "I got money. I wanna try it."

Arley studied her face. Then he gave a small nod. "Tomorrow, eleven o'clock. Yuh go to di island wid di oil storage tank, near Rattlesnake Island."

"Rattlesnake Island?" Marla raised a brow. "You're sending me to a place named after rattlesnakes? I'm guessing it's got plenty of them."

"Not dere. East, on a smaller spoil island, 'bout five hundred yards."

"There's a lot of those little islands in the lagoon. How am I supposed to know which one?"

"Look for di two flags—Jamaican and US."

"That's a little strange. Why all the way out there? Why not here?"

Arley's stare hardened. "Only a few get dis. I tell dem yuh coming."

"Who's 'them'?"

"Eleven tomorrow morning. Only you. No one else." His eyes flicked to Festus. "No dog. Now, gwan. Move along."

With a dismissive wave, he disappeared through the back door of the CBD shop.

Marla walked a block and called Standish. "Got a possible connection to the fenethylline."

"Yeah? Where?"

"A spoil island with an oil tank east of Rattlesnake Island. Do you know the place?"

"Sure. Don't know why, but someone dumped it there years ago. The tank is empty and rusting away. I can meet you there."

"I'm supposed to go alone," she glanced at Festus, "not even my dog."

"Okay, but call me if you need help. By the way, my buddy at the Mobile Port gave me more info on salt content. Several ships from East Africa ran a wagon train through the Gulf to Houston. One stalled from engine trouble and dumped a bunch of ballast full of high-salinity water. He said there was a large number of dead fish. How about we meet with your Dr. Hernandez from NOAA and find out more about that? Oh, I almost forgot, there were several cargo ships coming from a Syrian port in the last few weeks."

"Syria is the most interesting to me," Marla said. "I talked to the vet a few hours ago, and he told me they could track all their tagged fish, and both tiger sharks had been tagged. But he's in Galveston."

"That's four hundred miles from here," Standish said.

"True. He might FaceTime us or something similar."

"Call him back and let's meet up at the station."

After Marla contacted Dr. Hernandez again, he was eager to help. Even though the office had already closed, he'd return and get online. With most of the police staff gone for the day, Marla and Standish sat beside each other in her office, facing the computer screen that displayed the NOAA logo, with the doctor's face in the upper corner.

"Tell me again what you want to see," the doctor said.

"Not sure," Marla said. "Can you show us the activity of the two sharks?"

"Sure. Let me type in their tag numbers and a timeline for the last two weeks. Or do you want a longer time?"

"Two weeks is good with us," Marla said.

The screen changed to a map of the United States eastern seaboard and the Gulf of Mexico. "The lines are the two sharks. They stayed close to each other." Blue lines followed along the coastline before slowing near Houston for a day, then headed farther south near the island. "You had asked about whether there were any international ships in the vicinity of the shark movements. I found one that had problems." He typed in where a ship had entered the Gulf, and a red line appeared on the monitor. "You can see a place fifty miles from the Port of Houston, where the blue and the red lines crossed." He zoomed in on the area. "They reported the captain released part of the ship's ballast here. We are still investigating why he did this. What we do know is that in this area, fishing boats reported partially eaten tuna, grouper, and snapper in their shrimp nets."

Dr. Hernandez proposed, "My initial theory is that the ballast water carried toxic chemicals, potentially with a high saline content unfamiliar to the fish. This led to their death, and the sharks took advantage of the situation by feasting on them."

"What about the sharks?" Marla asked. "Why did they live through it and have a heyday with the dead, toxic fish?"

"Sharks are tough. Tougher than any fish out there. Most importantly, we're not a hundred percent sure if the two dead sharks mixed into the contaminated water or were the ones eating the dead fish. It could be other sharks that we have not tagged."

"Can you zoom in around the area where they beached on the island?" Marla asked.

He zoomed in and watched the blue lines close to the northern edge of South Padre and unexpectedly turned multiple times in small circles. They swam away for a brief period until they slowed to a drift.

Hernandez tapped his finger on the blue lines on the screen. "From the two necropsies and timing of death, I'm estimating they died somewhere within this five-mile radius."

"That's close to a seventy-five square mile area," Standish said. "Can you get a more accurate location?"

Chapter 20

A little after six in the morning, Marla entered the shooting range. The night contrasted with the bright indoor lights. By now, the person at the desk recognized her and didn't ask to see her law enforcement credentials. With her being the first customer of the day, she had her pick of the empty stalls and laid her 9mm pistol and two boxes of ammo on the shelf at the center stall. After adjusting her glasses and ear protection, she fired at the paper target ten feet away, then twenty-five feet.

Moments later, Ricky pushed the door open and stopped two stalls away. Close, but not too close. She wondered if he had taken time to work on his accuracy...and his fast draw. Ricky shot several times at ten feet before changing shooting patterns from two and three shots to one at a time. The bullet holes were a little closer to the x-ring this time. When Marla leaned back, she heard the familiar sound of a gun sliding in and out of a holster—his fast draw.

Marla couldn't stop herself, so she holstered her weapon and stepped out from her stall. "Better," Marla said from behind Ricky.

Without turning around, he said, "Been working on it."

"May I make a suggestion?"

"More? Thought you told me everything."

"Some things. Not everything. Try this." Marla eased beside him and gave a couple of tips using her gun.

After a few moments, Ricky gave a half smile when his aim improved.

Marla asked, "Do you know anything about two helicopters landing and taking off from the other side of the bridge?"

Ricky holstered his gun. "It's not against the law to own helicopters."

"Right, but it is if they cross the Rio Grande and bring drugs into the States."

Ricky paused before answering. "There's a guy that runs a helicopter feral hog hunting business. You know, they take people up and shoot as many as you can for an hour or two. The company butchers the small ones for the meat."

"Is there more than one company that does that close by?"

"How would I know? If it's outside of the city limits, I don't care, and you shouldn't either."

"Yeah, probably right. Oh, by the way, are Standish and the team ready for later this morning?"

Ricky tossed the rest of his ammo into a sack and walked away. He reached for the door and said, "You ask too many questions. And don't worry about our team, just make sure yours doesn't blow this thing wide open."

❖

An hour later, after a DEA agent from the Brownsville office gave Marla a handheld radio to communicate with all the other DEA agents on the planned bust, Marla joined Standish in her office. "Are your vehicles ready?"

"Yep," Standish quipped back. She was embarrassed about her total disregard for the desalination plant trucks driving through town every morning, crossing the bridge, and heading farther into Texas. It never occurred to her that there could be any problems. "Three unmarked vehicles on Padre Boulevard, with an officer on the beach watching the desal plant."

Marla held the DEA radio to her mouth. "Sun is up. Expecting a truck leaving the desal plant any minute. Everyone set?"

"All set," a voice said on the radio. "Drone up and above town," another voice stated. "Vehicles positioned on Padre Boulevard, and agents stationed along the sidewalks," another said. "Only one way to get off the island by truck—the bridge crossing the lagoon. There is no place to escape."

Marla looked at Standish and said in a low voice, "Overconfidence will get you nothing."

❖

Inside the desalination plant fence, Nico stood next to the truck and closed the driver's door. He gave a reassuring smile. "First time by yourself, right?"

The driver wore gloves and held onto the steering wheel. "Si."

"If the cops pull you over, they'll send you back to Mexico, so don't do anything stupid."

"Si."

"Remember, turn off your phone. The Feds can track you if it's on. Go straight through town and stay five miles under the speed limit. And whatever you do, don't run any red lights." Nico handed a short-range two-way radio to the driver as two men opened the gate. "Cheapie set. Leave it behind, when...if there's a problem. And speak English to me."

"Si. Yeah, okay."

"Take it nice and easy." Nico held his radio up. "I'll be with you as far as these will let me. After that, you're on your own. And no names."

Marla spoke into her DEA radio, "Still waiting."

"Go through your plan again," Standish said.

Marla placed the radio down and leaned forward with her hands pressed on the desk. She felt the nub of her little finger. "The truck drives through town—"

"Not my part. I know my part. Your part...the DEA."

"The Port Isabella Police and the DEA will block traffic on their side of the Queen Isabella Causeway Bridge when the truck is halfway through Padre. That way, the bridge will be empty. A DEA vehicle will wait at the Padre side of the bridge, ready to follow the truck once it turns onto the bridge. There's nowhere for it to go. We just want you and the police to keep Padre Boulevard empty and safe."

"Everything will be. Ricky is sitting in his car near the bridge," Standish added.

Marla paused before asking, "Why Ricky?"

"Just in case the DEA doesn't get the truck for whatever reason."

"Keep him right where he is. I don't want him any closer."

"Why?" Standish asked.

Marla remembered his mood change when she asked if the police were ready. "Just keep him back."

The police radio crackled. "Truck leaving the building."

The transmission whined as the truck driver shifted gears. He spoke into the radio. "Everythin' smooth."

Nico held the radio close to his mouth. "Nice and slow," he cautioned.

The driver spoke in a heavy Spanish accent. "First red light. Malditos turistas."

"English. Sit and wait."

"Green. Moving." The driver gazed up into the sky. "Don't see nothin' above me."

"Don't worry. You wouldn't," Nico said.

The driver shifted again. His seat bounced as the truck hit a pothole. "Second light. It's green. Damn tourists on the sidewalk."

"Follow the plan," Nico said. "Just stay steady."

◆

A DEA agent leaned against a parked car on Padre Boulevard. He called in as the vehicle passed by. The gears shifted and the motor groaned as the truck drove through an intersection with the light still green. Two blocks from the bridge, another agent reported it passing by.

◆

The driver spoke again. "Everythin' good." When Nico didn't respond, he repeated his message. Again, no response. He was past the range of the radio, so he dropped it on the passenger's seat and stepped on the accelerator. A horn honked as the truck ran a red light. He tightened his grip on the steering wheel as a car skidded to a stop.

◆

A DEA agent on the sidewalk, wearing shorts and a T-shirt, spoke into his phone. "The idiot ran a light and almost hit a car."

Marla glanced at Standish. "Your officers know not to stop him, right?"

"Yeah, of course."

A police vehicle with its emergency lights flashing pulled out, obstructing the truck a hundred feet from the bridge and stopped. Ricky opened his door, stood with his pistol aimed at the driver, and yelled, "Get out of the truck! You're under arrest."

The driver smiled before opening the door and running into the mix of tourists.

The officers in the police station heard Marla yelling from behind Standish's door.

"You've got to be kidding me!" Marla slammed her fist on the desk. "What is Roberts doing?" She glared at Standish. "You said he was at the bridge. He blew up this entire op!" She picked up the radio and yelled into it, "Get the driver!" She flung the radio at the floor when they reported the perp got away.

Ricky opened the back doors of the truck and pulled a fifty-pound sack onto the ground. He split the sack open with a knife to reveal nothing but sand. A DEA agent stopped behind Ricky to see the contents. "That stupid Adams," Ricky said. "She doesn't know shit from shit."

❖

Nico stood inside the fence and smiled. While his helicopter hovered in the air and reported the incident as planned, he changed the frequency on his walkie-talkie and uttered one word. "Go." A generator hummed from within the building. After several minutes, the captain of a forty-foot fishing boat waved his hand, and the boat eased clear of the dock at the desalination plant.

After returning inside the building, Nico sat down at the dining table, where Harlow placed a breakfast plate of scrambled eggs, wild hog bacon, and two fried quail in front of him.

"Did everything go okay?" Harlow asked.

He took a bite of the bacon. "Yep." He forked the quail meat and held it up in the air. "Those cops don't gotta clue what's going on." He stuffed the meat into his mouth. "Wow, these are good. You sure you don't want one?"

"I told you, I don't like gamey meat." She sat down across from him. "But I'll go with you to the manicure and massage place today."

He scooped up scrambled eggs and put them in his mouth. He nodded. "This soon, again? You must have liked it the last time. We'll have fun."

She rolled her eyes back for a second. "Right." She swept the longer side of her green hair behind her ear. "Your fun and my fun are different."

Chapter 21

Hours later, Harlow gazed out the side window of the truck as Nico drove down Padre Boulevard. "Which one are we going to?"

"You said you didn't like the one we went to last time, so we'll go to the other."

Harlow cracked a smile for a moment. "Sure. Whatever you think."

When the two entered the shop, a thin, middle-aged Asian man smiled and made a subtle bow. "Mr. Palermo, so pleased to have you." He turned his attention to Harlow. "And your sister, we are so happy to have you accompany him." The man clapped at a curtain covering an entrance. Two women passed by the curtain and smiled at their customers. "Mr. Palermo? Raylene is eager to see you again. Ms. Palermo, I have April for you, if that is okay with you."

Harlow made sure not to look at Raylene. "Doesn't matter to me. Anyone is fine."

After sitting at a long table, Raylene, wearing gloves, sat across from Nico, dipped her fingers into a jar of white cream labeled NICO PALERMO, and massaged his hands.

Raylene was Jax's live-in girlfriend, and Nico asked a question to which he already knew the answer. "How's Jax doing?"

"Jax is Jax. You talk to him more than I do."

"Doubt that. You live with him."

Raylene scrunched her nose. "We fuck more than talk."

Nico smiled as he changed the subject. "This stuff's great. The sea salt in that gives me a really fresh tingle in my hands for a long time after I leave."

"Thank you. I'm sure the sauna and massage will help, too."

"I should come every day."

Raylene smiled back. "Oh, that would be nice."

He glanced at Harlow. "Are you liking this?"

"Sure. Great."

Nico noticed something about April. "Why aren't you wearing gloves?"

Raylene answered before April could. "My hands become chapped when I don't wear gloves. So sorry. Want me to remove them?"

"No. Not if it hurts you."

She smiled again. "Thanks. We are ready for the sauna."

Raylene gestured toward a hallway. "Men's changing room on the left, women's on the right. Nico, you are such a great customer here. I'll give you fifteen more minutes for the sauna. Just don't tell my boss. Please enjoy, then come out wrapped in a towel, and someone else will do the massage."

April headed to the front while Raylene directed Nico and Harlow down the hallway. She stopped at the men's door and let Nico enter, then turned to Harlow and nodded. "Forty minutes, and you get your ass back here."

Harlow high-fived her before rushing down the hallway, where Raylene's brother waited upstairs for her. She didn't need to knock on the door. When she entered the room, his back was against the headboard and legs stretched out while strumming his guitar. The sheet covered half his body. He patted the mattress twice. "I'm ready."

Downstairs, Nico stepped out of the sauna with a thick white towel tied around his waist. His hand swept his wet hair from his forehead as he leaned against the wall to catch his balance. "That was too much time for me." His pulse raced and head ached. When he entered the massage room, he snatched a bottle of water from a table and chugged it. Harlow walked in with her towel wrapped above her breasts. He couldn't help but notice her long legs protruding from the short towel and wondered if she wore anything underneath. He ran his hand over his face, trying to wipe the image from his mind.

An hour later, they drove back to the desalination plant. When Harlow closed her bedroom door behind her, she smiled as she rubbed the inside of her thighs. "This has been a good day."

Chapter 22

Marla sat in the rented flat-bottom aluminum boat five minutes before eleven in the morning, wearing the sweatshirt and shorts she bought at Goodwill. Perspiration dripped from her armpit down her side. The sun and humidity were catching up with her. When she tapped the DEA necklace, her phone dinged with a message from the Brownsville office, *Gotcha.*

She touched the holster against her lower back before adjusting the wig. The outboard motor hummed as she spoke on her phone to Standish. "I see a warped, weather-beaten dock on an island with two flags. Have you been here before?"

"No, but I see where you are with your phone location on my screen." Standish sat at her desk and watched a blue dot near the spoil island. "We never island hopped, only backpacked along the shore when we trekked up and down the lagoon. Do you see the broken down oil storage tank?"

"Not yet." Marla killed the engine and let the boat float. "I'm fifty or sixty feet from the dock, and it doesn't look safe enough to walk on, so I'm turning toward the shore." Her shoes sank a few inches into the wet, sludgy sand. "There's nothing but mud, sand, and grass here. Any idea how big this island is?"

"Probably a couple of hundred feet long and just as wide. Most are very small," Standish said.

"Hold on."

"What?"

"I see a small craft pulled up on the shore around the corner."

Jax waited on the far side of the island, listening to their phone conversation.

Marla glanced behind her several times as she stepped along the shoreline. A rusting ten-foot-tall storage tank leaned slightly against a tall pile of dirt. The scent of metal and stagnant petroleum filled the air.

Marla saw something move. "Got to go. Someone near the tank."

Marla slid the phone into her front pocket before patting her gun again. She called out, "Hello?" She waited for an answer. "Hello? Arley sent me." She recognized Jax from the drone pictures at the desalination plant as he pointed a pistol at her and held his finger up to his lips. She stopped and raised her hands. "Hey. No need for that. Arley sent me here. I got money."

Jax reached over, yanked the necklace from around her neck, and before saying a word, flung it into the lagoon. "Seems you have met several new people in town. Bucky and Viggo, the waitresses at the Water Taxi and the Ocean View, and my friends at Pier 19 and the CBD shop."

Marla swallowed hard. Her cover was blown.

Jax took two steps closer to Marla. "And Standish and Roberts."

Why did he mention two cops? Marla swept the wig's hair from her face and glanced both ways, looking for a way out.

Jax asked. "What do you want, Narc?"

The man clearly hadn't bathed recently. Could she anger him and have him do something stupid? "Take a bath." She stepped toward him. "You smell like a—"

"Shut up!" Jax stepped back while pointing the gun at her. "Pitch your phone over here."

She reached into her pocket and dropped it near her feet. "Now what?"

"Back up. I'm not stupid enough to reach for it while you're there."

When she stepped back, Jax pitched it several feet away and yelled, "We don't want you here!"

"We? If you know who I am, then you understand you're in big trouble."

Jax waved the firearm toward the storage tank. "Let's go." She pulled the back of the sweatshirt below her gun and then walked around the side of the tank, with Jax several feet behind. With the phone on the ground, a text from the DEA read on the screen, *Lost connection. Trouble?* Jax ordered her to stop at the cutout section of the tank. The sides were jagged and rusted. A small pile of dead grass rested at the entrance. "Get in."

"Let's talk about this. We can work out a deal for you."

"Inside!" he yelled.

"I don't know what's in there. Do you?" She tried to break his attention. "You've got the gun. Why don't you go in there and make sure it's clear?"

"Get in, bitch, or I'll shoot."

"You won't shoot me because your boss doesn't want me dead, right? Kill a DEA agent, and a dozen more will drag your ass to prison hell."

Jax reached for a flashlight in his back pocket and pitched it near her feet. He still aimed the pistol at her. "Look for yourself."

She turned toward the tank and shined the light inside, revealing inch-deep puddles of oil mixed with water and flakes of rust reflecting a rainbow-like sheen on the floor's surface. Remnants of dried black oil streaked along the walls. From the ceiling, a drop of moisture plunked into a puddle. *How am I going to get out of this mess?*

From the rafters hung a long chain ending three feet above the ground, with a pair of handcuffs connected to the last link. The other cuff was open. "Nope. Don't think so." Marla turned in his direction. For a fleeting second, she saw the gun butt coming toward her. Everything went dark when it slammed against her head.

◆

Marla woke sitting on the ground with her right arm raised above her shoulder and a metal cuff clamped around her wrist. Her vision was blurry, and on the far side of the tank, the wig lay in a puddle of oil. A musty scent of dirt, rust, and petroleum filled the heavy air. Jax's silhouette stood facing the opening of the tank, with a pile of dead grass at his feet. She jerked her arm, and the chain rattled. With her free hand, she rubbed her eyes before asking, "What do you want?"

"I want you to go away forever."

"You would've killed me by now if you were going to, so why am I here?"

He reached inside his shirt pocket, removed a rolled joint, lit it, and took a deep drag before blowing it into the air. "I can kill you whenever I want."

Marla scooted back until the tank's metal wall pressed against her back, and so did the pistol still in her holster. *He's an idiot. He didn't pat me down when I was unconscious.* Her left hand was free, but the holster held the gun for a right-handed draw. "But you won't. You can't do anything, can you? You've got a boss who told you not to. Tell me, who's your boss?"

Jax pointed the gun at her. "Shut up. I can do any damn thing I want." He took another drag from the joint before stepping closer. "I might just kill you right now."

She was a fast-draw champion standing in front of a target with the holster at her side, but not while sitting and the gun behind her. She needed a diversion. "The Cameron County District Attorney's office knows who you are, Jax Whitmore."

He stepped back.

"You know what you get for killing a law enforcement officer? Death. Death by lethal injection. I watched men die. It burns when it crawls in your veins. Big men scream and cry. They cry for their mamas." She shuffled her feet. "And when you die, they dump your cold, dead body in a grave—six feet underground. Is that what you want?" She had no idea what they did with the bodies, but it sounded good as she made it up.

Come on. Do something stupid so I can reach for my gun. "Sometimes you wait ten years before they kill you. Every day, stuck inside a cell, just wide enough to take three steps. All alone. Each day you wake up. Will it be today? Tomorrow? And while you wait, they don't let you talk to anyone. Isolated from everyone and everything. They slide your food tray through a slot, and no one speaks to you. They do that until you beg them to put you out of your misery." The story had a grain of truth, but she would never admit which part. "And that's when they surprise you and drag your sorry ass to the chamber."

"Are you finished with your stupid story?" He scoffed with the joint between his lips. "Remember the bearded guy at the restaurant? Did you ever wonder why he hung around you for no reason? He did it to hack into your phone, and we've been listening to all your conversations."

"Then you know Standish will be here with a busload of cops any minute. And who's *we*? You and who?"

"Standish ain't comin' here. She's waiting for your call. And the GPS on your phone? When I take it back to your beach house and drop it at the front door, she'll just believe you wandered back with no problems." He reached for a burlap sack sitting on the ground near the entrance. "But I don't need to shoot you." He lifted the sack and pitched it between the two of them. It landed with a thud on the metal floor. "If you die from a rattlesnake bite, that'd be considered natural causes, wouldn't it?"

Marla jumped up onto her feet. "Let's not go crazy here. It's still murder. Your fingerprints are everywhere. And your footprints." When three rattlesnakes crawled out of the sack and slithered in different directions, she thought history was repeating itself. *Been there, done that back in Hildebrandt, and don't want to do it again.* "Forensics is good at matching them to your shoes."

Jax scooted part of the dry grass near his feet, dropped the rest of the joint onto the pile, and backed out. "Thanks for the heads-up. I'll wipe everything down and brush away my prints in the dirt." The grass smoldered. "Which will kill you first, snakes or smoke inhalation? I'll come back tonight and uncuff you. Poor little DEA agent...she died by snake bites. See ya."

Her left hand reached behind her, fingers fumbling for the grip of her Glock, and drew. The rattle to the left, a sharp and menacing sound, shattered her concentration as she fired at Jax. The shot echoed, deafening her momentarily from the sound similar to a loud church bell. Jax ran away, leaving behind a bullet hole in the metal shell.

She coughed from the smoke curling inside the tank as the grass caught fire. A chorus of rattles filled the air as the snakes emerged from three directions, hissing and slithering away from the sudden heat.

Marla pulled hard on the chain, trying to break it free from the rafter. The clinking metal only attracted a viper, which slithered closer to her, its forked tongue flicking the air. Her pulse thundered as she aimed again, this time gripping tighter on the gun handle. She exhaled and fired with her left hand. The bullet missed, and the echoes sounded like she was trapped inside a pounding cathedral tower. The snake turned away for a second before turning back toward her. She fired once more. The snake's body jerked and flipped backward.

Before Marla could catch her breath, a second rattle sounded near her other side, coiled and ready to strike. With all her strength, she grabbed onto the chain with her right hand and lifted her legs off the ground. With white fangs protruding, the snake struck. Marla felt the fangs hit the sole of her shoe. She coughed and her eyes stung from the smoke engulfing the interior.

Only feet away, another snake tried to climb the wall of the tank, slithering left and right against the oil-slicked sides. With her left hand, Marla fired off another shot that pierced through its thick body, dropping it to the ground. The recoil spun her around. Her ears throbbed from the sound.

The last snake lay under her feet, tail rattling. Still gripping the chain and swaying above the ground, she had to spin around. Her cuffed arm weakened, muscles burned. Her legs ached from holding them elevated. She fired and missed, pinging the metal floor. She fired again, hitting the snake near the tail of the body. With one last hiss, it slithered away to die.

Marla dropped to her feet, coughing and rubbing her eyes. Her ears hurt. The tang of gunpowder and smoke filled the air. The smoldering grass blocked her exit.

"Leave nothing to chance," she whispered as her foot slipped out of her shoe with the handcuff key inside. "Thank you, my love."

Crosby's words echoed in her memory, as clear as if he stood beside her. She could hear him chuckle. "Always carry a hand-cuff key. To be found handcuffed would be embarrassing for a cop. He had been gone for months now, but his lessons had imprinted in her mind, his voice constantly reminding her of how to stay alive in a world that seemed determined to take her out.

Marla uncuffed her wrist and touched the torn skin, painful, but she was free and still alive. The tank was stifling, and the heat clung to her flesh. Raising her arm and breathing through the sweatshirt at the crook of her elbow, she coughed as the burning grass withered. Slipping her shoe back on, she stomped the grass until the embers disappeared. A fire inside an oil tank, no matter if abandoned for years, might explode, throwing a thousand pieces of hot shrapnel in every direction.

If she stood on the highest part of the tank, maybe she could see where Jax went. Marla gazed outside and wondered how many more rattlers were out there. She had only one choice—climb straight up the chain to the rafters. The only drill at the DEA training center in Quantico she hated, and they made her climb the rope every day. When she reached the top, she pushed open the hatch on the roof, releasing a plume of gray smoke in the air, and hauled herself out. Her wrist throbbed, her ears rang, her arm muscles burned from the climb, and she praised the instructors whom she once cursed on a daily basis.

Marla scanned the lagoon, focusing on the distant water where Jax was now making his escape. Heading south, he was a shadow against the horizon as he sat in a boat with hers in tow. She looked for her phone on the ground, but it wasn't there. He took it.

Her hands tightened into fists, hating the helpless feeling and knowing she had no way to give chase. Standish had told her the waters weren't deep but treacherous between the spoil islands, so she sat down on the roof and waited for help.

The waiting gnawed at her insides, adding to the slow burn of anger. She hated it—the man had slipped away. Jax thought he had won—thought she'd die down there in the dark, surrounded by venom and death. But she wasn't dead. And she wasn't done.

The heat from the sun eased, and the smoke had cleared as the calm late afternoon winds whispered through the grass. At least her ears stopped ringing. She scanned the horizon again, squinting for any sign of a boat or passerby. Time had stretched forever, each second grinding in her mind. If forced to stay the night, she'd have to wrap herself onto the roof with the chain. The ground level was too dangerous, and there were more snakes down there, somewhere. As half the sun sank in the western sky, birds lit on the lagoon's surface, and faint sounds of the water lapped against the dock. And then—there it was. The low hum of a motor.

Chapter 23

Marla leaped to her feet, her eyes locking onto a small aluminum boat moving at a slow pace that had seen better days. A fisherman or someone from one of the neighboring islands? She cupped her hands around her mouth, then stopped. Was this an innocent passerby or a person Jax sent? If she yelled, would he respond with a gunshot? There was only one way to leave the man-made island—on that boat. Marla shouted, her voice tearing through the still air. "Hey! Over here!" She kept her gaze fixed on the man for any movement of a gun. "I need help!"

The boat continued its slow approach, and for a moment, Marla wasn't sure if the person heard her. When she yelled again, her raw throat burned from the smoke she'd inhaled. Waving her arms, relief surged through her body when the craft turned in her direction. An older man was at the helm, his sun-weathered face squinting as he steered toward the island.

Marla slid down the chain to the ground and raced to the dock.

He pulled up to the weather-worn pier, eyeing her dirty clothes and dried blood smeared on her hand and wrist from where the handcuff had bitten into her skin. "What happened to you?" the man asked.

"Long story." Marla latched onto the metal railing. "But I have to get back to the other side of the lagoon at the bridge. Someone took my boat and left me to die."

The man looked out toward where she pointed, then back at her, his eyes widening. "You got a score to settle with him or somethin'?"

Marla nodded. "You could say that. I need a ride."

His wide smile showed pinkish gums with most teeth missing. "Name's Jim. Hop in. Can't say no to a lady in need of revenge."

Marla climbed in and pushed away from the spoil island, knowing Jax had made a critical mistake.

The engine droned, cutting the craft through the still waters and leaving a gentle wake behind. Jim navigated the boat with ease, though he kept shooting curious glances in her direction. Marla didn't care. Her eyes remained locked on the waterline, waiting for the bridge to appear. Every second that passed was a reminder of how close she had come to dying in that tank.

Marla patted the hull. "Can you crank the engine up? I need to get to this guy."

"Gonna have to sit at the bow. If I go faster, my engine digs deeper."

Marla climbed over the seat and knelt at the bow of the boat. "Let's go."

Jim's grip tightened on the throttle as he increased their speed. "Gots to be careful."

"Pick it up. I'll cover any damages."

Marla felt the speed increase more, and the wake widened. She expected Jax's boat to be moored in one of two locations that night. Either way, cameras at the shops should record his image. The boat jerked forward before slowing down.

"Musta hit something," the old man muttered.

She glanced back at him. "What is it?"

"Boat's actin' funny." Jim reached down to tinker with the engine, but as he did, the sputtering turned into a loud cough before it stalled, leaving them drifting in the open water. He leaned over the back corner of the boat and saw the propeller. "Too much grass 'round the prop. Have ta pull it off 'fore we can go any further."

"Sorry, Jim. My fault. I just wanted to catch up."

He knelt closer to the water. "These grasses can clog the motor good if you're not careful."

Every second wasted meant Jax was getting farther away. "Can you fix it?"

Jim gave her a grim look. "Won't be easy out here. I ain't a young man anymore, and reaching around the engine and pullin' grass out is tough."

Marla cursed under her breath, her eyes darting back to where Jax's boat once was. She needed to think—which dock?

Jim reached into the water close to the propeller as Marla noticed something that worried her—a second boat moving fast straight toward them. "Jim? Do you have a gun with you?"

"Me? Nah."

The glint of sunlight off the distant boat's hull caught her eye, and her gut told her it wasn't a friendly fishing vessel.

"Get down!" Marla barked, grabbing Jim by the arm and pulling him below the boat's gunwale.

"What?" His eyes went wide with panic. "What's going on?"

Marla drew her pistol. "That boat coming toward us isn't here to help."

Jim's face drained of color as the approaching boat came into clearer view. Two figures were visible now, one in back next to the motor and the other crouched at the bow, holding what looked unmistakably like a rifle.

Marla ducked lower as the boat sped closer. "Stay down. Intruders." Peering over the edge while calculating the distance, she could take a shot, but their boat bounced on the water too much. She checked the magazine in her Glock—three-fourths full.

The man with the rifle raised it to his shoulder.

"Damn it," Marla whispered.

The first shot rang out. A high-pitched crack with an echo. Water splashed a few feet in front of them.

"What the hell?" Jim yelled.

"Stay down!" Marla eyed the oncoming boat again, bouncing against the waves. It'd be pure luck if he hit their boat. The rifle fired again, with the bullet ripping against the side of the hull and through the other side. So much for her luck. Jim yelled as he wrapped his hands around his head and curled his legs.

Marla took another look. Not close enough for her pistol. She had to do something—swinging around and firing twice, she missed. The recoil from the gun sent a jolt of pain through her injured wrist. At least their boat slowed. The rifleman stood and took aim once more. His third shot splashed short of the bow. Marla fired again. Blood splattered from the left thigh, and the man dropped to his knees, but held onto the rifle.

Jim peeked from his hiding spot. "Holy hell, lady. You're pretty good with that thing."

"Not good enough. I was aiming for the chest." Marla glanced over the side at the murky water. "Jump in."

Jim rolled over the side and splashed in the water. Marla followed just as the rifle shot again, echoing across the lagoon. A bullet ripped through the stern of their boat where Jim had been. "You stay down!"

They both ducked when another rifle fired. The echo sounded harder, louder. A bigger caliber bullet. Marla glanced up to see the intruder holding the rifle jerk before falling out of the boat. The weapon bounced once on the boat's gunwale, then disappeared into the water. Marla smiled as another boat fifty yards back headed toward them. *Has to be Brownsville DEA.*

The second intruder gunned his outboard motor and veered away. Another rifle shot fired, knocking the man out of the boat.

"You okay?" Marla asked.

Jim nodded, his hands shaking. "Yeah, think so. I kin get ta the prop now." He ripped away the grass.

"All right. Back in." Marla helped Jim roll into the boat, her mind already turning to Jax. As the outboard finally came to life, Marla sat down and motioned to the other craft. "Go over there."

Jim swept water from his face. "You sure about this, lady? What about those others?"

"Don't worry. They're with me." As Jim's boat edged closer to the two DEA agents, Marla called out, "Thanks, guys. I owe you."

Special Agent Adrian Allison laid his rifle inside the boat. "You're welcome."

Special Agent Chris Miller said, "When your necklace went blank and you didn't respond to the text, we knew there was trouble. Just glad to get here when we did. Who's your buddy?"

"Jim," Marla said. "Jim...uh, what's your last name?"

Jim smiled as he slowly shook his head. "Nothin'...anythin', anythin' you want it ta be."

Chris jumped out of his boat. The water stood knee-high. He rolled one of the dead men over to see the face. "Ah. I know this guy. Cartel." He checked the pockets, empty. Chris slogged to the other body and rolled it over. "Yep. Cartel too." He dug into the pockets and found folded money. "Two Franklins, here." He gestured to Marla. "How'd they know you were out here?"

"Jax Whitmore tried to kill me on a spoil island back there. Guessing he sent these two to make sure I was dead."

"Do we need to hit where he lives?" Adrian asked.

"Probably, but don't know where that is. I can get Sergeant Standish to help with that."

"Your call," Chris said as he loaded the bodies back into the intruder's boat.

"Yeah." Adrian pitched a rope to Chris. "We'll drag this boat back to the shore."

"I'll call Standish and have someone meet you," Marla said and then turned to Jim. "Do you have a phone on you?"

"Nah. Never needed one." He pointed to the motor. "But I got the prop cleaned off."

"No gun? No phone? Are you just a crazy old man?"

His toothless smile gave it all away. "Oh, yeah. That's me. Come out and catch a few, watch the sunrises and sunsets. Mornings are better. More fish, less skeeters. I tell you, lady, this is the most fun I had in twenty years. Guessin' it might be another twenty 'fore something like this happens again."

Marla shook her head and grinned at Jim. *Some people's lives are hectic and others just never make waves.* She caught Adrian's attention. "Mind if I use your phone to call all this in?" She called Standish and reported the incident. "Do you have my phone's location on your screen?"

Standish glanced at her laptop on her desk. "Looks like you are heading down Padre Boulevard. Just turned off and onto the beach near your rental. Are you there?"

"No, Jax stole it."

"Well, he's there. Where are you?"

"Middle of the lagoon. Need assistance with two bodies. I'm using another agent's phone, so I'll ping you where I am."

"I'll send two officers. How did Jax know you were there?"

"He hacked into my phone and heard our conversation. Thinks I'm dead at the spoil island. Give you the details later, but you need to get an arrest warrant for Whitmore ASAP. And you need one for Arley at the Jamaican CBD shop. He set me up for the ambush."

"Got it."

After Marla gave the phone back to Adrian, she asked for one of the hundred-dollar bills. She thanked Jim for the lift and handed the wet money to him.

Jim meandered back to the center of the lagoon, a hundred bucks richer and a fun memory for life.

Chapter 24

Marla parked her truck next to the beach house, and Festus came sprinting from behind the sand dunes to meet her. Crouching down and expecting him to dash around her as usual, instead, he leaped into her lap. She toppled back onto the damp sand, catching him in her arms. "Festus, hold on, boy." When she let go, he ran circles around her until she told him to stop, then sat with his tongue hanging out, panting heavily.

Marla's phone buzzed on the porch. *Standish was right. Jax had dropped it near the front door.* With sand brushed from her clothes, she checked her phone, revealing a long-forgotten number she wished to remain forgotten. Apprehension and childhood remembrances evoked recollections she had long suppressed. Caught between her aversion to the caller and a curiosity that gnawed at her insides like a hungry tiger shark, she winced when she answered. "Hello?"

"Come see me," said a familiar voice on the other end.

Marla was already annoyed with the caller. "Why would I ever do that?"

"I haven't seen you in a while."

"Maybe I don't want to."

"Maybe you should."

Her grip tightened on the phone. "Why now? What's this about?"

"If you come over, I'll tell you."

"I'm busy."

"In South Padre? Doubtful." The tone was casual, but the words made her pulse race. "I hear it's a nice time for spring breakers. Oh...I understand you took scuba lessons. Planning on diving in the Gulf? I'm able to arrange something for you."

Her stomach dropped. *How does he know about the lessons?* "I don't want your help," she snapped back before ending the call.

The phone buzzed again before she had a chance to stick it in her back pocket. She answered. "What?"

"Come to the house." The voice was as calm as ever. "I have information you need."

"Where are you? In Texas...the US...Europe?" She paused. "And besides, what makes you think you know what I need?"

"You're asking the wrong question."

"What's the right question?"

"I've been watching you."

Marla spun around, looking for anyone suspicious.

"I know what you want."

Marla reached for the DEA necklace, but remembered Jax threw it in the lagoon, then capitulated with a shrug. "I'm armed."

"I'll have someone pick you up at your place in five minutes."

"Fifteen minutes. I stink like a redneck on an oil derrick. And how do you know where I am?"

"Still asking the wrong question."

The call ended before she could respond, leaving her standing there, torn between dread and curiosity.

◆

Marla showered off the lagoon water and changed into her white shirt, black pants, and windbreaker. It wouldn't have bothered her to dish out the rancid odor to the person she was meeting, but she couldn't stand to smell herself.

After an SUV stopped beside the beach house, Marla contemplated her options should the driver jump out after her. The top of his unkempt hair scraped the headliner, scraggly beard, bear paw hands, and shoulders wider than the seat were more than she wanted to tangle with. He said nothing as he glared at her. Reluctantly, Marla climbed into the four-wheel-drive vehicle, with Festus hopping into her lap. They crossed the Queen Isabella Causeway Bridge as the sun had started its downhill slide in the sky. She asked, "Where are we going?"

"Might as well sit back and relax." The driver glanced at the dog, who stared back at him. "Another fifteen or twenty minutes."

Repetitive whups in the air made Marla look out the side window. Two private helicopters lifted higher in the distance before moving forward. "What are those for?"

"Hog killing machines."

"What?"

"Those take people out to hunt feral hogs. Big business around here. A hoard of twenty or thirty can ravage a farmer's field at night."

"They're called a sounder, not a hoard," Marla said.

"Whatever. All I know is, they're worse than any locust plague in the Bible."

Marla's palm rested on top of Festus's back as he sat in her lap. "Those ever cross into Mexico?"

The driver glanced at Marla again before returning his eyes back to the road. "To hunt hogs?"

"No. To pick up contraband."

"You're asking the wrong guy."

"I'm guessing you know Leo Searcy. So, maybe I'm asking the right guy."

He glanced at her one more time, but didn't respond to the question. "We'll be there shortly."

When the driver slowed, Marla noted the time on the dashboard clock—eighteen minutes on a highway traveling at seventy miles per hour after they crossed the bridge. They had to be about ten miles from the Rio Grande—and Mexico. After passing a long stretch of white wooden fencing that bordered a pasture with a few cattle grazing, the driver turned into the gated property. Marla estimated the lot to be twenty-plus acres, reminiscent of a nineteenth-century Gentleman's ranch where affluent men raised cattle or horses at their pleasure. They pulled into the driveway of a modest, one-story house, the rough gravel crunching beneath the tires as the vehicle parked near the front steps. A cement truck sat about eighty yards from the house, with three men working around it. The truck's drum spun, and a gray slurry slid down the channel from the back end and onto the ground. *A new foundation for what?*

When she opened the vehicle door, Festus jumped over her lap and onto the ground. The driver remained behind the wheel. The front door of the house opened, and two young women in scanty clothes and high heels ignored Marla while rushing to jump into the car.

Okay. Two from the oldest profession. What else is not right here?

Two men in work clothes exited the house and closed the door. They stepped away too fast for Marla to read the logo on the left chest area. They jumped into a van ahead of the vehicle she was in and sped away. The SUV with the two women and the driver followed close behind. Both vehicles turned, headed toward the Gulf, and soon disappeared down the road. "Kinda limits our chances of getting back to town, Festus."

After Marla stepped to the front door, she knocked twice. A young man in his early twenties, with a rough appearance and a hardened expression, opened it. "Adams?" He asked in a flat tone.

"Yes." Her windbreaker hid the gun and holster attached to the waistband. "I'm expected."

"Have to frisk you."

With a flat expression, Marla stared at the man. "I'd let you talk to the last man who tried that, but he's dead."

The young man paused a long moment before stepping aside. "You know where to go?"

She nodded and entered, with Festus following close behind. The house had an odd stillness to it as she made her way through the corridor. Expensive light fixtures and furniture gave the place a sense of luxury—different from the deceptive blandness of the outside.

When Marla reached the door left ajar, she knelt beside Festus and stroked his fur. "Be good," she whispered. "I don't trust this person one bit, but I need you to stay calm."

Festus wagged his tail once, then sat silent but alert.

She rapped twice on the door, then pushed it open. An aging man with salt and pepper hair, wearing an expensive business jacket, sat behind an old desk cluttered with papers. He looked up, and despite the wear and tear of time, he still exuded an aura of calculated control.

Marla entered and took a seat in the only other chair in the room. "Hello, Uncle Leo." Her voice dripped with sarcasm.

Leo reclined in his chair. "It's been a while since you called me that."

"Not since I uncovered the truth."

He rose and stepped around the desk. "We could rehash the past or have a drink and talk about the future. Follow me."

Like a pensive cat, Marla sat in the chair as Leo walked out. He peered at the dog sitting still before turning down the hallway. The heel of Marla's shoe tapped a steady rhythm against the floor before she stood and exited the room. Festus escorted her through the hallway. She entered a room with a polished mahogany bar and several floor lamps casting soft incandescent light. A stainless steel sink and shelves of clean glasses were along one wall.

Leo stood behind the bar and reached for two glasses. "What'll you have?"

"I'm not here to drink," Marla shot back. "Let's just cut to the chase. After what happened in Hildebrant, you left me...you left the family."

"Didn't see a need to hang around."

"No reason to stay after Searcy died?"

"You still call your father by his last name?"

"My father? It was always clear to you I wasn't truly part of his family...your family. You knew Searcy wasn't my real father."

Leo poured two glasses of whiskey, setting one on the bar in front of her. "You want to talk about my brother? Fine. But I wasn't aware of all his actions—not until it was too late."

Marla narrowed her eyes. "Too late, my ass. You were close by the whole time, watching me grow up, knowing I didn't belong."

"I didn't raise you," Leo replied. "I wasn't the one who made those decisions."

Marla raised her voice. "But you didn't stop him either."

Leo took a slow sip of his drink. "I told the police everything when my brother died. After you...never mind. My conscience is clear."

"Well, good for you," she said with a bitter slash of her tongue. "You should have done more."

His gaze never left her as he took a drink. "Perhaps. But that's in the past, Marla. Dwelling on it won't help you now or ever. Move on and come work for me."

Marla rested her elbows on the bar. "Work for you? Is that your solution to all the death in my hometown?"

Leo smiled, though it never reached his eyes. "My business ventures could be mutually beneficial to us both. You're smart. Capable. Time to move on with your life."

Marla's voice sharpened. "Yeah? Well, you're a great visionary."

Still holding his glass, he raised his voice, "You can't live in the past forever, Marla. Wanna be the big hero? Then you'll die like the rest of the hero Feds."

"Maybe," she said.

"I've seen your little ranch you play with during your two seconds of downtime from your...work."

Marla slapped the glass off the counter and spiraled across the room. Bourbon sprayed the air. "I'm doing the best I can!"

"Are you looking to spend the rest of your life doing what? A DEA agent until you're forty?" Leo laughed. "That's when they give you a desk and you wish you were anywhere else in the world except there." Leo shrugged. "Or run a tiny ranch with a hundred cattle? It's a losing business, both ways...but I could make things better for you."

"So, suddenly, you want to dish out charity. I don't want your charity!"

"I'm trying to help you out, so listen."

Marla waited a moment. *He's dirty. I know it. Come on, Uncle Leo, tell me how dirty you are.* "So, what exactly are you offering?"

Leo leaned back, scrutinizing her. "I've got plans, lots of plans, and one is to expand into a cattle business bigger than your LEGO like playhouse of a ranch."

Marla let it go. She knew he wanted to see her lose it, but she wasn't going to let that happen. She gazed out the large window on the back wall. In the distance were several cattle. "How many head do you have?"

Leo scratched the front of his neck. "Sixteen here, close to two hundred about a mile away. We could increase your herd, make it a thousand head."

"I don't have that much land for a thousand."

"We could buy out your neighbors."

"I don't know anybody who wants to sell."

"Leave that problem up to me. Listen, Marla, it's a business deal for both of us. I'm sorry about all that happened in Hildebrandt, and...maybe this is my way of making amends."

She stared at him. *Don't trust him. Don't do it. Bad blood always pools at the bottom of the family tree. But the money to expand an all-woman ranch? Would Leo be a silent partner and let that happen?*

"But what's important is you'll need more than Cassie and Trixie." He sipped his drink again. "Trixie's not so dependable, is she? She might leave someday."

"How do you know anything about my employees? You damn well better leave them out of any of your doings!"

"So, we agree to expand? A thousand head? And more help?"

Is he a godsend, or will he take everything away from me? Show me your true colors, you son of a bitch. "Tell me how exactly that might work." Marla's tone grew more pointed. "Where's the money coming from, and what else are you involved in?" She paused, hoping her next question would throw him off. "Last night at the outside concert in Padre, I saw you on stage talking to what looked like a Jamaican. He handed you a small package. What was that about? Are you a big man with a backstage pass? Are you the one who's fronting the bands coming into town by selling drugs for them? To them? And the city councilman on stage beside you—slipping a little something to him to keep things nice and quiet around the island?"

Leo's smile faltered, and a chill crept into his voice. "Don't know what you're talking about."

"I'm just asking questions." Marla held Leo's gaze. "You're asking me to be involved in this, so I deserve a little clarification. What exactly do you do?"

Leo poured himself another drink. "I run a cattle business and a hog killing business with nothing to hide. Borderline Hog Hunters is the company name, and I have two helicopters."

The helicopters? She continued her unwavering stare. "What does killing hogs have to do with cattle ranching?"

Leo finished the whiskey while ignoring her question. "You're getting a chance to start fresh. Leave behind your past and create something bigger than what you have imagined."

Marla glanced at a roach skittering along the baseboard. "And all it'll cost me is my integrity, right?"

"Integrity's a funny word." Leo drummed his fingertips on the counter. "Wanna keep chasing ghosts? Or do you want a future?"

"You make it sound like you're doing me a favor," Marla shot back. "But we both know this is about more than just cattle. So, what's your angle...Leo? Are you involved with the recent fenethylline outbreak in this town? Mexico? Syria? Russia? That's at least fifty years in prison."

Leo took a step toward her before stopping and regaining his composure. "Is that what you think?" He shook his head. "I have always run legitimate business ventures."

Marla forced a tight smile. "Legitimate? I remember several instances when I was a teenager and Searcy had to get you out of trouble."

Leo replied calmly. "He was a good man and a good father to you."

"He kidnapped me and killed people! I'm as much related to him as I am to that roach on the floor."

"You've done your share of killing." He swirled the ice in the glass. "Do you intend to kill it, too?"

"No. I'll leave it amongst its friends. Among your—"

"Let's start with your ranch, and if it does well, we can move on to bigger projects."

Marla's phone rang. She was glad for the interruption. "Hello?"

"Marla," Cassie's voice came through with an urgency. "The calving's started, and I need help."

Irritated by the call, Marla was paying Cassie to run the ranch. "I'm busy. Where's Trixie?"

"She's gone," Cassie replied.

"Where'd she go?"

"Who knows? I'm out here all alone and need help."

Marla lowered the phone from her ear while glaring at Leo. "What the hell did you do? Where's Trixie, you son of a bitch!"

He shook his head. "Not sure what you're talking about."

Marla unzipped her windbreaker and placed her hand on top of her gun.

"You going to kill me, too?" Leo asked.

"What did you say?" Cassie asked on the phone.

"I'll leave your cockroach friends to do that for me." Marla lowered her hand from the gun and returned the phone to her ear. "I'm two hundred and fifty miles from there, Cassie. That's hours away. Ask around for help in town."

"I can't leave and make a dozen phone calls. I'm busy with the herd, and I need you here. Understand? Here, now!"

Leo overheard the conversation and raised his hand. "Take my helicopter."

Marla lowered the phone again. "What?"

"Told you. I run a feral hunting business with helicopters."

Like a bolt from the blue, it hit her. *The cement truck outside is for another landing pad.*

"Whatever I can do to help," Leo said.

Marla shot him a disdainful look. "I don't need your help."

Leo placed the empty glass on the bar. "Family takes care of family...and new business partners. I can get you there in a little more than an hour. Without an extra hand there, you could lose several of your herd."

"Did you do something to Trixie? Where is she?"

"I heard your conversation," Leo said. "If you want, I could call your boss in San Antone and tell him you have to rush back.

I'm sure he'll understand whatever you're doing here can wait a few days."

Chapter 25

The helicopter was a sleek black machine with a logo of a dead hog on the side, and the company name underneath—Borderline Hog Hunters. Blades whirled above Marla's head in a steady rhythm as they headed for the ranch. Her ranch was five minutes away. She left her position in Padre and hadn't told her boss. How deep a hole had she dug herself into? AWOL without a chance of parole if they found out. Festus fidgeted in her lap, almost as if he smelled home.

Marla's heart jumped to her throat when she remembered Standish could track her phone. Was she watching Marla's location on her computer screen? Turning it off wouldn't stop the tracker. Dropping it in a bucket of water might work, but then nobody could reach her, leaving an animated voice on the other person's phone, *This phone is not accepting calls*. An answer Tillman or Standish would not appreciate. Too late to do anything now.

The weight of Trixie's sudden disappearance loomed over Marla like a dark cloud. Gone without a trace, and Marla couldn't shake the gnawing feeling that Leo had something to do with it.

Cassie stood tall, with a determined expression on her face, while holding the reins of two saddled horses with one hand. The familiar whup whup whup sound grew as a black dot in the sky moved closer.

As the ranch came into Marla's view, cattle grazed in the distance along rolling hills with tall trees surrounding the perimeter. She gripped the cool metal grab bar for balance as the helicopter's landing skids hit the ground with a jolt. She flipped the headphones off, opened the cockpit door, and helped Festus out before she ran while ducking her head.

Cassie tilted the bill of her cap down to shield her eyes from the blowing dirt. Her work clothes were crumpled and dusty, and strands of hair whipped across her cheeks as the helicopter engine revved higher and lifted off the ground into the blue sky.

"Where did that come from?" Cassie asked, gesturing toward the helicopter.

"Don't ask any questions about anything." Marla's hand swept along Daisy's smooth coat. The animals were well-groomed, ears alert, and eager for work.

Cassie held a cap in her hand for Marla to take. "I've got most of the heifers showing signs in the calving barn. Four delivered so far this morning, three on their own, and one I had to use a calf puller. We have twenty or so still out in the pasture, and it's time to go check on them. Saddle up, Boss."

Marla took the cap and rubbed her thumb over the heart logo with the female symbol in the center before slipping it on her head. She grasped the reins and mounted her horse. "I'm ready."

"Let's go," Cassie said as she mounted her horse.

Marla's phone rang in her back pocket. "Hello?"

"I glanced at my computer," Standish said. "Your phone is near San Antone."

"I'll explain later. Keep it to yourself for now. Got to go." Marla slipped the phone into her back pocket. "Okay. Ready."

Cassie adjusted her cap. "I just don't get it. One minute, I have help, and the next, the girl vanishes."

Marla swallowed hard. "I've thought about that, too."

"I mean, it's possible she could've left on her own," Cassie shook her head, "but...she didn't give notice or ask for her wages, and I just don't think Trixie's the kind who'd walk off and leave me alone. And besides, if she just up and left, she stole one of your horses."

The breeze carried a scent of grass and earth, mixed with a faint hint of exhaust fumes from the helicopter. I branded my horses, and selling them at an auction might be difficult for anyone. We can't waste time thinking about that now."

"Right," Cassie snapped the reins.

They rode out to the pasture with the steady rhythm of the horses' movements beneath them. Cows lay scattered over the field, some resting, others grazing.

"Over there." Cassie pointed toward the far end of the pasture. "I missed that one, a new calf. Let me go tag it real quick."

After an hour, they returned to the calving barn to inspect the heifers. Marla knew Cassie had much more experience in calving than she did, so she let Cassie take the lead.

Marla watched a restless heifer in a pen, its tail whipping. "That one looks just about ready, but the water bag is still intact."

Cassie briefly checked the time she wrote on the sheet taped to the railing when the cow went into the pen. "Looks like it's been almost three hours. Too long. She needs help."

They approached the laboring cow. It groaned and strained with contractions. They positioned themselves and waited for the next contraction. The calf wasn't making much progress.

Marla said, "I should get the chains ready."

"Yep. I'll make sure her head is safely in the stanchion."

Cassie cut the water bag and felt inside. "All good. Head and legs coming out first. Let's get the chains wrapped around the calf's feet."

"Ready?" Marla asked, and Cassie nodded. "Pull."

The calf's head emerged. They pulled again with the uterine contraction.

"Come on, girl," Cassie said. "Last time." And with one last pull, the calf landed on the hay-covered ground.

"Good job!" Marla exclaimed, relief washing over her as the mother instinctively started cleaning her newborn.

Several hours later, Marla sank to her haunches in exhaustion. "What just happened? These cows have a fire sale on calves?"

"Yeah. That's been more than I have helped deliver in a day. But it's not done yet. Got the last mother two pens over. I checked on her just a short time before this last one delivered, and it's breech."

Marla stood and stepped to the pen. "She's tired. Think we need to call the vet?"

"Let me try to turn it around first. I got a good feeling about it." Cassie laid the chains on the railing. "Just in case."

After a few moments, Cassie stopped. "Calf is too big. I can't get it turned, but got the legs out in the birthing canal. We can wrap the chains around the hind legs and pull it out."

They each wrapped the end of a chain around the calf's legs. "This one will be harder. The calf is bigger. We do this together. Ready?"

Marla nodded, the moment settling heavily on her shoulders. "Can't afford to lose her, or the calf."

"We do what we have to do," Cassie replied with a steady voice. "Pull."

They both pulled on their chains. Marla's knuckles whitened as she held her breath, her body straining with every ounce of strength. The tension mounted as they pulled with all their might against the calf stuck tight in the birthing canal.

"Come on, come on!" Cassie pulled harder, but the calf didn't budge. The cow let out a distressed moan.

"Go!" Marla yelled, and they pulled together again. With a final effort, the calf slipped free, landing in the hay with a soft thud. The relief for all was immediate.

"Got it!" Marla rushed to clear the calf's mouth and nose.

As Cassie removed the chains from the newborn, she thought of Trixie and couldn't shake the feeling that something wasn't right. "Marla," Cassie said. "What if something happened to Trixie?"

Marla paused. She knew more than what she was willing to say...or not say. "What do you mean?"

"I'm thinking maybe she fell off her horse and broke a leg."

Marla's voice trembled a little as she mumbled, "Leo." *The son of a bitch better not have done anything to her.* The spark of their achievement vanished. "You really think so? I don't imagine it's anything bad, do you?"

"And no calls from her. Maybe someone took her."

"Why would someone take her?" Marla asked.

"I don't know. Why *would* someone do that?" Cassie could see Marla's resolve hardening. "No surprise if someone doesn't like the idea of a bunch of women bustin' cattle. One of us might be next. We can't just ignore it."

"All right," Marla said. "I'll call the sheriff's department to look for her, then let's finish up here and go check the rest of the cattle. We'll keep an eye out for her and her horse. We can't afford to let our guard down, especially if you think someone's out there. I was going to say we split up and cover more of the herd, but I think it's best to stay together for now."

"Agreed." A sense of urgency settled over Cassie.

They moved to check on the other cows as the sun eased closer to the hilltops. Together, they patrolled the pasture. Marla couldn't ignore the possibility of one of Leo's men out there watching them just beyond their sight.

The night was busy, with them checking the herd every few hours. As a yellow sun rose above the tree line, warming the morning air, the sheriff's department called with nothing new about Trixie.

Marla yawned. "We've been up too long. Need sleep."

"No. Not yet for me," Cassie said. "I'll head back out and look for Trixie."

"Let the law search for her."

"The law? What do they do around here..." Cassie realized she was talking to a former Hildebrant police officer and current DEA Special Agent. "Oops. Sorry."

"Don't worry. Think you can handle it out there?"

Cassie nodded. "Sure. Easier to see intruders and cattle in trouble during daylight."

"Keep your phone close and call me with anything."

Upon reaching the house, Marla dismounted Daisy, removed the saddle, and placed her horse in the barn stall. As she headed for the house, she called the San Antonio office. Festus followed behind.

"Tillman here."

"This is Adams, sir."

"Jeez, Marla. Until this week, we were just regular ol' Special Agents. Don't give me this 'Adams, sir' stuff."

Marla chuckled. "Thanks, Sam."

"What's up?"

Festus stopped on the wooden porch and sat as Marla entered the house. "Two things. The veterinarian at NOAA said they were not able to get the name of the recipient of the orthopedic shoulder joint yet. He sent me photos of the joint and the number. Unfortunately, it has a deep scratch from a shark tooth halfway through it. Maybe the DEA forensic lab can figure out the number and once we have it, we should have more influence than NOAA in getting the person's name. I'll forward them to you."

"I'll have the lab get on it. What's the second?"

She hesitated before saying. "I'm reporting I am back home. Part of my help at the ranch quit just before the cows started calving. One person can't manage all of them by herself. I'll try to return to the island as soon as possible." She chuckled. "And the fantastic odor of two decaying sharks."

Tillman said, "Already knew you were home."

Marla blinked a few times. "How could you know that?"

"Someone called and informed us...me, that you had left."

"Who?

What's the reason behind someone calling the office? Tell me who called."

"You know I can't say. But you need to get back there sooner than later."

"Okay. Is it Leo Searcy?"

"What do you know about him?"

She scoffed. "Sam? You haven't reviewed my file, have you?"

"Marla…I will be in this office only until Borland returns from vacation. I am definitely not diving into any agents' personal files."

"That's good to know. Leo Searcy is my so-called, somewhat uncle."

"I had no idea."

"So, he offered me a job, leave the DEA, run the ranch, and, I'm certain, other things if I said yes. Of course, I said no. That is when my ranch hand, Cassie, called me and needed me back here. Leo offered his helicopter so I could get here in an hour, instead of driving four hours. *Did Leo just get me fired? Was that his motive?*

After Tillman didn't respond to her, she said, "At least give me a response. A clearing of your throat means yes." She heard nothing. "Are you sure?" She heard nothing. "And Standish?" Again, nothing. "Oh, holy cow! Is it Ricky Roberts? How could he know?"

Tillman spoke. "I have to go, and you should get back to work before someone above me finds out."

After Tillman ended the call, the last twenty-four hours caught up with her. With her eyes burning and head hurting, Marla rested on the couch and fell asleep.

Chapter 26

Festus barked once and woke Marla. She sat up and swept her hands over her face and hair. "What are you, my alarm clock?" The dog barked again.

Okay. Better call Cassie. "Cass? Anything from Trixie?"

"No. Nothing. Maybe she really did leave us."

"Maybe. Any more new calves?" Marla asked.

"Sure," Cassie said. "So far, all good."

"Where are you?"

"On the west side."

"Okay," Marla said, "I'll head out to the east. Come back to the house, rest up, and get breakfast."

Cassie smirked. "Are you actually cooking something?"

"If you want me to leave peanut butter on toast for you, otherwise, you better make it." Marla smiled as she disconnected the call and trekked to the barn to saddle a horse. In separate stalls, Daisy and Blackie pranced on their front legs. "Good morning, almost afternoon, to both of you." She rubbed Daisy's head and handed her a carrot. "I'm taking your boyfriend out today. Hope you don't mind. I'll let you rest for the day."

Marla saddled Blackie. Just as she started to head out, a few hundred yards away, she noticed a horse ambling toward the barn with a person bent forward. Marla hopped on her horse and raced out. Trixie had slumped over the saddle horn, her clothes ripped, cap pulled down tight on her head, and feet bare.

She looked nothing like the last time Marla saw her: vibrant, purple hair stuck out from under the baseball cap, with a clean, crisp denim shirt and pants, and purple boots. Marla jumped off Blackie and helped Trixie off the horse.

"What happened? Can you stand?"

Trixie looked up, wearing a half smile with dried blood on her swollen lips. "I didn't tell them about my money."

"What are you talking about? You look bad. Here, sit. What money?"

It all flashed in Trixie's mind, before being hired by Marla, the Saddle Horn Bar with a Jabba the Hutt-sized owner, his attempted blackmail, and her stealing his hundred thousand after the office caught fire, with no one the wiser. She swung her arm away. "I'm fine. I've been in worse fights."

"Where have you been? What fights?"

"Those pansies. They took me to an old barn somewhere, thinkin' they're tough when I'm tied to a chair. They even stole my boots off my feet and started hitting me with them. Then one asshole got a call, and they untied me. That was a big mistake, thinking I was a wimpy little girl. I had been eyeing a hammer in the corner for hours. One won't walk for a long time, and the other won't ever talk again."

Marla's phone rang in her back pocket. It was a number she recognized. "What do you want?"

"Got your help back?" Leo asked. "We should talk about your new job."

Marla glanced at Trixie before replying. "Did you do this?"

"Me? No. I'm always here when anyone needs help, and you need help."

"I don't want your help. Not after someone beat the bejesus out of my ranch hand, but this was no secret to you, was it?"

"Bullshit on that!" Trixie said. "I don't need any help with anything." She grasped the saddle horn and mounted her horse. "See? I'm ready."

"Sounds like she is just fine. I'll send the helicopter for you."

What does he want? Keep your friends close and your sort of nieces closer? "If you're involved in this, I'm…"

"We're family. I do what is best for the family," Leo said.

Marla scoffed. "That's not what your brother did. Send your copter."

◆

Marla, Cassie, and Trixie gathered near the house and barn and discussed the plans for the rest of the calving season. "Four or five days, six at tops to finish all the birthing," Marla said. "Any problems, call the vet. I have already contacted him and told him Cassie is lead on all of this. What she says goes."

Cassie asked, "Trix? You good?"

Her lips swollen, blue discoloration across her left cheek and around her right eye. "Hell, yes. Nothin' bad happened to me."

A repetitive whup grew louder as the helicopter came closer. Cassie closed the barn door to keep the wind from blowing inside and spooking the horses. The chickens scurried into the coop as the helicopter eased toward the ground, with the dust and dirt swirling.

Marla texted Tillman, *Returning to the island. No need to ask how.* She texted Standish, *Pick me up on the north side of town at Edwin King Atwood Park in an hour.* After handing her dirty cap back to Cassie, Marla climbed into the two-man cockpit, buckled up, and put on the headphones. She patted her thigh for Festus to jump into her lap and then nodded at the pilot.

The engine surged with power, and the blades spun faster as the helicopter headed south. Neither spoke for forty minutes.

When the familiar landscape of the ocean came closer, Marla adjusted her headset. "Drop me off at the Edwin King Atwood Park."

The pilot continued to look straight ahead as he pulled the microphone connected to the headset closer to his mouth. "My instructions are to land on Mr. Searcy's pad."

Marla drew her pistol from the holster. "I will shoot this instrument panel if you try to land there."

"And kill both of us?"

The gun edged closer to the panel. "As soon as this touches the ground, I'll shoot, and you'll be out of a job. Leo Searcy will send you back to whatever rock you came from."

"We're about ten minutes out. I need to contact him about the change."

She pushed the gun muzzle against his thigh. "You do, and I'll shoot you before I destroy this piece of flying crap."

He eased the stick left as the copter headed toward the island's north side. Marla glanced over the instrument panel to see Standish's vehicle parked sideways on the highway with the emergency lights flashing.

"There," Marla said.

"I can't land on the beach. Too soft. And there are cars in the lot."

"Over there. On the road."

After landing and the engine slowed, she swung the door open. Festus jumped from her lap to the road and waited for her. "Thanks for the ride."

"If I lose my license over this, I'm saying you kidnapped me at gunpoint."

"Didn't realize you had a license, but I may look into it."

Marla closed the door and covered her face when the engine revved and sand flew in the air. As the helicopter lifted off the ground, she ran to Standish's Bronco, with Festus following.

"Welcome back," Standish said when the door opened.

After the two climbed into the vehicle and closed the doors, they headed for the beach house. With a stern voice, Marla asked, "How long have you known Roberts?"

Standish stuck a piece of gum in her mouth. "Since he was a kid."

"Is he in debt? A gambler? Divorce lawyers sucking all the money out of his account?"

Standish turned off the road toward the beach. "What's going on?"

"He called my office and reported I left the island and returned to my ranch. There is only one way he could know that."

"How?"

"You."

"Whoa there, girl. Just what are you saying?"

"We talked when I was at my ranch. You are the only one who knew."

Standish stopped beside the beach house. "I sat in my office when you called. I told no one."

"Anybody else sitting in your office when I called?"

"Every two minutes, someone walks into my office and gives or takes from me. Ricky came in while we spoke, but a half dozen others did, too." Standish rolled her window down and spat out the gum. "I'm not worried about my end. What about your end? After you climbed into Leo Searcy's helicopter at no charge, did he tell someone to call and pretend to be Officer Roberts? Did you think about that?"

"No, I didn't."

Standish held her hand in the air to change the subject. "The judge signed off on the arrest of Jax Whitmore and a search warrant for his place."

"Where's that?"

"Another spoil island. You up to it?"

"Oh, hell, yes. I'm all in."

Chapter 27

Jax's phone rang while helping to wrap the fenethylline tablets in waterproof plastic. He lifted the mask from his face. "Yeah?"

Ricky spoke into his phone while standing alone in the police station bathroom. "Need to speak with you."

"All right. Go ahead."

"Not on the phone. I'll meet you at your place in forty-five minutes."

"I'm busy," Jax said. "Tell me what you want."

"Busy doing what?"

"None of your business what I'm doing."

Ricky heard a voice outside the doorway. "Hold on a minute." He muted the phone, entered the toilet stall, and locked the door as someone came in and used the urinal. After the water cut off from the sink and the door opened and closed again, he spoke. "Okay, clear."

"Did you not hear what I just said?" Jax asked. "Did you just mute me?"

"Had to. I'm at the station."

"I ain't got time for this, just tell me."

Ricky raised his voice. "You need to hear what I found out about Leo, and not on the phone. Your place or face the consequences."

Jax pulled his disposable mask off and crumpled it in his hand. "What are you talking about? I'm calling Leo."

"No. You call him if you still trust him after I tell you what I know."

"This better be good or I'm kicking your ass. Forty minutes."

When Ricky returned to his desk, Standish asked, "We're ready for the Whitmore raid." She held the paperwork in her hand. Arrest and search warrants. "You're sure your informant said he's there?"

"Yeah. Said so."

"Good. I got room for one more on the Whitmore raid. Want to come?"

Ricky shook his head. "Nah. Got too many things going on here. I'll just be happy when you lock him up."

"All right. We'll be back as soon as we can."

❖

A pair of fifteen-foot flat-bottom boats launched from the east side of the lagoon and headed for the long line of spoil islands, one of which Jax Whitmore lived on. The first carried two officers, and the second held Standish and Marla. Each person wore an armor vest with POLICE on the back and carried an assault rifle. Standish held the warrants for Jax in her hand.

Marla noticed Jim, her rescuer from the spoil island near Rattlesnake Island, sitting in his small boat near the middle of the lagoon. His fishing pole hung in the air, waiting for a bite. She tapped Standish on the shoulder. "Let the other go. We have to stop for a sec next to that boat."

"Why?" Standish asked.

"That's Jim. The guy who helped me out when Jax tried to kill me. Pull over."

Standish eased off the throttle, and the boat slowed.

When Jim recognized Marla, he smiled and waved. As the boat closed in, she latched onto the gunwale. "Jim, good to see you."

"Howdy. Looks like all y'all going somewhere impo'tent."

"The spoil island where Jax Whitmore lives. Remember? The guy who tried to kill me."

"Oh, yeah, but you goin' da wrong way."

"What do you mean?" Marla asked.

Jim pointed at an island different from the one pinpointed on the map. "There. That's da one. You headin' the wrong direction."

Marla glanced at Standish. "Who told you which one to go to?"

Standish pulled out a map of the line of spoil islands, with a red circle around one. "Ricky did. He said this one."

"Who are you going to believe?" Marla asked.

Standish glanced at the map and then at Jim. She called the radio on the other boat. "Turn around and head back to me. Wrong island. Repeat...wrong island."

The boat veered and headed back toward them.

"Thanks, Jim. I owe you one," Marla said.

When the bows of both boats slid onto the muddy shore of the island where Jim had pointed, the four jumped out and charged ahead. It was an old, short, one-bedroom, single-wide trailer with a ten-foot-tall palm tree at the corner. The officers circled around the back. Marla and Standish stepped past the heavily worn plaid couch with twenty-plus beer cans scattered on the ground. They stopped on each side of the front door.

Standish used the crowbar to pound on the door twice. "Police! Jax Whitmore, we have a warrant for your arrest!" She leaned away, waiting for a shotgun blast to blow a hole through the door.

Marla held her rifle with both hands. *Come on out, asshole. I want you to see my face.*

When no one answered, Standish hit the crowbar on the door several more times. "Police! Jax Whitmore! Come out with your hands up!" She clicked the microphone on her shoulder epaulet. "See anything in the back?"

An officer replied, "Quiet."

Standish glanced at Marla. "You ready?"

When Marla nodded once, Standish jammed the tip of the crowbar between the door and the trailer and snapped it open. They waited a moment for gunfire before the two rushed in. Trash and dirty dishes were piled on the floor. Standish cleared the bedroom. Marla checked around the kitchen counter and opened the refrigerator, revealing beer cans, leftovers, and baby bottles filled with what looked like formula. She opened the freezer on top to find it empty.

Standish opened the sliding glass door on the opposite side of the trailer and let the two other officers enter. "Did you check underneath?"

"Yeah. Nothing but junk under there."

"I cleared the bedroom and bathroom for people. You guys check for any drugs or money."

Standish called the station, and the dispatcher answered.

With a stern voice, Standish said, "Find Ricky and put him on the radio."

"Yeah, boss."

"There's nobody, and the place looks like a garbage dump. You said your informant told you Jax would be here at the trailer house."

He briefly looked at the dispatcher before turning his back. "That's, um, yeah, that's what my guy said."

"Well, your guy is full of it. Send the forensics team out here and have them comb this place for anything. Now!"

Ricky exited the building and stood by a police vehicle. He had to call Jax and give a reason for the raid.

"Listen, asswipe," Jax yelled into his phone. "Someone just told me two boats full of cops landed on my island. You're dead meat."

Ricky spoke on the fly, fabricating a story as he went along. "I had everything set for you, Raylene, and the baby. Get you out of this mess...immunity and a big bag of money. I got the Feds to offer you a sweet deal. When they ask the question about what's going on, all you had to say was one word...LEO! That's it! Leo, and life would be good for the rest of your life. But you blew it by not showing up."

Jax's tone became curious. "How much money?"

Everyone had a price. Everything came at a cost. Ricky had to remove Jax. He could never get what he wanted as long as Jax stood in the way. "Five hundred thousand! You hear me? Five hundred!"

Jax sat down on the concrete near the drying bins. "Wow. You shoulda told me. I'll meet 'em."

"So, where are you now? At the desal plant?"

Jax stood. "Why do you care about that?"

"I don't just want to help you and Raylene."

"Don't worry about where I am."

Ricky leaned against a vehicle when the phone disconnected.

Chapter 28

The sparse exercise room in the desalination plant had mirror-lined walls, a rack of hand weights, mats rolled beside each other, and two hanbos, three-foot wooden staffs used for offensive and defensive moves. Harlow wore a low-cut, sleeveless black top and tight-fitting black pants. Her hands adjusted her grip on the staff, with fingers curling around the smooth wooden surface and her eyes fixed on her brother. The green colored hair, cut longer on one side, brushed her forehead. The vented room meant no need for their masks.

Nico wore a white undershirt and red bike shorts, attempting to accentuate his manhood. He stood opposite her, his stance wide but stiff, shifting his weight and glancing at the instructor. Carl, a retired Mexican Marine in his forties, hair a quarter inch long and a clean-shaven face, with arms and chest not small but not large, filled a tight T-shirt, and stood off to the side with his arms crossed. Once a week, he arrived on one of the Mexican boats to teach self-defense with them.

"Nico! Keep your focus!" Carl blurted. "Your sister ain't waitin' for you to think about your next move."

Harlow smirked. "I never do."

"The hell with that. Let's just do this."

Harlow raised the hanbo, sliding one foot forward. Nico mirrored her, slower, less gracefully. Carl clapped his hands. "Go."

Harlow struck first, a quick jab into Nico's midsection. He blocked the second attempt, the wooden staffs clacking together, but his counter strike was slow. Harlow spun, ducking low, and swept the hanbo toward his thigh. He sidestepped but faltered.

"Stop!" Carl yelled. "Nico, you're acting like an old woman. You're too predictable." Carl paced around them. "She's your enemy, and an enemy will give you no mercy. Fight like this is for your life." His voice eased a bit. "Your movements need to flow, not react. Ready? Go!"

Nico lunged forward, swinging the staff at Harlow's leg. She dodged with a pivot, blocking his next maneuver and snapping the end of her hanbo against his ribs. Nico grunted in frustration.

"Point to Harlow."

"Big surprise," Nico snarled. "She's too close. Back up! And I shoulda worn looser pants, or something."

"Jesus! Excuses won't help you in a fight," Carl said. "You're stronger, but not using it to your advantage. Power means nothing without precision."

Leaning on her staff, she glared at him. "He's right, you know. A weak little girl is kicking your ass."

Nico glared back. "Don't start with me...little sister. I'll stick you back into your room and lock you up tighter than a nun's virtue."

She swung her hanbo and knocked Nico's staff from his grip. It clattered on the floor as she rushed him, knocking him on his back. Harlow held the stick against his neck. "Try, and I'll stick this pole up your stupid asshole!"

"Enough." Carl tapped Harlow on the shoulder, signifying for her to step away. "I don't give a rat's ass if you two argue all day, but not on my time. You're here to train. Nico, get up and reset."

They moved back to their starting positions, and Harlow saw the tension in Nico's shoulders, the way his grip tightened on the hanbo. He was trying too hard, and she loved it.

Carl stepped back, gesturing for them to continue. "This time, focus on control. Power without control is chaos. Go."

Harlow let Nico make the first move. She expected his lunge, his strike more measured, aiming at her chest. That was when she parried the hanbo and countered with a quick thrust at his armpit. Nico stumbled back.

"Point to Harlow. She makes you look weak, Nico," Carl said. "Don't back away. Hold your ground."

She pressed the advantage, faking a thrust to the left before sweeping her staff low. Nico jumped back. Harlow swung wide, holding the end of her hanbo an inch from the side of his neck.

Carl clapped once. "Point to Harlow. Again."

Nico cursed under his breath, stepping back and lowering his staff. Harlow gave him a small, tight smile. "Come on, big bro."

He didn't respond, but the flush in his cheeks was answer enough. Carl's voice cut through the silence. "Break for five. And Nico, use the time to figure out what you're doing wrong. Harlow, good work."

Harlow leaned against the wall as Nico dropped onto the mat, rubbing the back of his neck. She didn't say anything, but the satisfaction of besting him was clear in her faint smile.

Carl took Nico's staff from his hand and gave him a measured look. "Next round, don't focus on beating her. Focus on not beating yourself." He took a stance opposite Harlow. She swung, and he countered, sweeping her feet off the floor. "See? You can do it." He reached for Harlow's arm to help her up.

Nico glanced up, his jaw tight. "Yeah, sure."

Harlow twirled her hanbo absentmindedly, her eyes gleaming with amusement. "Whenever you're ready, big brother."

Nico grabbed the hanbo and stood, making sure Carl was far enough behind him not to hear what he had to say. He whispered, "You got a sweet little ass, sis."

When Harlow blinked, Nico slapped his staff against her ribs before swinging around and clipping her ankles. After falling on her back, he said, "Point to me."

Chapter 29

Inside the kitchen, Harlow still wore her workout clothes as she wiped the sink dry. The water in the dishwasher agitated in a constant back-and-forth motion while she gazed out the window of the building to a view of the birdcage, concrete, drying bins, and Texas heat.

Nico entered with a handful of papers and snapped out a command, "Two eggs, meat, and one slice of that swirly rye bread." He sat in his usual chair and glanced across the table. "Where's my plate and fork?"

Harlow spun around. "What in God's name are you talking about?"

"Where's my breakfast?"

"You've been up for hours and ate twenty minutes ago, after our hanbo lesson." She pitched the dish towel over her shoulder. "Did you forget about our class this morning? You should go back to bed and get some sleep."

"I'll sleep when I get all this done. Pacheco called again, and you know what happens if he doesn't get what he wants. The Mexicans turn against us." Nico's fingertips tapped the table like he was keeping time to music. "My head is killing me."

Harlow's finger swept green hair behind her ear. "Let me see what's going on." She stepped to the table and placed her hand on his shoulder, then his neck. "Your veins are pounding, and they're way too fast. Are you snorting any of the stuff we're making?"

He slapped her hand away. "Hell no. You know better. I don't do that...at all."

Harlow raised her brow, unconvinced, but decided not to push it. "You're stressed to the max. Let me help. I can work the numbers on the pages. Go lie down for a bit and take a nap.

"I can't sleep. Haven't had a decent night for weeks. All I think about is," he held the papers up in his hand, "this! And sometimes it all just turns into a pot full of confusing numbers. I need to go to the control room and resume work."

Harlow eased the papers out of his hand. "Let me help you to the couch in your room." Nico stood as she wrapped her arm around his waist.

Jax entered the kitchen and slid his blue mask under his chin. "Nico? We need you out here."

Harlow covered her mouth and nose with the dishtowel. "Good God, you stink. Go back to your pigsty and take a bath."

"You look pretty fuckin' hot in those clothes, girl. How about you and me—"

She flung the dishtowel at Jax before pulling the shawl from the chair's back and wrapping it around her shoulders. "You got Raylene, so shut your stupid eyes and mouth and go get cleaned up."

"Can't leave here. I heard there's an arrest warrant out for me."

"Then get away from here. We don't want the cops here looking for your stinkin' ass."

"Screw that. I'm staying. What do you plan to do with Nico?"

"He needs to go to his bedroom and lie on the sofa."

"He can't go there. I need him out there to help with the drugs."

"I know the numbers and the correct mix," Harlow said. "Put him on his couch. I know how to run things."

"You nuts? Nico's always done it."

"Stop arguing!" Nico yelled. "Give me a little time." He motioned to his sister. "She's right. Harlow knows how to mix. Have her do it for now, and I'll be there soon."

Harlow laid a blanket over Nico on the couch. He blinked a few times before his eyelids closed.

"Fifteen, twenty minutes. That's all I need," Nico said.

She plumped up the pillow under Nico's head. "When you wake, come take over."

With their masks on, Harlow and Jax entered the main room and turned the corner to reveal a reverse osmosis desalination unit much smaller than expected for the size of the building. They ran the ocean water through the system twice to ensure the very clean, salt-free water didn't go to the community—it went to fenethylline production. Two towering, twenty-foot-tall conical silos stood side-by-side, labeled AMPHETAMINE and THEOPHYLLINE. Harlow joked that if the Feds came in and saw the names, they'd be busted, but if there was a raid, it wouldn't make any difference if they'd named them Mickey and Minnie. Each silo had a large opening at its base as wide as a man, with a hard plastic tilt truck capable of carrying hundreds of pounds of material sitting beneath the cone.

While wearing a disposable mask, Harlow rapped her knuckles on the metal, and it clanged. "When will the next shipment come in?"

Jax adjusted his mask over his nose again. "It's scheduled to be here within the hour."

"Scheduled? So, you're saying you don't really know. Just hoping for the best?"

"Shut up! It'll be here."

"Make sure it's not late." Harlow knocked on the second silo, producing another clang. "And what about the mixing room? All good in there?"

"Why you asking all these questions?"

"Just answer, unless you've got no idea what's going on around here."

"I know everything about this place." Jax pointed to a long rectangular window on a cream-colored wall, revealing two men in Tyvek protective suits, wearing respirators and operating stainless steel machinery, which made round, nondescript tablets. A slight haze of the powder floated in the air. "Don't worry about anything. Everything is on schedule."

"And everything can go bad in a second." Harlow tightened the shawl around her shoulders, wishing she had the carving knife from the kitchen in her hand. "I worry as much as Nico...just manage it better. We should bump up production after the next batch. I'm going into the control room to make that happen."

"I'll come with you. Nico always lets me inside the control room."

She stopped before unlocking the door. "That ain't happenin'. He never lets anyone inside. The mixture percentage is a secret; only Nico and I know the formula. So, you and your rank stank can wait outside."

Once in, Harlow snapped the lock shut and sat at a desk. The oversized monitor screen allowed her to oversee all activity in the mixing room. The door stood between her and Jax, but he kept trying to sneak peeks through the large window. She pivoted her back so he couldn't see what she was doing on the keyboard.

The keys clacked as her fingers typed Nico's ID and password. If her mix went bad, she didn't want any timestamp of her entering the site. She wanted it to be Nico's fault, not hers, but when the site asked for facial recognition, she aimed the camera at the wall. FAILED. It wanted Nico's face with his ID. "Damn!" She accessed the photos on her phone, pulled up a picture of Nico, zoomed in on his face, and aimed it at the monitor camera. FAILED. "Damn!" Halfheartedly, she typed her ID and password. When she looked straight at the camera, a green PASS popped onto the screen, and the website opened.

Harlow motioned for Jax to go to the silos. Her fingers typed on the keyboard, and the soft buzz of a small electric motor sprang to life under the towering conical silo labeled THEO-PHYLLINE. White granules flowed from a large mouth opening on the bottom and into a waiting tilt truck below. Without missing a beat, Jax pushed the truck to the mixing room and swung the heavy metal doors open. Machinery on the left side hummed as it made fenethylline tablets from the finished powder. On the opposite side of the room, four identical seven-foot-tall stainless steel mixing containers stood side by side.

The noise of the machinery and the faint smell of chemicals filled the room. Intense heat emanated from the four containers in the various drug manufacturing stages. The process was straightforward: mix theophylline with a bromide solvent, cook it, then cool it before adding amphetamine, producing one hundred percent fenethylline. Nico's precise measurements and planned schedule ensured the production flowed around the clock, with each container producing five hundred pounds of the product twice daily, equal to four thousand pounds of finished product—three million tablets each and every day.

Harlow was aware of every detail and adjustment needed in the control room, watching the production move like a fine-tuned engine. An alarm, sounding like a vintage egg timer on the computer, signaled the completion of the product in one container. After draining and recovering the bromide solvent, Jax transferred the damp product into another tilt truck and took it outside to the drying bins hidden in plain sight under the hot Texas sun. An hour later, it was ready for tablet production and packaging.

A knock on the door interrupted Harlow. She turned to see Nico gesturing for her to unlatch the lock. As soon as she snapped the deadbolt free, Nico burst in and checked the monitor screen for production numbers. The doorway shut behind him.

"I'm better. Where are we in today's production?"

"You should wear a mask."

Nico shook his head. "No. Can't breathe with them on."

Harlow gestured at the computer screen. "I finished the one batch and I'm adjusting the temperatures in numbers two and four. Don't worry, I know what I'm doing."

Nico relaxed after reviewing all the numbers were correct. "Okay, fine. Good." While rubbing his temples with the palms of his hands, he muttered, "Damn headache."

"I could take you to get another massage."

"I am stressed to the hilt, but...I don't know."

"You can be back in two hours, maybe less," Harlow said.

Nico nodded. "Yeah, okay. Jax can take me to town."

Outside, near the drying bins, Jax waved at Nico.

Nico opened the door and spoke to Harlow as he exited the control room. "But I'm waiting for the guys to finish making tablets from the previous batch. Call and tell them I can be there in thirty minutes." He walked out toward the drying bins.

"Hey!" Harlow rushed out of the control room and grabbed her brother's arm. "I'll take you. I want to go downtown."

"No," Nico said. "Slats will take you to your room."

When Slats came around the corner, Harlow shoved him in the chest, but he didn't move. "Jax can't take you, Nico. He has a warrant out for his arrest. If the cops pull him over, both of you will go to jail. I'm your sister...the only one who gives a rat's ass about you, understand? I'll drive."

Nico scoffed. "I'm already stressed enough without you behind the wheel. Go to your room, get comfortable, and watch the batch on your computer. Be a good little supervisor for all this while I'm gone."

"Watch nothing for six hours until the timer goes off?"

"Of course not. Watch the temperature, pressure, and time...make sure they bring it in when the stuff dries."

"Then I need free access around here. If something is off, I have to come to the control room and fix it."

"Okay, choose...your room or the control room. You stay in one place until I get back."

Harlow sighed heavily. "So, which place are you going?"

"I don't know. Not sure."

"You're not going to that stupid CLEAN U UP, are you? Every time you go there, you say you don't feel as good as the Padre Massage place. As bad as you feel right now, go to the best place in town. I'm calling to tell them you need to see Raylene in fifteen minutes."

"Fine. Jax can drive me there."

"I told you, Jax can't be seen in town. Give me the keys, and I'll let you be beside me in the massage room."

Nico smirked. "You can't wear clothes in that room."

"Don't be gross."

◆

Harlow parked near the front door of the Padre Manicure and Spa. She killed the engine and said, "I'll wait for you."

"I don't think so. Is that why you brought me here? So, you can gallivant around town while I'm inside?"

"Gallivant? Where did you learn such a big word? Cross-word puzzle?"

"Go inside. You get a manicure and a massage with me, or we head back right now."

"I already got one this week. Don't need another, but...I'll sit next to you."

"Good enough." Nico opened his door and waited for Harlow at the entrance.

The nail salon manager had a warm smile. Her curled hair fell in perfect waves around her shoulders. "Mr. Palermo, nice to see you again." She held a cup of hot herbal tea for Nico to take. "When your sister called, we hurried to have everything ready for you. Please sit, and I will have Raylene here very soon."

Nico sipped the warm liquid, soothing his throat as he studied the framed posters on the walls, young flawless hands with bright colored nails, headshots with smooth facial skin and vivid red lips, a relaxed woman on her stomach with a white towel draped over her buttocks and a female therapist's hands on her back. The scents of lavender and eucalyptus oils filled the air, accompanied by soft, peaceful music playing in the background.

Moments later, they sat across from Raylene in plush chairs, with cushions soft enough to sink into. As her gloved hands massaged Nico's fingers, he felt the warmth of the sea salt compound, coarse yet invigorating, melting away the tension in his body.

Harlow rested her elbows on the table with her fingers intertwined while glancing at the mirror reflecting a narrow entryway leading upstairs to the stud she wanted to get naked with.

"You might want to add a flavor," Raylene said.

Harlow turned back to Raylene. "What?"

"*Some* men like the smell of fresh strawberries."

Nico almost choked. "A man? What the hell is going on?" His eyes turned toward Harlow. "She isn't seeing anyone." He turned back to Raylene. "She's not seeing anybody."

"No, of course not," Harlow raised an eyebrow at Raylene, "but...are you able to do that?"

"For you? Sure." Raylene pulled a small bottle from a drawer next to her leg. "I just apply a thin layer on your nails. It won't bother the color."

Harlow smiled. "Okay. Do it."

"What? Wait. What is going on here?" Nico asked.

"Nothing. You made me come to this place, so now I'm doing something."

Raylene slipped her gloves off and painted a layer on each of Harlow's nails, much to Nico's chagrin.

After placing the bottle back into the drawer, Raylene motioned Nico to the men's facilities to change. "Our massage therapist is gone today, so I will meet you inside the room."

Nico smirked. "You want me to take all my clothes off?"

Raylene faked a surprised smile. "Nico."

"Fine. I'll wear a little something under the towel." He glanced at Harlow, hoping for two women in the same massage room with him. "You're going in there with me."

"I am not going into any room where you have *a little something on*. I promise," she crossed her heart with a finger, "I will not leave this building."

Raylene waited until Nico entered the men's room before turning to Harlow. "I told my brother you were coming up there." She said with a touch of sarcasm, "Be gentle."

"Ha! That is not what he wants," Harlow said. "You told me he wants the smell of strawberries, and he's gonna get it."

After they high-fived, Harlow jaunted up the stairs and knocked on the door. She didn't wait for him to answer and entered. "Get those clothes off!" Her hands pulled her T-shirt over her head. It landed on the floor as she kicked her shoes off. "Haven't got much time before my stupid brother finishes downstairs."

"Strawberries? I love the smell of strawberries."

Thirty minutes later, Nico emerged dressed and smiling from the men's dressing room. Harlow sat in a chair against the wall, one leg crossed over the other, and a smile that wouldn't go away. She uncrossed her legs and stood. "Feel better?"

He took a deep breath and released it. "Yeah. Headache is gone, but I'm tired and jittery at the same time." He gave a once-over to Harlow. "You look flushed, happy."

"Am I? Hmm, don't know why. Let's go back."

As they left, Harlow smiled, then nodded once at Raylene, who gave a small wave to her. Harlow bumped into a person and almost fell to the floor.

Junior, Jax's fishing buddy, caught her before she fell. "Sorry, miss. My fault."

Harlow paid little attention to him and exited the store.

Raylene stood with her hands on her hips. "Junior? What's up?"

"I just wanted to, um, ask you out for a beer or something."

"I'm Jax's girlfriend. What are you doing?"

Junior shuffled his feet. "I don't want to get him in trouble or nothin', but he said it was all right if I asked."

She crossed her arms. "He did?"

Junior crossed his arms for a second before uncrossing them. "Yeah, yeah. I really kinda like you and all. Maybe we could go down to the bar down the street and split a beer. You got really nice...uh... you're nice looking, and I'd like to—"

"To what? You mean take me to a bed and fuck my brains out?"

He mumbled to himself, then stopped. "Oh, I mean. How about a beer first?"

"Why do we need a beer? We have tables in the back."

He nodded. "Okay."

"Okay?" She shoved him back. "Get your slimy little ass out of this shop!"

After Raylene watched Junior slink out past the door, she called Jax. "You're nothing but garbage. Did you send Junior over here to fuck me?"

Jax laughed. "Did he really do it? He asked me if it was okay, and I said sure, go for it."

"All right, asshole, get your crap out of my trailer today!"

"Your trailer is on my land, so get it off my land!"

"You don't own that land. Nobody owns that. It's nothing but a pile of mud."

"I claimed that island for myself, like that guy who climbed to the top of a mountain and claimed it."

Raylene rolled her eyes. "It's not a mountain. It's a mud pile scraped off the bottom of the lagoon. If you're not out when I get home—"

Jax scoffed. "Good luck with that. You didn't hear? The cops raided your trailer today. You ain't got no home to go to, and you and I are done."

"What about your kid?"

"I'll come visit sometime, but I'm moving into the shack out back of the Borderline Hog Hunters business. Headin' there now."

Harlow closed the car door and wondered who Raylene was arguing with on the phone. She turned her attention back to her brother. "See. You feel better than that other crappy place, right?"

"Yeah." He rotated his shoulders and his neck. "Everything feels better." When they stopped at an intersection, he said, "Pull over there at the restaurant. My stomach is kinda cramping. Hurry up, 'cause I gotta take a dump."

"Got a bug or something?"

"Don't know. It's been bothering me for a few weeks. All the stress, I guess. The Mexicans want thirty thousand pounds by the end of the week." He pointed again. "Hurry up."

Chapter 30

Jax and Leo waited as the helicopter descended onto the concrete pad behind Leo's dwelling. The blades slowed, and the pilot emerged from the cockpit, making his way toward the house.

Jax glanced at Leo. "Did he forget to pick up Adams?"

Leo shook his head in response. "I didn't receive any calls from him, so I assumed she was already on board."

"Well, you know what they say about assuming," Jax snorted, a hint of sarcasm in his voice. "It makes an 'ass' out of 'u' and 'me'!"

The pilot stormed in through the front door, his face red with anger. "I never want to see that woman again, do you hear me? She is not setting foot inside my helicopter ever again."

Jax furrowed his brow in confusion. "So, where is she?"

"Probably back at wherever she's staying," the pilot replied with a sharp gesture of his finger toward the island. "She threatened to shoot me and the instrument panel if I didn't fly her there."

"You can't just land a helicopter on a beach," Leo interjected.

The pilot shrugged. "I landed further north by a park. A cop was waiting for her."

Leo nodded with approval. "Clever move on her part." He turned back to the bar and poured three glasses of bourbon. "Jax said he found the fenethylline leak. One of the workers snuck it out and sold it."

"What does that have to do with me?" the pilot asked.

Jax aimed his pistol, equipped with a suppressor, at the pilot.

"Whoa, whoa, whoa. I had nothing to do with it." He pointed at Jax while looking at Leo. "He said *he* gave it to a friend." He glared at Jax. "You son of a bitch. You're trying to throw the heat on me." The pilot turned to Leo. "I promise. Nothing at all."

"I found your fingerprints on a packet," Jax said.

"You can't run fingerprints. Only cops can do that. Who do you know that's a...oh! No way." The pilot grabbed a glass and flung it at Jax. The bourbon flew through the air over an expensive chair as the glass shattered against the wall.

"Hey!" Leo yelled. "That's a one-of-a-kind fabric."

The pilot pointed at Jax. "Blame that asshole with the gun. He's the one who did it." Turning to Leo, he said, "Jax is the one. He stole it and set me up because that couple, you know, the ones that died a few days ago in the lagoon. Leo, you've got to believe me."

Jax gun butted the pilot from behind, knocking him down. "Get your sorry ass out and get in your helicopter and leave."

The pilot raised his hands and rushed out the door.

Leo glanced at him and nodded to Jax. "Go ahead."

The pilot hadn't made it halfway before he fell forward with two bullets in his back.

Jax smiled as secrets stayed secret. "That was fun."

Leo closed the door. "Clean that up before you leave."

"I'll drop him off near the feral hogs, and in an hour there'll be nothin' left."

When another man entered the room from the hallway, Jax set his pistol on a table beside a chair. "You understand what happens if you steal from Leo?"

"Yes, sir. Is that chopper mine now?"

Leo poured another glass of bourbon for the new pilot.

Jax grabbed his glass and downed the drink in one gulp.

"Learn some manners," Leo said. "This is high-quality sipping bourbon, not something you chug like cheap beer."

"Got it."

Leo poured Jax another as the pilot took a small sip from his glass.

"Tomorrow, the Mexicans are bringing another shipment," Leo gestured toward the new pilot. "You stay up there and keep a lookout for any trouble." He then turned to Jax with a serious look. "And you make sure every last bit of that load is delivered. I don't want a repeat of when the cartel ambushed my boat going to Houston."

Chapter 31

Standish dropped Marla off at the beach house. Her phone rang moments after she plopped down into a plastic chair on the porch. It was a well-deserved one minute break. Dr. Hernandez's name lit up on her screen. Her fingers scratched behind Festus' ear as she answered the call.

"Adams here."

"Agent Adams, you made me think about the sharks a little more. I can't imagine why anything like this would happen. It appeared senseless until I thought about you and why you are here, so I said, okay, I'll do it. I called my boss and told him about the fenethylline you are trying to find."

"And?"

"He agreed and said to run more laboratory tests."

"Okay. Like what?"

"The test I ran was for drugs. We don't normally do drug tests on animals, but I did, and it came out positive for amphetamines."

Marla stopped scratching Festus and sat straighter in her chair. "Amphetamines? Where in the hell?"

"And when I told my boss the results, he said to test for theophylline. That was positive, too. Those are the primary components used to make fenethylline, right? I'm sorry, but my initial cause of death in the tiger sharks was incorrect. They didn't die from elevated salt in their system. It was from an overdose of fenethylline. Oh, and by the way, the two dozen fish beached near the restaurants are all positive."

Marla's mind raced as she tried to process this new information. "Thanks, Dr. Hernandez. I'm not sure what this all means, but it's something."

After hanging up, she immediately called the San Antonio office. Stepping over the two-foot porch fence, the sand crunched under her shoes. She stopped beside her truck and felt the warmth of the front quarter panel against her palm. In a situation like this, she'd prefer to talk to Borland, even SAC Davies, but he said to call Tillman.

"Tillman here."

"Sam? This is Adams...Marla."

"How's it going down south?"

"I have new info about the fenethylline."

"Okay, what is it?"

"Remember the sharks beached near my place?"

"Sure."

"They're both positive for amphetamines and theophylline—fenethylline."

"I don't understand how that is possible."

"Me neither. How can fish get the drug?" Marla paused, gazing out at the ocean where two windsurfers zigzagged between each other until one rammed into the other. A surfer fell off the board, and the sail dropped into the water. "Unless...are you aware of any reports of cartel activity near here along the shoreline?"

"No, but I can check with the Coast Guard."

"Thanks. That'll help."

Marla called Standish. "I need a favor."

"Sure. What's up?"

She climbed into her pickup after Festus jumped up on the seat. "Can you get three couples with ATVs, and you too, to meet me at the beach house in an hour? Everyone in beach clothes, and no cops except you."

"Easy enough. Why?"

The engine started, and Marla headed toward town. "It's time we do a little visit right outside the desal plant. And don't say anything about it at the station." After Marla dropped the phone in a cup holder, she drove down Padre Boulevard and turned onto the Queen Isabel Causeway while Festus sat quietly in the passenger seat. She glanced over at the KOA campground, where the remains of Pier 19 were being scooped up by a front loader and emptied into a dump truck. The once lively spot was now a desolate sight, leaving Baldy no place for his midnight business, and any chance of her getting fenethylline from him.

After crossing the tranquil waters of the Laguna Madre, the truck picked up speed on the highway to Brownsville. Marla tapped the number of the DEA office. When Special Agent Chris Miller answered, she said, "Special Agent Adams here. I'll be there in fifteen minutes, tops. While I have you on the phone, I need one six-foot outdoor folding tent, two ice chests with beer and water, that surveillance camera I saw over in the corner, and the battery pack that goes with it."

"Got it," Chris said. "Adrian is here with me, and we'll have it ready."

Marla pulled into the Brownsville office and parked behind the building. She held her palm down at Festus. "Stay right there. This will only take a second."

Chris and Adrian emerged from the back door with the equipment in hand. Marla lifted her truck bed cover and gestured for them to place it beside the scuba gear.

Chris asked, "Setting up a party? Shouldn't drink and *dive*."

Marla threw a sarcastic smile at him. "Funny, drive-dive." She pushed her wetsuit to the side. "Surveillance."

"Of course. Planning on using the scuba gear while here? Beautiful blue water out there."

"Yeah? I'm sure it is."

"Well, take a couple of hours off if you can. It's worth it."

Marla hadn't had two seconds of free time since arriving in town. "Right."

Half an hour later, Marla pulled up to her beach house, where couples in summer attire stood beside their ATVs, laughing and joking. Amidst the crowd stood Standish.

When the truck door opened, Festus jumped out and ran around the crowd. The girls oohed, and the guys laughed. Marla dashed into the house and changed into shorts and a T-shirt while the group loaded all the DEA equipment on the ATVs. When Marla came outside, Standish handed her a pair of sunglasses and a floppy beach hat to cover her face from prying eyes.

Standish laughed when Marla recognized the confiscated four-wheeler. "I don't have an ATV. Not supposed to do this, but I took a wheel from one and put it on this one. I'll write it up as official police work."

"Good enough for me." Marla climbed on behind Standish, with Festus in her lap.

✦

Two guards stood inside the desalination fence and watched a group of young adults riding ATVs stop on the beach. They unloaded ice chests and a large tent. It took less than five minutes to unfold the canvas, blocking much of the view of their activities. Several ran in and out of the water, while others sat along the shoreline drinking beer. Moments later, a line of smoke rose, accompanied by the smell of toasted marshmallows.

Marla waited an hour to let the guards pay less attention to them before grabbing a small bag, then eased over to a grouping of grass growing on a sand dune. She leaned back on her elbows and studied the angle needed for the surveillance camera position. Positioned between the equipment and the watchmen, she unzipped the bag and pushed the camera with the battery pack into the sand and grass. A clear image of the pier showed on her phone screen. Marla lingered another hour before rounding the group up and leaving the premises.

Chapter 32

Harlow's parents lay lifeless in the front seat of their VW Microbus, blood seeping from multiple gunshot wounds. She felt the muzzle of a revolver push against her forehead. "No! Don't, please!" A thumb pulled the hammer back with a click she had never heard so close before. Harlow begged, "No. I promise not to say anything." She stared at the finger pulling on the trigger. The gun fired again and again and again.

Harlow jolted awake from a midday nightmare and sat up on her bed, wiping the sweat from her damp green hair off her face. "Holy crap."

It was never her fault what happened. She had nothing to do with her parents' murder after their house had burned down. The police found both parents dead two days later, shot multiple times in their Microbus. Murdered, and the cops didn't care because they said her mother and father were just another set of mid-level drug dealers. They had more important duties in law enforcement. Sure, she was a teenager, but Nico went crazy over the top in protecting her.

Harlow scooted off the bed, stepped to the compact refrigerator, and opened the door before grasping a bottle of water. After twisting the cap off, she peered at her fingernails in disgust. "So stupid what my brother does." After rubbing her fingers on her black pants, wishing the smell and the polish would miraculously disappear, she moaned. Thanks to Raylene, they looked shinier. She guessed it was a worthwhile price to keep Nico going, and for her seeing the boy upstairs.

After replacing the cap on the bottle, she walked to her door and pulled, but it didn't budge. Pulling again with all her might, it remained closed. Nico had her room locked again. She pounded on the door with her fist. "Open this damn thing, Nico. I want out, now!"

Harlow threw the bottle against the wall and screamed, "Goddamn it! I want out!" Yanking a drawer open, she pulled out a long screwdriver. "You can't keep me here forever! Let me out!"

The guard stationed outside her door tried to tune out her screams, but he couldn't help but hear every word she yelled.

Harlow paced back and forth in her room, searching for a way out. She slipped her ankle-high boots on, tied them tight, and returned near the door. "Who's out there? Let me out, just for a minute. I get cooped up in here and need a breath of fresh air. You understand, right?"

The guard, wearing his mask, stood motionless and spoke with a Tex-Mex accent. "Can't do that. Nico would have my ass."

Her hand tightened around the screwdriver handle. "Your voice, I remember you. The cute one, right? Why don't you come in, and we can talk about it? I've always liked you and should have told *you that*." She didn't know who was out there and didn't care. "If you join me, we could keep this private between the two of us. Could be fun."

On the opposite side of the door, the guard dropped his hands to his sides and glanced around, making sure no one was looking. Since her return from town, he had caught a whiff of her strawberry fragrance. He fantasized about the color of her toenails. He liked painted toes and bare feet. While standing outside her door, he fantasized about what she was wearing and what he had to do to get her to take it off. The temptation was too much. He couldn't wait, pitched his mask on the floor, and unlocked the deadbolt. Pressing the handle down and cracking open the door, he saw Harlow smiling with her hands tucked demurely behind her back. He checked again to make sure the hallway was empty before pushing the door open farther, then grinned as he entered. He was ready.

The guard was short and thin, with baggy clothes. This would be easy. Harlow took a step closer and wrinkled her nose at him. When he turned his head to shut the door, Harlow swung her arm and plunged the screwdriver into his chest. He slapped at her hand, but missed. Harlow yanked it out and stabbed him again.

Confused about what had happened, the guard slid down to the floor, clutching his wound. Words never came out of his mouth.

"You pathetic loser. Get out of my way, you rapist. She kicked him in the face. "I'm telling Nico you tried to rape me in my own room. You're a dead man." She closed the door with him inside and locked the deadbolt.

Harlow slipped a mask over her mouth and nose as she stormed through the hallway, her boots thudding against the concrete floor. She stopped in an open area, her eyes searching for Nico. "Where's that worthless brother of mine?" Her voice echoed off the walls. No one answered. She yelled again, "Where is Nico?"

A man she didn't recognize answered with the same Tex-Mex accent, "Outside." He waved his hand toward the back. "He go to dryin' bins."

"Who are you?"

"Nadie…no one."

Harlow gazed over at the man before brushing past him. She yelled as loud as she could, "Where the hell is—"

A hand the size of a bear claw latched onto her shoulder. "He needs help."

Harlow turned to see Slats beside her, his face partially obscured by a mask.

"He's confused." Slats pointed his finger at his temple. "Messed up."

Nico stood outside between two drying bins, maskless. "I said, mix it. Use the shovels and turn it over. We need to dry this faster."

A worker slumped his shoulders. His mask muffled his words. "Yes, sir, but you told us never to touch it once it is out here."

"I don't care what you heard before. I said turn it."

"Pacheco not like this."

Nico grabbed the shovel from the man's hand. "Forget Pacheco." He swung it, hitting the man across the side of his knee. "I said, shovel it!" The tool clanged on the concrete when Nico pitched it away.

"Nico?" Harlow called out as she tentatively approached. "What are you doing? You can't beat on Pacheco's men."

"We have to get this out of here. They're up my ass because Pacheco bumped the amount he wants," Nico gestured out at the ocean, "and we lost a shipment." He snatched Harlow by the forearm. "I can't do this. He has to understand." He grabbed Harlow's other arm. "You don't know what the Mexicans can do to us. There's no place to hide from them."

Harlow twisted her arm away. "You're hurting me." Nico turned around and pressed the heels of his hands against his temples. She glanced at Slats. "Do we have enough for another batch?"

"We can't start another one until we dry and sack these."

Nico's eyes were wild, and his hands were shaking. "There's no time!" He rushed away as he yelled, "They'll kill us if they see we're behind!"

Harlow pointed at a stack of bins leaning against the fence. "Get two more and load them with the product."

Slats shook his head. "Can't. Those are not clean—dirt, sand, and salt covering them. It would contaminate the drug."

She glared at Slats and said in a low tone, "Do I look like I give a rat's ass about contamination? I don't care who it kills. I'm going to the control room and starting another batch."

"What about Nico? He's not acting like himself."

Harlow nodded. "Give him a Valium or something and help him to his room."

❖

The following morning, Harlow stood outside the birdcage. After shaking a limb from the flowering plant next to the cage, the seeds dropped into a large pan. She scooped up a handful, opened the door, and scattered them on the floor. The quail fluttered as she grabbed two and snapped their necks.

Moments later, Nico entered the kitchen, sweeping his hair back from his face. He sat down in the closest chair and watched her clean and prepare the birds. Harlow pushed two thick slices of wild hog bacon to the side before placing the meat in the frying pan, which erupted in sizzles and pops.

"I'm a mess," Nico said. "Did somebody give me something?"

In a second pan, two fried eggs were almost done. "Slats gave you a Valium or something."

"I don't want none of that stuff."

Harlow grasped the bacon with tongs and flipped it over, causing more sizzling in the pan. "You have got to get control of yourself." An English muffin popped up from the toaster while she slid the eggs from the second pan onto a plate. "You can't do what you did yesterday."

"What? I don't remember what I did."

"You almost turned over the drying bins, that's what." Harlow turned off the stove and placed the meat beside the eggs. "Come on, what is wrong with you?"

"Too much stuff going on." He scooted up closer and rested his elbows on the table.

Harlow laid the plate in front of Nico. "Eat this. You need your strength to handle all the problems today."

Nico pushed his fingers against his carotid artery. "My pulse is booming. What did Slats give me last night?"

"Not sure. Something to let you sleep."

He cut a section of bacon and forked half of a quail breast before swirling it in the broken egg yolk. He stuck it in his mouth. "You're right. I have to be on it today. Pacheco is coming."

That's news to me. Why haven't you told me, and how's he getting here?"

"The same way they always do, on one of our fishing boats on the pier."

"When?"

Nico stuffed the rest of the bacon and quail into his mouth. Chewing while talking, he said, "Why do you care? None of your business. Oh man, I feel bad. Whatever Slats gave me, I don't want it anymore." Nico swallowed the last bite of meat and egg, slid the plate away from him, and pushed back from the table. When he stood, his legs gave way, and he collapsed back down in the chair. "What in the hell is going on?" He squeezed his hands against his temples. The taste of bile rose in his throat. "My head...it fucking hurts." He felt the room spin before falling off the chair and vomiting on the floor.

Harlow rushed over, pushed the chair away, and turned him on his side. His skin felt cold and clammy. She yelled for help as Nico convulsed, arms and legs jerking back and forth.

Harlow stood and stepped away when Slats ran into the kitchen. "Nico is sick. Take him to his room. I have to call a doctor."

Slats shook his head. "Leo doesn't want outsiders in here."

Harlow knew Leo would be furious if he knew about the hanbo instructor at the building every week. "Then I have to call him."

Chapter 33

Harlow sat in the control room, her eyes fixed on the drug production numbers scrolling across the monitor, when an outside surveillance camera drew her attention. Leo Searcy's Toyota Land Cruiser eased up near the fence.

A guard with an AR-15 hustled to the gate, exchanged a quick word with Leo out of the vehicle, and unlocked it. Dressed in a blue pinstriped suit with no tie, Searcy moved with the confidence that made Harlow uneasy. The gate clanked shut behind him, locked again.

She shifted to another screen as Leo entered through the front door. Without a word, she powered down the monitors, stood, and exited the room just as Leo approached her.

❖

Marla's concealed camera, positioned in a sand dune outside the desalination plant, captured the same Land Cruiser with Leo Searcy at the wheel and slowing near the fence line. The camera couldn't catch the gate itself, but Leo's arrival was unmistakable.

❖

"Where's Nico?"

"You should put on a mask," Harlow said.

"I'm only here for a few minutes. Where's Nico?"

Harlow gestured behind her with her thumb. "I told you on the phone he's in bed, sick or something. He needs to see a doctor right away."

"What do you mean, sick?"

"Not sure. He threw up breakfast and said he had a headache, so I put him to bed. How am I supposed to figure that out? I'm no doctor. You could let one come over and see him."

Leo shook his head. "We don't need any outsiders in this place. What other symptoms does he have?"

Harlow shrugged. "He gets mad easier now. Anxious, doesn't sleep anymore. Says his pulse was too fast...and then he almost fell to the floor when he tried to stand from the kitchen table. I asked him if he's back on drugs again. What do you think is going on?"

"What do you mean, again? We chose him because he was supposed to be clean—no drugs, no alcohol, no weed, nothing. Said he didn't even smoke cigarettes, but sounds like he's been dipping his finger in the finished product. We'll need to clean him up. I'll take him out of here for a few weeks."

"I can run the place while he's down, but keep him here. Even with him sick, he might help."

"Yeah? How so?"

"Just stuff he knows about. Keep him here and let him rest."

"So, you wanna be the boss?"

"I don't get paid enough to be the boss, but yeah."

"You want a raise, too?"

Harlow stared at him for several seconds. "I want what my brother is getting...and...twenty percent more because you need me to finish this job by the week's end, right?" She took a single step toward Leo. "If I deliver, then I take control. Just me, and Nico does what I tell him. Agree?"

"No. He's done well here, making millions of tablets and keeping the Mexicans happy. Sounds to me like you're trying to steal your brother's job. You finish, but if you can't do what he did...well, let's just say bad things can happen to little girls."

"Fine. Keep Nico as the boss, but he's staying here until he fucks up again."

"Lock him in his quarters and let him go cold turkey till he's clean," Leo said. "Just keep him away from the product. Now, get in the control room and finish the job." Leo spun around and walked away. "Don't mess this up."

Marla's motion camera captured the Land Cruiser as it left the plant.

❖

Junior called Jax's phone. He almost didn't answer, but slid the mask under his chin and said, "I'm busy, Junior. What do you want?"

"You set me up."

"What are you talking about?"

Embarrassed almost to reveal the truth. "You set me up. Raylene turned me down, and you knew she would. Why'd you let me do that?"

Jax scoffed. "Idiot. You wanted that piece of ass, so I let you try. Not my fault she said no."

"You knew she'd say no. You knew it!"

"Yeah, probably. What are you going to do about it? Not let me go fishing with you?"

"You're an ass." Junior hung up.

Jax laughed as he came around the corner and stopped beside Harlow. Both wore their masks. "Where's Nico? I have to talk to him about the next shipment coming in."

"He's sick, and Leo put me in charge of the operation until he recovers. There are enough chemicals to make one batch, and that's all. Tell me when the boat is close to the pier."

"That was what I was going to tell Nico. The federales wanted more money before they let the boat leave the Mexican harbor. It won't be here until late tonight."

"We've never had a shipment come in at night. With no lights on the pier, how will anybody see what to do?"

Jax nodded. "I can have spotlights brought in."

"A bright spot along a dark beach? That could bring trouble. The cops, the sheriff, that DEA agent. I don't like it."

"So, what do you suggest?"

Harlow paused, deep in thought. "Put red lights on the pier. That could guide the vessel in. Have a couple of guys with Maglite flashlights ready when it arrives...and have everyone armed. I don't want anybody killed or anything like what happened to that kid who worked here, wherever he is. What was his name?"

"Steven McCale," Jax said. "After the boat left the dock, I found out he had brought an unexpected guest on board."

"Wait," Harlow said. "You let an outsider on a drug run to Mexico?"

"I said I had no clue until the boat was out in the Gulf. It was supposed to be a side job. I set it up to sell to a guy from Houston who'd pay double. The plan was for them to meet at a specific spot, but the Mexicans must have found out.

"Why didn't you tell me this sooner?"

Jax held his hand out, facing Harlow. "Nico knew about it and said it was okay."

Harlow swept her green hair away from her face. "No wonder the Mexicans are coming here. They think we've double-crossed them. *You* double-crossed them! If they find out what really happened, they'll kill us all."

Jax shuffled his feet. "Are you sure Leo is okay with all this? You being the temporary boss and all."

Harlow tilted her head a tad and narrowed her eyes. "Do you have a problem with me running things?"

He ran his hand through his hair. "Maybe I should call Leo and tell him you're nothing but an idiot."

"Maybe I should drag your ass out and use it for target practice!"

"Try and see what happens."

Harlow offered him a sliver of fake goodwill instead of a bullet to his head. "Hey. Listen, I'm sorry about all this. Take the night off and go see Raylene."

Jax scoffed, scratching at the grime on his neck. "Yeah, sure. Let me just stroll into town with a warrant on my ass. Trying to kill that DEA bitch wasn't the best idea, so I'm not leaving this place."

"She knows that?"

"Hell, no. She only knows what I feed her and not a lick more."

How much of an idiot can you be? "You oughta be with her...and the baby. That whole mess is your fault."

"Bullshit," Jax snapped. "It's her fault. She knows what can happen when she jumps in bed with me. She wanted it. Now she can deal with it. I'm done handing over cash just 'cause she begs for it."

His grin was pure grease as he looked her over. "But you? You got more sense. How 'bout you and me head to your room, and you show me what you're good at. Then tomorrow you whip up one of Nico's breakfasts. Wear somethin' sexy while you do it."

Every part of Harlow's skin crawled. Her thoughts were cold and full of venom, imagining a fork jammed in his throat. She wanted to kill him where he stood.

"That's not gonna happen. Not in a million years. Now go check the drying bins. Nico almost flipped one over, acting like a psycho."

When Jax left, she called Raylene. "I want a jar of Nico's hand cream, and I need it now."

"I opened my last jar during Nico's last visit. You can have it, but I'll need to make more before he returns, and I don't have time to go to the smoke shop. Jax is being difficult again and threatening me and the baby, so I need to work and earn more money to get away from him."

There was no question. Harlow wanted to kill Jax for herself and for her close friend. No doubt he was cheating on Raylene. "Don't worry about going to the nail salon anymore or seeing Jax."

"What do you mean?"

"Just bring the cream over to the desal plant in ten minutes."

A voice came from the overhead speaker. "Boat docking in thirty minutes."

The Mexicans were coming.

A small SUV stopped near the fence line of the desalination plant. Harlow jogged down to the gate and opened it. The driver's window rolled down, revealing Raylene as the driver.

"Whose car is this?" Harlow asked.

"Mine. Didn't have enough gas to get here and back, so I borrowed one of the other manicurists' cars." Raylene held out a twelve-ounce jar, three-quarters filled with hand cream. "Slap some of that on Jax."

"Jeez. Thought you wanted to keep him around. I'm doing my best to keep him alive for you. What happened?"

"That wimp-ass Junior tried to hit on me, and he said Jax was all right with it. I want that jerk out of my life."

Harlow snatched the jar from Raylene's hand. "Well, that's a bitch. You want him to leave you alone?"

"Yes."

"I need all this for Nico, but don't worry, I got something else for Jax."

"Promise?"

"Yep." Harlow patted the roof above Raylene's head. "Now, get out of here. Trouble is coming."

When the vehicle turned around and left, Marla's camera captured the automobile's motion, but with the dark tint on the windows, the driver was unrecognizable.

Harlow rushed inside the building and checked to make sure Jax was out in the back with the bins, filling the dried fenethylline into the sacks. Another one of Pacheco's men pushed a handcart with three sacks into the mixing room and poured the powder into the machine, making the final tablets. She chuckled when a cloud of white powder surrounded the man, who wore a respirator covering only his mouth and not his nose. He might not live until tomorrow.

When Harlow entered Nico's room, she eased the door closed and locked it behind her. Nico rolled on his side before sitting up in his bed. His feet hung down.

"Did I wake you? I'm sorry." She stepped closer.

Nico swept his hand over his unkempt hair. "What happened? How did I get here?"

"You got sick and threw up in the kitchen, so Slats carried you in here to rest."

"He didn't give me a Valium, did he?"

"No. I asked Raylene if she could send over that soothing hand cream you like." Harlow held the jar up for him to see. "She rushed right over with a jar. You want some?"

"Um, yeah. Might be good, I guess."

"Raylene told me to warm it in water so it could soak in more thoroughly. I can spread it on your hands, but to make you feel better, I could also rub some on your arms. If you remove your shirt, I could put it on your chest." Harlow brushed her green hair from her face, making sure Nico watched. "I'm a little hot. Is it okay if I take this off?" She slipped her sweatshirt over her head and dropped it on the floor, revealing a tight-knit, sleeveless top and no bra.

Harlow gazed at Nico in the mirror. She watched him stare at her ass as she stepped to the sink. *Watch, you pervert.* Harlow's hips swayed from side to side as she let the hot water beat down on the glass jar. The water stopped, and she set the jar on the countertop. *No need for a towel. Let's see if you like this.* She rubbed her hands over her buttocks several times.

Watching Nico still staring at her every move, Harlow could tell his head throbbed as he pushed his thumb and fingers against his temples. She laughed inside when he had taken his shirt off, knowing he had high hopes. "All right, sit on the edge of the bed." She knelt facing him and then squeezed closer between his knees. The tip of her tongue licked her lips as she inserted her fingers into the cream and lathered a glob on the back of his hand. She felt him staring at her cleavage and her erect nipples as she dipped into the cream again, rubbing his arm up to his shoulder and over his upper back.

He complied without a word when she gestured to his other arm. He closed his eyes as the warm balm covered his skin. Her hands were smooth, cloudlike. He hardly heard her when she asked him to lie down. The sheet felt cold against his back, and the warmth of the cream over his chest. Her fingertips lowered to his stomach. He wanted her to go lower. And then she stopped. He opened his eyes when he heard the water running in the sink.

Harlow washed the last traces of cream from the jar, watching it swirl down the drain, then dropped it into the wastebasket. It shattered like his life, her life, once whole, now worthless.

She scrubbed her hands longer than necessary before drying them on a towel. With Nico still lying on the bed, she checked his pulse—fast. "Were you thinking of something good?" She slipped the sweatshirt over her head, covering her breasts. *Theatrics are over, pervert.* "I'll come check on you in about ten minutes." *That should be long enough.*

A haze surrounded Nico's mind as he heard the door close and the deadbolt lock. Moments later, his stomach churned and cramped. He turned to his side, fell off the bed, and vomited on the floor. The putrid odor made him turn on his other side. Pushing himself up on his knees and gripping the mattress for support, he tried to steady himself. Nico's eyes flipped in and out of focus as he lost his balance and fell onto his back.

Chapter 34

The overhead speaker announced Pacheco's arrival. Harlow slipped a disposable mask on while walking down the hallway and straightening the sweatshirt before greeting the Mexican entourage at the front door with a smile. Pacheco had refused the mask, didn't smile or offer his hand, so Harlow gestured to Nico's office.

With a pock-marked face, a thick Fu Manchu down to his chin, and black hair slicked behind his ears, Pacheco stepped straight to the mini-bar and dropped a sack of American dollars on the counter. "Nico's cut." He poured himself a shot of tequila, took in a deep breath of the aroma, and drank it in one gulp, then poured another. The two men accompanying him stood close by.

"Shall we sit?" Harlow asked.

He studied her for a moment. "My men tell me you're the sister."

"Yes, sir. I am. I'm Harlow."

Jax entered the room wearing a mask. "Sorry, I'm late."

Pacheco faced Jax. "Who the fuck are you?"

"Jax." He pulled his mask down for a moment for Pacheco to recognize him. "We met once before."

Pacheco turned back to Harlow. "Where's Nico?"

She asked again. "Would you like to sit?"

"No. Where's Nico?"

"He's been very sick the past few days. I'm the only other one who knows the correct calculations, so nothing has changed in production. Our tablets are far superior to that Syrian crap from the past few years."

Jax moved closer to Pacheco. "We can produce as much as you want."

Pacheco glared at Jax. "As much as I want? Looks like you're making more. Why were you selling to Houston?"

Jax took a step back. "No. That batch was not for you—"

Pacheco leaned into Jax. "Everything from here is for me."

Jax backed away. "That was a bad batch. We had to get rid of it, so I thought—"

"That's where you get in trouble," Pacheco said. "People die when they think they know more than me. You understand?"

Harlow interrupted. "Excuse me." She hit Jax on the shoulder. "We don't have bad batches, and what is this about Houston? Is that what happened to Steven? You told me the boat sank because of a mechanical problem." Turning to Pacheco, she said, "Did this Houston person do something?"

Pacheco narrowed his eyes. "You don't know?"

"Know what? What don't I know?"

Pacheco turned to Jax. "You know, right?"

Jax waved his hand dismissively. "Listen, I was trying to dump a bad product. Get it out, you understand. Can't just throw it in the dumpster, can we?"

"You must think I'm stupid. It didn't take long for your little Steven boy to talk. A few fingers bent backward make most people give all the information they have. You loaded the bottom of the boat with my pills, right?"

Harlow turned her head when the butt of a rifle struck Jax in the back of his skull.

Pacheco bent down and leaned into Jax's face. "Stealing gets you killed."

The rifle muzzle pressed against Jax's head.

"No!" Harlow cried out. "Please, not here. He won't do anything like that again. I promise."

"You're right about that, little girl." Pacheco motioned toward the man with the rifle, who grasped Jax by the collar and picked him up. Pacheco pointed his finger inches from her face. "Where's your brother?"

Harlow nodded several times. "Yes, of course. This way."

Pacheco gestured with his head, and one man shoved Jax in the opposite direction.

"Where are you taking him?" Harlow asked.

"Better you don't know."

While walking down the hall and holding the sack full of Nico's money, Harlow thought, *You damn well better be dead.* She unlocked the door and opened it. Nico lay motionless on his side, surrounded by vomit. Harlow's lips broke into a small smile. She rushed in and dropped the sack on the bed. Shaking him a few times, she whimpered a fake cry. "Nico? Wake up!" She slapped his face. "Wake up." She put her fingers on his neck. "Oh, no! I think he's dead."

Pacheco stood in the doorway. "What happened?"

"He started taking the drug and couldn't stop. I begged him so many times, and he said he was going to quit for good."

Pacheco stepped into the room and latched onto a handful of her green hair. "I should kill everyone here and burn this place down."

Harlow wiped her cheek as if there were a tear and then put on a determined expression. "I can run this place. I will make as much as you want. Bring the chemicals to me daily, and I will make a perfect drug for you—one hundred percent pure."

He pulled a knife out from a sheath on his belt, forced her to the floor, and pressed the tip of the blade against her cheek. Drops of blood appeared. "I can find another place."

Harlow clenched her teeth, promising herself not to give in to him. When the tip twisted and blood oozed down her cheek, her breaths hardened. "That...that would take months, maybe years to set up. You need it now. You need me. I've been running this place for the last week, and I ran it perfectly. You didn't even know I was doing it."

Pacheco yanked Harlow up and backhanded her, rolling her across the floor. He grabbed her by the hair again and pulled her head back, then sliced her sweatshirt down the middle. His eyes lingered on her tight, low-cut top, her breasts heaving with each deep breath.

She felt a cold blade against her skin as he sliced her t-shirt from neck to stomach, exposing her breasts. Terrified for the first time in her life, she forced the words out, "I can do this for you."

"Lucky for you, they're too small for me." He threw her back to the floor. "Can you do anything, pendeja?"

Still crouched on the ground, Harlow turned to look at him. "If you want us to run this place 24/7, then leave Jax here with me. Nico didn't run this place by himself, and I can't either. You want four thousand pounds a day? Ten million tabs each and every day? I can do that, but I need him here." Harlow stood. In defiance, she let the cut shirt fall open, revealing her breasts to him. "You just make sure the boats from Mexico get here twice a day, with enough amphetamines and theophylline to make the product."

Harlow cringed when Pacheco's hard finger thudded against her chest. It hurt, but she refused to show the pain to him.

Pacheco aimed the tip of the knife at her face. "I give the orders around here." He glanced at her small breasts. "Just as soon cut your throat and take over now."

"None of your men know how to mix the product. With Nico dead, I'm your last hope to keep this place running. Give me a week, and I'll show you what I can do." She swallowed hard before continuing. "I want double what Nico was making. Cash, American dollars, no drugs, and no pesos."

Pacheco stared briefly before nodding once. "For that, I'll send more boats, and I want the finished product in three days...twelve thousand pounds, or everyone dies. And don't forget, chica, I have eyes watching your every move."

Once Pacheco disappeared around the corner, Harlow snatched the sack of money off the bed and glared at her dead brother. "This is mine now, you pervert. You locked me in my room and made me a prisoner. You ogled me and wanted to fuck me." She kicked him in the head once and then pointed at herself. "I'm the smart one."

Through the surveillance camera in the sand dune, Marla observed Pacheco marching toward the forty-foot boat. Upon boarding, two men threw Jax off the vessel onto the pier, hands and feet bound with zip ties. Several men from the building hurried down the pier and severed Jax's restraints before helping him to his feet as the boat left.

❖

Harlow grabbed a pullover from Nico's dresser and put it on. She knelt beside her brother's lifeless body and searched his pockets for the key to her room. She rolled her eyes when she found it dangling from a gold ring with a heart charm. "What an idiot! Did he think this would make up for everything?"

Inserting the key into her door's keyhole, she snapped it off. "No one will imprison me ever again."

"What do you want to do with Nico?"

Harlow turned around and glared at Jax. "Speaking of an asshole..."

"Screw you, bitch."

"Sprinkle some of the fenethylline on his clothes and a little in his mouth and nose, then dump him outside of town near the border. Let the coyotes feast on him."

"During the day? Are you nuts? Someone might see us and call that in."

"Then I guess you better drop him and get out of there. Do it."

Jax stood still, arms crossed. "No. Tell someone else to do your dirty work."

Harlow leaned into him. "It's because of me that you're alive. Pacheco wanted to throw your lazy, thieving ass in the ocean, but I convinced him not to. You do what I say, or I'll call Pacheco."

"What is this, a coup? I have too many here who are loyal to me."

"You lost all respect when they saw you tied up like a helpless little lamb and thrown on the pier like garbage. You got no one on your side." Harlow turned and walked away. "Now go do what I said, or die by tomorrow." She stopped and turned back. "And call Leo. Tell him I want to meet with him tonight, not tomorrow...here, not there."

Chapter 35

Jax and two of Pacheco's men pitched Nico's dead body inside a service van with no markings, connecting it to the Palermo Desalination Plant. Jax took the precaution of removing the license plates. Driving along the sandy beach, they hit the paved road back to town. The two men sat in the rear and spoke Spanish to each other while Jax drove, wishing he knew more Spanish.

"Hey!" Jax yelled. "Shut up back there. I can't concentrate." Jax stopped at one of the last traffic lights on Padre Boulevard when he caught a cop car in his rearview mirror. "Shit, shit, shit. We have a cop behind us. Don't say a word." Jax glanced at both men as they pulled their knives from the sheaths attached to their belts. "Whoa, guys. We are not killing a cop in the thick of town with a hundred witnesses. Put those away." When the light turned green, Jax eased through the intersection, and the police car behind him turned left. He took a deep breath. "Okay. Clear."

Jax felt a bump against the driver's seat, then a knife against his throat. "Hey, puta. How 'bout I cut your throat? We get rid of the body." The side door slid open. Cars passed the van in the right lane. "We ditch it here."

"Wait. You do, and we're dead." Jax glanced back again as they rolled it closer to the edge. "Oh, come on, man. Don't do it!" Jax turned hard left to avoid hitting a vehicle. Cars honked. The two men lost their balance and fell out, hitting the street along with the body. Jax floored the accelerator and headed back to the plant. In the rearview mirror, he watched the two men run away, leaving the body in the middle of the road. "Oh, this is so fucking bad."

When Jax returned to the desalination plant without Pacheco's two men, Harlow questioned him about their whereabouts. After Jax gave a feeble excuse, she knew the trouble ahead. If those men survived, crossed the border, or ended up arrested, they would inform Pacheco what happened, sealing her fate. She was not safe inside the building with ten of Pacheco's men close by, and dangerous outside with Nico found dead on the street and the cops soon looking for answers. Strapped for cash and Pacheco controlling the finances, she found herself trapped. Jax was her last pawn to play. Convince the man not to run and keep him in the building—trade Jax's life for hers.

Her ambition burned bright to control her life, helm the business, and churn out thousands of pounds of fenethylline every day. She knew the formula and had perfected the process. She was willing to work 24/7 for a guy who punched a hole in her face, yet that act paled in comparison to what Pacheco might do if she didn't produce. Yet doubt lingered, gnawing at her insides. Crazy? Maybe. Stupid? No. Going forward in a brainless direction wouldn't get her what she wanted, which she hadn't decided on. Is it money? Power? Fame? The infamous *girl* who fought for what was hers and outsmarted the Feds and the cartel? Despite Pacheco's physical threats to destroy her. Despite betting her life on everything that needs to go right, but rarely does at that plant, maybe she should just pack up and run.

❖

Ricky sat at his desk, dressed in a pressed uniform with a badge on his chest and a telephone receiver next to his ear. He wrote an address down on a piece of paper. "Yes, ma'am. Thank you for the call. I will have a unit over there very soon." After hanging up, he walked to Standish's office and knocked twice on the open door. "An individual called in a dead person. Said someone dumped it on the street."

Standish tossed her empty coffee cup into the wastebasket. "When?"

"Just now. Here's the address." He placed the paper on the desk. "I'll dispatch a unit immediately."

"On Padre Boulevard? The middle of the tourist section?" Standish stood and stepped around her desk. "I'll meet them there."

"Can I go with you?"

"Yeah. Come on."

Two police cars had already arrived at the scene, their emergency lights flashing, trying to block curious eyes. When Standish stopped, she noticed a single white male lying on his side, clean-cut, dressed in nice clothes, and didn't appear homeless. "Ricky? Grab the reel of yellow tape in the back seat and mark off the area. I'll check the body."

Standish gloved her hands and stepped over to the other two police officers standing nearby. "Dead?"

"Right, Sarge. Thirtyish white male. No obvious bleeding. No restraints, but, as best as I can tell, without moving it, there are a few scrapes on the face. I checked for a pulse. Nothing. The body is not warm, so it's been dead for at least an hour. Here's the strange thing, there's a powder covering the facial area, almost like someone sprinkled it after the fact. A junkie wouldn't squander a drug like that, not a live one."

"Good to know. Do we have the witness here?"

Yeah, standing by my unit, who said a van slid the side door open and two men and the body fell out. The men ran away. We're looking for them now. No one got a license plate or a photo."

"There's a thousand tourists here, and no one had their phone out taking pictures of whatever?"

"No one owns up to it."

"So, of course, you thinkin' murder?" Standish knelt and checked the body lying face down with one side of the face against the asphalt. She recognized the face. Her fingers touched a pulseless neck. "Definitely dead."

The cop scoffed. "Looks that way, Sarge. We need to get the coroner here."

After wrapping the perimeter with yellow police tape, Ricky stopped beside Standish. "Who is it?"

Standish stood. "Look for yourself."

Ricky bent his head near the dead man's face and gasped. "No way. This is bad." His hand brushed over his cheeks as he glanced side to side and behind him.

"What's bad?" Standish asked.

"It's, um...it's Nico Palermo."

"I know that...the guy who runs the desal plant. Changes everything."

"Who is it?" Marla asked.

Ricky turned. "How'd you get here?"

"My truck. Why?"

"No one at the station called you," Ricky said.

"I listen to the police band, and when I heard about a dead person on the street, I came over. Why are you so nervous about it?"

Ricky fidgeted with the phone in his pocket. "Me? Not sure what you mean."

"You've seen dead people before, haven't you?" Marla asked.

"Yeah. All the time."

"You sound like this is New York or Chicago."

"Well...no...I mean, of course, I've seen a dead person before." He turned to Standish, who stood there and let Ricky dig a deep hole for himself. "This is someone I know...I mean, acquainted with. Others were just random people." Ricky pulled his phone out of his pocket. "Listen, I should call for more help."

"No calls. The coroner is on the way," Standish said. "And we need no more cops out here. It's disruptive enough for the tourists and traffic."

Ricky shoved the phone back into the pocket. "I'm going to take a minute." He stepped away.

"What is that about?" Marla asked.

Standish shrugged. "Haven't a clue."

"He's seen a body before, hasn't he?"

"Yeah."

"Many?"

Standish scoffed. "This is Padre. Except for the recent ODs, the answer would be a big fat no."

Ricky stood with his back to them fifty feet away and his phone pressed to his ear as he spoke in hushed tones. "Leo? We just found Nico dead on the streets...how am I supposed to know how...nothing big, no blood, no obvious gunshots...nothing...maybe...it could be drugs, but I thought he was clean...yeah, of course, they'll do a tox on him. With all the other ODs in town, that will be priority one. This looks like stupid ass Jax's work. He's an idiot, and you should get rid of him. After all this, we're done. I'm not crossing any more lines for you."

"Who's Leo, Ricky?" Of course, Marla knew the answer but wanted to see how he responded."

Ricky disconnected the call and shoved the phone into his pocket. "Who? No, no. I was talking to, um, Theo, not...who did you say?"

"Leo. I heard the word, Leo."

"No, you're mistaken. Theo is a buddy, and I called about something kinda personal. I don't want to discuss it. He stepped away from Marla, but she moved back in front of him.

"How about Leo Searcy?"

"I can't speak about official police business."

"Oh, I understand that," Marla informed him with a coolness in her voice. "But just for your information, Leo Searcy lives outside of your jurisdiction, about twenty miles beyond the Queen Isabella Causeway. Why call someone outside the city limits about a death here?"

Ricky shifted. "We interact with other cities, so I'm not sure who or what you're talking about. But, like I said, official police business is not your business."

Marla let him go without further discussion. Now was not the time to interrogate a police officer in the middle of a death scene.

She called the San Antonio office and spoke to Tillman again. "Sam? Time for another update. Someone saw Nico Palermo thrown from a van onto the town's main street. He's dead. He was a person of interest, well, until a few minutes ago. This smells more like a cartel killing. I'm going to need your help. The police department will investigate the Palermo case as a murder, and I sure could use confirmation if his blood is positive for fenethylline as soon as possible. Tomorrow would be best."

"You understand that's not happening. There's a backlog everywhere with city detectives, state troopers, and a multitude of federal agents who want their results an hour before you get yours."

"What if I can get the tox done in Bexar County tomorrow?"

"We must follow protocol, and Bexar County is not the location for the tests or autopsy. Courts could throw that out."

"Okay. Understood, but what if I accidentally acquired a little blood and urine and *unofficially* had it run at the Bexar County Crime Lab tomorrow? We couldn't use it as evidence, but my case, our case, could jump into the stratosphere with a positive result."

"Marla, you're asking a lot. I'm just here until Borland returns."

"Right. Of course, Sam...unless you are hoping to secure your spot as the next Assistant Special Agent in Charge somewhere in the United States. Locking in on the beginnings of a fenethylline outbreak before anyone else *could* do that for you, but only if you take a chance...unofficial chance if you understand what I'm saying."

Tillman took a moment to reply. "I don't know what you're talking about, so I'm forgetting this conversation. Do you understand what I'm saying?"

Marla made a fist. *Yes.* "Understood." She ended the call and made another.

"Bexar County Crime Lab. David Weidman speaking."

"David, it's Marla Adams."

"Marla? Great to hear from you. What's going on in your world?"

"I'm working down in South Padre. Hope all is going well with you."

"Oh, yes. This place is rocking full tilt every day."

"Hmm. Well, that's why I called. I need a favor, an unofficial favor."

"Sounds interesting."

"We have a death here today, and the body will go through the protocols of tests and autopsy, but it could take weeks for the results. I really need to find out if this person had fenethylline in his system."

"Fenethylline? The stuff from Syria? Wow! I had no idea it was here."

"Yep, it is. The police department called us in to help after several overdoses. If I sent you a blood and urine sample, could you, unofficially, of course, run a tox report?"

"Remind me what is in that."

"The two main chemicals are amphetamines and theo-phylline."

"Okay. Just those two or a full tox?"

"Everything, please."

"Just between you and me, right? Nothing official." David confirmed. "When can you get it here?"

"That's where the problem comes in. I'm not sure how to obtain them. They're taking the body to the county office for the autopsy, so I, or someone else here on the street, can't just stick needles in veins and bladders before they take the corpse away. How do I convince the doctor at the autopsy to give me the specimens?"

"The crime labs and the medical examiner's offices are a pretty close-knit group in Texas."

"David, I don't wish to get you into trouble."

"I have a fraternity brother who works in South Texas. Let me see what I'm able to do. Okay, if I text you if he can help?"

She couldn't help but smile. "That'd be wonderful. Thanks, David."

Chapter 36

The next morning, Harlow observed the fishing boat edging near the dock from the control room. When the captain and a deckhand pitched the coarse fiber of the ropes from the deck, two armed men from the plant tied a bowline knot to each cleat hitch. Everything looked good to her so far.

Jax knocked on the control room door and called out to Harlow, "Boat's here. Delivery of the products and transferring the Mexican plant workers should begin soon."

Harlow wanted to lock the front door and not let Pacheco's men inside, but that wouldn't go over well at all. Nico's paranoia ran deep about the Mexicans, Pacheco in particular. After what Pacheco had done to her the previous day, she felt the same way. People who looked at her would see a scar on her cheek and wonder what happened. Leaders have scars...losers are dead. With her brother out of the picture, Harlow charged into the leadership like she had practiced her battle plan for a long time.

She snapped back, "I can see them on the monitor."

Before the DEA agent arrived, Pacheco sent his men in their regular clothes, rotating a dozen in twenty-four-hour shifts. He worked them hard, kept them from being comfortable, and checked each before they left the building, making sure they didn't steal any drugs. Twelve men in, twelve men out, each group passing the other on the pier, but that suspicious activity couldn't happen anymore with Adams in the mix.

Harlow stepped out of the control room, making sure the door closed behind her since Jax was somewhere close.

"Your crazy idea better work," Jax said.

"And what did you come up with? Nothing, that's what." Hoping to appease Pacheco if push came to shove, Harlow proposed having the Mexican workers wear uniforms from a cleaning company. After all, every business has outsiders clean their building, and the Palermo Desalination Plant is no exception. Still, anyone peering through binoculars or a drone would question a dozen men arriving and leaving simultaneously on the pier.

"We'll see if the Feds or ICE charge the pier and arrest everyone," Jax said. "I gotta go back where the stuff is drying."

"Good." Harlow waved her hand in dismissal. "Go."

Harlow planned to increase the prodrug deliveries from Mexico to two boats a day, not one, and run the cooking containers at five hours, not six, thereby increasing production by twenty-five percent. She didn't care if the final product was not perfect, not anymore. She needed numbers, bigger than what Nico produced.

The first-morning boat drops off the incoming crew from Mexico during a covert drug exchange, swapping prodrugs for finished tablets, then departs without men. A few hours later, with the next delivery, the outgoing crew, wearing the same coveralls, boarded the boat for the return trip, making the daily cleaning operation appear routine.

Meanwhile, Festus chased seagulls while Marla rested on her porch chair and stared at a forty-foot vessel beside the desalination plant dock on her phone. The odor of the decaying tiger sharks had become secondary. The reception from the hidden camera in the sand dune just twenty feet from the pier was excellent, revealing an ordinary, unassuming craft. Unlike other charters, this one lacked the usual array of long fishing poles protruding into the air.

A dozen Hispanic men wearing dark blue coveralls disembarked and walked down the pier toward shore. Marla murmured, "What are they doing?" She zoomed in on the small logo on the upper left pocket, BHH Cleaning. "Where have I seen that before? Goodwill? The veteran's store?"

Panting, Festus plopped down beside Marla. He was done with the birds. She leaned closer to him. "I guess even a desal plant has to be cleaned." She took a photo of the logo patch. "Is it easier to bring a crew by boat than by car?" Her fingers scratched the nape of the dog's neck. "Maybe Standish can find out what company that is." Marla exited the camera app and called.

Standish answered, "What's up?"

"I need a little info on a company. The name is BHH Cleaning. Ever heard of them?"

"B-H-H? Doesn't sound familiar. Why?"

"I've been watching the desal plant on my phone, and a dozen men wearing identical coveralls with a logo on the pocket climbed out of a fishing boat and entered the building."

"From the pier at the plant?"

"Right. So, they're not from here?"

"Never heard of them, but I could ask around City Hall. May not have much luck, though. After the warrant on the Whitmore trailer and the spoil island with nothing to show for it, the county judges have given me the cold shoulder, and I can't even get past the secretary of our city council member who owns the CBD shop you wanted to raid."

"What about the BBB or the Chamber of Commerce?"

"They're all in the same building, and all drink the same coffee…or Kool-Aid, if you know what I mean."

"Understand."

"It's as if everyone senses something is not right, but fixing it might run off the tourists."

Marla thought of Venice with hundreds of gondoliers and no automobiles. "Do people travel in boats rather than cars around here?"

"Sure. Transporting a dozen people on water from one end of the island to the other takes less time than driving…cheaper, too. Even from Corpus Christi to the island is shorter than driving. I can ask around about the cleaning company and let you know what I find."

◆

At the dock, the seemingly innocent fishing boat was a disguise. Hidden beneath the deck sat two thousand pounds of ivory-colored powder in vacuum-sealed bricks stacked on top of each other, a small mountain of contraband. The bricks, wrapped in black tape, contained amphetamine, while the other bricks, wrapped in green tape, held theophylline, which together served as the precursor to fenethylline.

The small fishing boat's rumbling engine hummed. A porthole, smudged with salt spray and rusty corrosion above the waterline, but below the level of the dock, blended seamlessly into the fishing boat's hull. Instead of a traditional glass pane, the porthole housed a reinforced rubber gasket fitted with a locking collar. The inside rim contained a quick-seal coupling similar to those used in industrial airlocks.

A deckhand crouched low near the bow, his eyes locked on the dock's underside. Tucked below the weathered planks, hidden from casual view, was a black tube. He reached down, attached the tube's end to the porthole, and secured the collar with a sharp metallic click, creating an airtight seal. The tube stretched out from the hull, dipping into the water before running underneath the pier to land and then burrowing beneath the sand, reaching almost a hundred yards underground to the desalination plant.

The setup dawned on Nico when he watched an outdoor leaf vacuum/blower commercial on television. Suction in, blow it out. His design was flawless, with no surface interactions, no suspicious cargo moved on the dock or pier, just a seamless covert transfer from the ship to the shore.

Once the transfer was complete, the deckhand disengaged the tube with a simple twist and replaced it under the dock. The gasket on the ship resealed, leaving no trace of its function. It was a perfect mechanism for invisible transactions.

Inside the boat and below deck, the captain knelt by the porthole where the opening of the tube connected. Under the dim glow of an incandescent light, he checked the contraband to be transferred before contacting the plant on a two-way radio. "Captain to control room."

Harlow responded. "Control room."

The voice took the captain aback. "Who is this?"

"Nico is not here. I am, so get the ball rolling."

"Put Nico on. I want to hear his voice."

"Nico's not coming, so get ready or get out of here."

The captain hesitated. He couldn't leave without unloading. Pacheco would not be forgiving. His only choice was to permit her to operate the vacuum system. "Ready."

Harlow flipped the switch and activated the generator, suctioning a long underwater pipe from the building to the boat.

Crouching next to the pipe, the captain double-checked the seals and tugged on the hose while listening to the faint hiss of suction coming to life. The tube hummed, a soft vibration traveling through the boat as the vacuum system came online. He fed one brick after another into the system.

Four men stood on the desalination plant's second floor, positioned at the opposite end of the tube system. Two pulled out the bricks with black tape while two others sliced them open with KA-BAR tactical knives and fed the powder into the silo labeled AMPHETAMINE. When the green taped bricks came, the men switched to filling the silo labeled THEOPHYLLINE.

Once the captain transferred all the bricks from the boat, Harlow reversed the airflow in the tube. "Ready to send product."

"Ready on this end." Hundreds of bricks filled with fenethylline tablets arrived every few seconds, and the captain stacked them on top of each other as quickly as he could. When the last one came through, he called to turn off the blower.

The deckhand disconnected the tube from the porthole and placed it back under the wooden pier. He untied the ropes from the hinge cleats and pitched the thick, coarse fiber onto the boat before boarding. Moments later, the craft slipped away from the dock, leaving behind ripples in the water.

Chapter 37

Marla called Tillman to explain the situation. "Not much activity. From the deck of the plant, a cleaning crew disembarked from a boat. A guy looked like he was cleaning something off the side of the hull, but I couldn't see what he was doing when he stooped below the level of the dock. Sam, I appreciate you being there in San Antone, but I do wish I could speak to Borland. His experience with crazy stuff is beyond anyone else."

"Someone in the lunchroom said he went to South Padre to visit his nephew. Did he contact you?"

Marla jumped up from the chair. "He's here? Why was I not told that?"

"I only found out a little while ago. I was going to call you."

"Where is he staying? A hotel?" There were no coincidences in the DEA, and if Borland had been in town, he should have contacted her. "Did he come here for the fenethylline investigation? Is he monitoring me?"

"No, Marla. Your mentorship ended long ago. The South Padre Police Department requested help the day after he left," Tillman said. "He didn't know anything about it."

"Can you find out where he is staying and call me back, please?"

"Why don't you try calling him? He might answer."

She ended the call and then dialed Borland's number. After the phone rang twice, it went straight to voicemail. She hung up and called again. It transferred to voicemail again. After three tries, she gave up. "Why don't you answer?"

Marla's phone rang once before answering. It was Tillman. "Took a minute to find out everything because when Borland left, so did his administrative assistant. He didn't fly to South Padre. He drove. Planning on staying a day or two and then driving to the Harlingen airport and flying to Los Cabos, Mexico."

The shoulder joint. "Didn't you tell me the story about Borland getting shot in the shoulder during a raid?" Marla asked.

Tillman paused before replying. "Not sure if I told you, but he did get shot. Are you thinking that the shoulder joint in the shark's stomach is Borland's?"

Marla returned to her chair. "My mind sweeps too wide sometimes with crazy thoughts. Check the airlines and see if he boarded a plane heading to Cabo. If he did, then the shoulder joint is back to an unknown."

Marla ended the call and proceeded to her FIND MY app. When she typed in Borland's number, an unfamiliar address several streets off from Padre Boulevard popped up. "So, he's here?" She hopped over the porch fence and opened her truck door, with Festus jumping from the sand onto her lap and into the passenger seat in a single fluid motion. Her phone served as a GPS, guiding her down a road that no tourist traveled, past a metal reclamation business, a fish processing plant, two used car lots with autos all twenty-plus years old, and a tow service company enclosed by a twenty-foot solid metal fence. She parked near the fence gate before leaning toward Festus and telling him to stay in the cab.

After opening the front door of the building and flashing her badge at a man sitting on the other side of a counter, she said, "I'm DEA Special Agent Adams, looking for a vehicle."

A male with a heavy black beard and tattooed forearms had lost his politeness years ago from obnoxious customers demanding their vehicles back at no charge. "Got a license plate number?"

"No." Marla turned her phone around for him to see. "It's this car where the blue dot is. Had to be picked up recently."

He leaned in and gazed at the screen. "Okay. Looks like the fifth or sixth row. What's the big interest?"

She had to come up with an excuse. "The owner is a missing person in a drug case, and this might be his vehicle."

He shook his head. "I can't just let someone wander through the yard looking at every car we got. What's the car model?"

"Go with me if that makes you more comfortable. Just let me look around, please."

"Maybe you need a warrant for that."

Marla sighed. "Don't make me call Standish to help."

He straightened up on his stool. "You know her?"

"Yes."

"Hmm, I'm not sure."

"Hold on a minute." Marla called Standish. "I need to go inside a towing service lot, and I'm getting blowback. Can you help and speak to the person at the counter?" She handed the phone to the employee. "She wants to talk to you."

He paused before taking the phone. "Hello? This is Bobby." He stood almost at attention. "Yes, ma'am, I can do that for you...yes, of course...yes, ma'am, whatever she wants...yes, ma'am, anything for you. Thank you, sir...uh, ma'am." He handed the phone back to Marla. "Follow me."

As they walked down a row of vehicles, Marla thought about which was Borland's. "Show me which one is the cleanest, not the most expensive, but the cleanest."

"Got several. Tourists wash their cars before coming here."

Marla dialed his number and heard a ring from an open window. "There. That one. The Lexus." Opening the door, she found the phone in the cup holder. After pressing the ON button, the device lit up and asked for a four-digit password. She didn't know it.

Borland always kept his iPad with him, as if it were attached to his hip. Marla searched between and under the seats, and the glove box.

"What are you doing?" Bobby asked.

"Looking for something."

"Listen, lady. You need to get out of the car."

After giving up, she closed the doors. "Do you have the fob for this vehicle?"

"No. Someone abandoned it on the beach."

"Where?"

"Out north, past the city limits. Near that gray building."

"The desalination plant?"

"Yeah, that's it."

Marla held Borland's phone in her hand. "I'm taking this with me."

"Can't let you do that. Private property. When the owner comes to claim the car, he or she will be pissed if the phone is not there, and we'll have to buy a new one."

Marla continued grasping the phone. "Do I need to call Standish again?"

He held his hand up. "No, no. Please. One ass-chewing is enough. Take what you want. You just have to sign for it."

Marla closed the truck door and patted Festus on his head. After checking the time on her phone, mid-afternoon, she called Tillman again to contact Borland's secretary for the four-digit password.

Moments later, Tillman called back. "Got it, 1776."

"Makes sense, considering who he is. Did you find out if he boarded a plane to Cabo?"

"No flight this week listed him as a passenger."

Marla typed 1776, and the screen opened. "Hang with me for a sec. I'm going straight to the Find My app. Thank God! I got the iPad number." When she tapped it, a green dot glared motionless in the ocean. "Oh, hell."

◆

Dr. Hernandez's phone rang in his office. "Hello?"

"Doctor, this is Agent Adams. I need a huge favor. Something I hope you can do in a split second."

He scooted his chair closer to his desk. "If I can, I will."

"You indicated the area where the sharks were together for a short time. I must find the exact location of that spot. If you can, please send me the coordinates to my phone."

"Yes, of course. What's going on, if I may ask?"

She couldn't tell him. "Not a hundred percent sure."

After Marla ended her conversation with the vet, she called Standish. "I need a diving buddy. Are you familiar with anyone who owns a boat on the Gulf side for an excursion tomorrow morning?"

"Damn right I do. You got a lead?"

"As big as a tiger shark."

Chapter 38

At dusk, Marla's surveillance camera captured a Toyota Land Cruiser crossing past the pier. She should have placed another camera aimed at the gate.

Leo Searcy stepped out of the vehicle by himself and walked to the fence. After the guard let him in, he entered through the front door. Slats waited as Leo shook the sand off his shoes.

"Mr. Searcy, this way."

They walked past the conference room and the bedroom hallway, stopping at the kitchen entrance, where Harlow and Jax sat at the table.

"I'm glad you took a shower," Leo said.

Slats left, and Harlow grinned at Leo's comment. "Come in, and thank you for showing up."

"This is not a leisure call. Why am I here?"

Harlow stood and offered her chair. "Absolutely. Please sit. I have a proposal. Since I don't drink, I thought I would fix a meal, and we can hash out the details of how to keep this place operational—breaking bread, so to speak."

The scent of garlic, black pepper, and lemon wafted through the air as she walked around the island to the stove, where rice cooked inside a pot and quail sizzled in a cast iron skillet. She pulled open the oven door, releasing the aroma of fresh bread and roasted mushrooms.

Jax nodded. "She's a knockout cook."

Leo sat down. "All right. You said not to eat before coming here, so I'm hungry."

"Excellent," Harlow said. "I suggest we do this every couple of weeks. But, of course, you can come anytime you want."

Harlow wiped her hands on a kitchen towel before opening a bottle of wine. "Stag's Leap 2019? I understand it's one of your favorites from California." Leo watched her pour the wine into two glasses and handed them to Leo and Jax. She held her glass of ice water up. "To a business that will flourish even more." The three sipped from their glasses. "I'll bring the plates to you. The birds are small, so each of you gets six." Harlow filled two plates with the meat before adding the rice, mushrooms, and bread, placing them on the table. She set her plate with a salad, mushrooms, rice, and bread between theirs.

"I do hope you enjoy. I love to cook."

Leo eyed her plate. "You're not eating the quail. Why not?"

"I don't like game meat. Next time I'll fix chicken or pork."

Leo forked one and put it on her plate. "Eat."

Harlow chuckled. "You want me to be the court taster?" She pulled a leg off and winced while eating it. "There. Satisfied?"

"Eat more."

She tightened her lips. "I don't enjoy eating game, but Nico insists...I mean, he insisted on it for himself every day. I hope you don't mind having his favorite."

Jax forked the rest of the quail off her plate and placed it on his. "I don't have a problem with them." He stabbed a mushroom. "This is fantastic. Leo, try it."

Leo sipped his wine. "This is good."

"I'm glad, but I want to talk while we eat." She scooped a few sliced mushrooms onto her fork and ate them. "I will do whatever it takes to keep this place running, work harder than Nico, make more product, anything you and Pacheco want."

Leo left his food on the plate. "Forget about Pacheco and his worthless cartel. I let him think he runs this op. I feed money to the city, county, and state politicians, and make the desalination plant legit."

"I think Jax and I can manage any problems. He's tight with the Mexicans, and Pacheco loves him. Right, Jax?"

Jax stopped eating and looked at her in surprise. "Um, sure. Right. Pacheco and I are tight." He finished his glass of wine. "Can I have some more?"

Harlow poured more into Jax's glass and then gestured to Leo.

He shook his head. "You do what I say. There's a chance Pacheco might have an accident soon."

Harlow banged the bottle on the table. "Do whatever to Pacheco. This place is mine, and I can run it without him."

Leo took another sip of wine. "You can't run this place by yourself. You'll need help without the Mexican workers, and I'm able to find that for you."

"Then I want more money."

"More?"

"Ten percent off the top."

Leo leaned forward in his chair. "Why would I do that?"

"I have to train the new guys. Takes time. Time is money, and besides, I'm the only one who knows how to make this one hundred percent pure."

"Jax can train. You sit in the control room and do your job."

Harlow scooped up a forkful of rice and ate it. "Don't give Jax anything. He's worthless."

"Hey?" Jax said. "I'm right here."

Harlow pointed at Leo's food. "Are you done *not* eating?"

Leo leaned back. "The wine is enough for now."

She picked up all the dishes and rinsed them off before placing everything in the dishwasher and turning it on. After checking the time, she said, "Finish the wine, and then I have a surprise for dessert, that is, if the two of you want it."

"What is it?" Leo asked.

"I'll wait," Jax said. "I think I ate too fast."

Harlow stepped to the kitchen counter and lifted a round cake cover, revealing several brownies cut into squares. "A little bird told me you like brownies." After handing one on a plate to Leo, she did the same for herself. Harlow reached over to his dish, broke off a corner, and ate it. "It's safe."

He turned the plate. "Take another bite."

Harlow leaned over, pulled a corner off, placed it in her mouth, and chewed. "Satisfied?"

Leo broke half off. "Eat that."

"I'm tiring of this bullshit, Leo." She stuffed it in her mouth, chewed, and swallowed. "Anything else?"

Leo took her other half and ate a bite. "Keep talking."

"I take control of the operation 24/7. All you have to do is get the amphetamines and theophylline here every day."

Leo placed his wineglass on the table. "Interesting thought, but not a subject to finalize tonight." He stood and walked out, adding, "Come to my place tomorrow, and I'll have a proposal for you."

After Leo left, Harlow grabbed a handful of Jax's hair and pulled his head back. "Loser." She released his hair. "I'll give you ten more minutes."

"I'm going to kick your..." Jax stood, only to fall to the ground with stomach cramps. "What's goin' on?"

"Get up and go to Nico's bedroom." She kicked him in the butt. "Go! You can use the bathroom in there."

Jax rushed from the kitchen to Nico's room and opened the door. Harlow followed and shoved him inside. He stumbled and fell. Struggling to stand again, he yelled. "Bitch, I'm going to kill you."

Harlow snatched Nico's hanbo leaning on the wall and twirled it in her hand. "I'm ready."

When Jax ran at her, she spun around and slapped the wooden stick against his lower legs, knocking him down. "You're nothing but a loser."

Out of breath, Jax struggled with the words, "What did you do?"

"Hemlock poisoning. The quail is an interesting bird. It can eat hemlock all day and not die. But the poison doesn't go away. It's in the meat. The meat you ate. Oh, and by the way, you treat my friend like dirt. Why? Raylene is a wonderful woman. She gave you a child, and all you do is dump on her."

Jax's arms and legs became weak. He vomited again before convulsing.

Harlow knelt beside his head and looked into his eyes. "You see, if I feed you one quail, or even two a day, like I did with my rotten, perverted brother, you get just sick enough to feel bad *all day long*. But you, oh yes, you, six will kill you in just a few minutes." She glanced at Jax, who was lying dead. "One piece of crap down." She closed the door and locked it. "Leo Searcy, you're next."

Chapter 39

Marla paced back and forth on the deck of the thirty-five-foot, sensing the gentle hum of the motor beneath her and smelling the familiar scent of burnt diesel. The weather had been cooperative so far, with a bright sun shining tall at nine o'clock. She tugged at the collar of her long-legged wetsuit, the thick neoprene hugging her skin. It was her only suit, and she had trained in it for hours at the San Antonio pool. There was no way she was changing into a different wetsuit for her first real dive.

Her phone rang. It was Tillman.

"Hi, Sam."

"The Mexican government reported they stopped a Russian-registered cargo ship originating from a Syrian port. Evidently, no country allowed it to dock, and the ship has been at sea for months. When it crossed into Mexican waters, they boarded it, confiscating weapons and several thousand pounds of fenethylline tablets. Looks like what's left of the Assad regime is trying to sell as much as they can before the supply is completely cut off."

"Any chance we could get a sample of the drug and compare it to what we found with the dead couple in the lagoon?" Marla asked. "Same? Different?"

"Working on it. At least the Mexicans informed us regarding the vessel, but doubt they are permitting us to view the contraband."

"Is there any intelligence on Russian or Syrian vessels potentially discharging fenethylline in the Gulf?"

"Still working on that, too. Dumping thousands of fenethylline tabs in the Gulf would be devastating to the fishing community."

"Right about that. Thanks, Sam."

Marla laid her phone on the bench and watched Festus stand firm at the point of the bow, the wind blowing in his face, tongue hanging out of his mouth. He rode the waves like a surfer on a giant swell.

Standish wore a short-legged wetsuit and approached Marla. She pinched the end of Marla's suit around her neck. "This is thick. A cold-water suit. You're going to get hot in that thing."

"Don't know, don't care, don't have anything else."

Marla stood on the deck; the boat swayed as the waves grew, bouncing more and making her a bit unsteady. With Borland's phone in her hand, where the FIND MY app was tracking the iPad, she hoped the battery wouldn't die before getting to it, and all this was for nothing. A green dot marked the location hovering on the screen, bearing witness to its own disappearance in the depths of the Gulf, the area where Dr. Hernandez said the two sharks were together.

Glimmers of light that once danced across the water faded with incoming clouds. She watched the captain of the vessel navigate toward the designated longitude and latitude, and suddenly felt uneasy. This would be a jump not into a pool with clear, smooth water and sides to grab if needed, but an endless, volatile ocean stretching infinitely in every direction, with no clear end in sight.

Standish stood relaxed at the side rail, ready for the dive. She should, she had done this a hundred times or more. She stepped around the helm, feeling Marla's angst. "Hey, it'll be fine—a shallow dive, fifty feet at most." With a sweep of the hand toward the ocean and then the sky, "Don't worry about what is up here." Her hand held up a diving mesh bag. "I always bring this: a knife, flashlight, a spool of red ribbon to mark things, and a jelly jar to collect stuff." She pulled out a retractable rod. "I carry this on my belt. I use all this on most of my recreational and wreck dives."

"Yeah, okay, but what's down there? Just an iPad in a watertight container, or a boat, drugs, sharks...bodies?"

"There won't be any bodies," Standish said. "Sea life ate everything days ago."

"Oh, thanks for that cheerful image."

Marla closed her eyes and tried to forget the dead sharks, dead people, and an unforgiving ocean. Festus' wet tongue licking her cheek brought her back to reality.

The signal from the iPad had remained steady, but Marla couldn't shake off the questions circling in her mind. What else was down there, and did Borland accidentally drop it in the water, or was it a clash with man or beast? Each thought nibbled at her conscience.

Standish glanced back at her. "You good?"

Raindrops hit Marla's face as Festus trotted back to the bow. "Just wondering what happened. It all feels a little...off." She held her hand out toward the clouds. "Even this. An hour ago, beautiful. It's as if something is saying don't go in."

Standish smirked. "Listen, Poseidon is nowhere near here. You're reading too much into it. This happens out here. You'll be fine."

Marla turned away and tapped the phone screen again, focusing on the green dot. The device had been sitting in the same spot for days, almost forgotten. The anticipation churned in her gut.

Marla's phone rang again. On the other end was Dr. Hernandez. "Hello, Agent Adams. I have good news for you."

"Excellent. I could always stand for a little of that."

"With the help of the DEA, the orthopedic company released the name to us. You know, the shoulder joint."

"Okay." Marla grimaced. She didn't want to ask. "Whose is it?"

"It belongs to a man named Lloyd Metheny."

Marla leaned forward on the padded bench. A drizzle splattered the deck. *Thank God it's not Borland.* "Say that again."

"Lloyd Metheny. I took the initiative and searched for the name. He has a Texas captain's license. He either fell off the deck or a boat had to sink for a shark to…get the shoulder joint in its stomach."

Like the iPad? Can you find out which boat he captained?

"No, sorry. Unlike larger vessels and ships, they don't have to register their captain's name. They could work for several fishing or charter companies and be on different boats each week."

The rain increased. Marla and Standish spun toward the wheelhouse as the captain slowed the engine to a crawl and the boat wobbled in the sea. "Thanks, Doc. I have to go."

Chapter 40

Three days before the first shark beached

ASAC DEA Agent Ronald Borland parked his Lexus SUV on the deserted northern stretch of South Padre Beach, where a solitary pier stretched out into the clear blue waters. Half-hidden by a chain-link fence with rust-streaked barbed wire looped at the top, a lone gray building loomed nearby, with "PALERMO DESALINATION PLANT" printed above the front door.

He sent a text message from his cellphone to his boss, SAC Davies, in San Antonio, *Keep the place rolling for me. I'll be back in two weeks.* After the message delivered, he placed it on his thigh. The phone dinged almost immediately. *Call me this afternoon.* He nodded to himself and set the phone in the cup holder before unbuckling the seatbelt.

Borland opened the back door and removed a backpack before checking the contents: a San Antonio Spurs cap, sunglasses, two protein bars, his Glock, and a waterproof pouch holding an iPad and a USB drive. The water bottle on the side still felt cold.

His nephew, Steven McCale, stepped out from the passenger seat with a strained smile. "Perfect, right? We got a boat for the whole day. It's set up for us—anything we need."

Borland slung the backpack over his shoulder, its weight not as heavy as the tension in Steven's tone. The faint warmth of the early morning breeze surrounded him, still remembering his nephew's insistence on bringing a jacket—the wind was always chillier five miles out. With a nod, Borland gestured for Steven to lead the way as the gray building loomed behind them. "Your buddy's connected to that place?"

Steven's expression turned blank for a flash before he forced a laugh. "Forget the building, Uncle Ron. Let's fish."

They walked down the wooden pier, Borland's steady steps contrasting with Steven's impatient strides. "All this seems a little too isolated for a commercial charter business."

Steven didn't answer.

Borland grasped the railing and climbed aboard a forty-footer with chipped white paint and a faint smell of salt and diesel. "Not much of a looker."

Steven waved it off. "Don't judge a book by its cover, Uncle Ron."

The captain stood at the helm, a wiry, unshaven man in his fifties with a cigarette stuck between his lips and a faded captain's cap pulled low over his forehead.

Steven patted the captain's shoulder. "Ready to head out, Cap?"

The man glanced at them, then shook his head. "Hold up. Need a few more minutes."

Steven's face tightened. He whispered to the captain, "Minutes for what? This is not a good idea. Not today."

A muffled noise came from beneath their feet. "I need to go below." The captain opened the two-foot-tall doors of the wheelhouse and disappeared below deck.

Steven stiffened, a tense smile straining from the sound of objects bouncing against the boat's hull.

The captain poked his head above the deck and flicked the end of the cigarette overboard as he blew smoke into the air. "Almost done." He disappeared below again.

Borland arched a brow, watching Steven stand tense, with a forced smile. He dropped the backpack at his feet, sensing his nephew was hiding something. The sound below deck ceased, and the captain appeared once again. "All set now."

"*What* is all set?" Borland asked, stepping closer to the helm while glancing inside the wheelhouse before the captain closed the doors.

The captain gave Steven a sidelong look before answering. "Just securing the fuel line. Lost a little fuel last time out." His voice was as flat as the water around them. "Come around here. Let me show you my new depth finder."

Borland remembered the man smoking while working around fuel.

The engine rumbled to life. "Just relax and enjoy the ride," the captain uttered while adjusting his cap. He showed the instrument panel to Borland and Steven while the man on the pier disconnected the vacuum tube from the boat's hull. Borland turned when the ropes hit the wooden deck with a thudding sound, thick coils bouncing across the surface like heavy snakes. As the captain eased the throttle forward, a growing roar echoed across the waves, and the boat sped forward.

The coastline blurred as they continued farther out to sea. The wind whipped their faces, carrying with it the salty, clean scent of the ocean. Steven continued to smile too much. "This is going to be great fun, Uncle Ron. I'm really glad you came to see me. The island is beautiful this time of year."

Borland gestured to a padded bench seat. "I'm just going to sit for a minute. Don't want to get seasick."

"Oh, yeah, sure. Totally understand. I used to get that when I first started."

Borland settled into his seat as they continued farther out in the water. As it picked up speed, he reached into his front pocket for his phone—it wasn't there. "No, I left it in the cup holder." He unzipped the backpack and pushed aside his Glock while opening the pouch and removing the iPad with a USB drive attached to the side. He typed a quick message to his boss, *On fishing boat in South Padre. Something suspicious under the deck, possible drugs. More info later.*

He pressed the send button and then glanced at Steven and the captain, who both stared straight ahead. He looked back at the screen, where the message on the tablet read 'undelivered.' They were too far out to sea. Borland scanned all around the water for any other activity, but saw only cargo ships miles away. After placing the iPad beside him and leaning back, he shouted over the engine's hum, "How far do we go?"

The captain gave a slight nod. "Thirty more minutes. I found a spot that's been good lately."

The outboard motor hummed as the hull bounced against small waves. A hundred feet to the side, a pod of dolphins swam alongside. Borland asked, "Do you see many dolphins out here?"

The captain ignored the question and asked what line of work Borland was in.

"I'm a DEA agent."

The captain faced Steven and muttered. "Your uncle is DEA? We have pills below deck?" He turned to Borland. "If you go to the back, you can see more dolphins."

Steven waited for Borland to walk back. "That's why I said on the dock that," Steven pointed down, "this was not a good idea. This was not supposed to happen."

"Is Jax aware he's with the DEA?"

"No. I mean, I don't think so. It never came up, so I never mentioned it."

"How am I expected to move the product with him on board? I'll have to cancel the exchange. Keep your uncle at the stern while I call Jax." The captain grasped the microphone and called Jax on the radio. The two argued for a bit. A team from Houston planned to meet them at the designated coordinates to collect the drugs. Jax had made the deal, exchanged money, and he couldn't back out. The captain grabbed his binoculars and peered through them—a boat about a thousand yards away, heading straight at them.

Their boat veered hard left, dropping Borland and Steven to their knees.

"What the hell?" Steven shouted, gripping the rail. "What's going on?"

The captain jerked his head to the right, where a sleek, black boat trailing them was approaching fast and kicking up a spray of water in its wake. "That."

Steven's hand gripped the captain's arm. "Who's that?"

The captain remained stoic. "Not sure, but there's chatter on the radio, speaking Spanish, something about they found the boat."

Borland made it back to the wheelhouse, eyes squinting, and a sinking feeling in his gut growing. "What is this about, Steven?"

"Uncle Ron, I...I should help at the wheel. You should rest up on the bench seats near the back."

"Steven?"

"Uncle Ron, I'm..."

"Did you set this trip up?"

"Yes...at least I thought I did."

The captain interrupted. "Jax added a little sideline before the fishing excursion." He glanced behind them at the fast-approaching boat. "Was supposed to meet up with someone out here in a yellow speedboat coming from Houston. That," he pointed at the vessel bearing down on them, "ain't it!"

Borland's voice cut through the rising tension. "Tell me you didn't drag me into a drop. I work for the DEA, and you think I wouldn't notice?"

Steven's face turned pale. "Forget it—get back to shore! Now!"

The captain spun the wheel more, and Borland caught his balance. He watched as the captain grabbed the radio, calling out on a static-laden frequency, "We've got company. Repeat: we've got company. Turning back in, but still loaded."

Borland's face hardened as the enemy boat edged closer, his mind already in survival mode and mapping out the few options. With nowhere to hide and only open water around them, any escape required split-second actions. In his head, he measured the distance between the boats, watching the wake pattern as the dark hull cut through the waves. A message sent now could be their only hope. He grasped the tablet and took photos of the boat edging closer as the steady rumble of its engine grew louder.

"Uncle Ron, I'm sorry. I didn't mean for this—"

"Save it," Borland snapped, his voice low. "Tell me, what exactly did you bring on board?"

"Nothing, really. I promise."

Borland turned toward Steven with a sarcastic voice. "What drugs are under the deck? What other reason would there be for," he gestured at the boat following them, "that?"

Steven glanced down and hesitated before answering. "It's not my fault. It was supposed to be a routine fishing trip, but Jax decided, without telling me, to run a small shipment."

"You didn't tell me who Jax is." Borland removed the Glock from the backpack and stuck it in his windbreaker pocket. "Routine fishing trip? Don't think so."

"Wait. Uncle Ron, let's see what they want."

"They want your boat, Steven, and everything in it."

As they sped over open water, Borland picked up his tablet. As the vessel drew closer, he typed while maintaining a neutral expression. *Captain hiding drugs below deck. Pursued by drug runners.* Borland grimaced after hitting the send button, and it didn't deliver. No Wi-Fi. The urgent message sat suspended in digital limbo.

He stowed the device back in the pouch. He kept his face unreadable as he watched Steven's increasingly panicked expression. The messages would go through when they got closer to shore, if they made it that far.

The captain checked their speed, with the throttle at full power, but the pursuing boat continued to close in on them with every passing moment, its bow rising and slapping against the waves.

Steven's voice shook as he pleaded, "Uncle Ron, they'll kill us. What do we do?"

Borland's gaze hardened. "We fight. That's what."

Chapter 41

Steven turned back to the captain, his voice shaking with fear. They're gaining. Do something." He was startled by how calmly his uncle was managing the situation. "Maybe we just slow down, Uncle Ron, and let them pass."

Borland placed the iPad on the seat, his face betraying nothing. "Passing isn't what they have in mind. You know that as well as I do, don't you, Steven?"

At that, Steven's face flushed, jaw tightening at his uncle's words. "I... I didn't expect anything like this."

The captain swerved to the left, his sweaty hands gripping the wheel hard as he shouted, "Hold on!" Steven and Borland staggered but held their ground. The turn bought them a little distance, but the gap soon narrowed. As it closed in, Borland typed on the iPad once more. *Pursuers close to boarding*. Once again, the message failed to send.

Steven tried to keep his voice steady. "Uncle Ron?"

Borland replied, his mind dissecting their few options as the vessel drew nearer. "Steven, they are going to board this boat. Just be ready."

As if on cue, a burst of machine gun fire ripped through the air, shattering pieces of wood and metal from the railings. They all dropped to the deck. Sweat poured from Steven's neck while his body trembled. He gripped the back of the captain's chair.

Borland typed as fast as he could, sending a quick, final message: *Engaged and returning fire.* He hit the send button without waiting to see what happened. He pulled the pistol out of his pocket to check the mag, then slipped it back into his windbreaker pocket.

Borland slammed into the railing as the boat jerked hard.

Behind them, the black vessel charged like a predator, surging forward until it closed within a hundred yards. Gunfire tore through the air—spitting and screaming through the air.

Vicious pops ripped cables, whipping them loose in the air. Wood splinters bit his face.A hammering burst ribboned through the hull. The captain hit the deck as another burst exploded the windshield, throwing glass in every direction.

Steven's voice cracked. "We're dead! We're dead right here!"

Borland's eyes locked on the shoreline, close to four miles out, and caught the faint blur on the horizon, a gray building. A long shot, but close enough if they could move faster. His gaze darted between the captain and the oncoming boat. "Go! Push it!" he barked. Still time. Maybe. "Harder! Faster!"

More gunfire tore into the bow. White powder clouded out of the holes. Bullets zipped past them, shredding the deck and the wheelhouse. A burst of gunfire ribboned across the stern.Metal shrieked. The engine roared and belched black smoke, a dying gasp as it surged forward before shuddering. The boat staggered, dead in the water. Stuttering gunfire spat and hissed, chewing the sea into froth. Nowhere to run.

Borland felt them sinking lower in the water and to one side, the cabin listing as oily smoke rose from the engine compartment. His face hardened as he watched the other boat sidle up alongside them. Holding the tablet close to his chest, he photographed the vessel and the men again, then reached into his backpack for the waterproof pouch and dropped the iPad and USB drive inside before sealing it. He placed the cap on his head and grasped the two protein bars.

The approaching boat was less than a few yards out, and a rough voice cut across the water, shouting from a megaphone in Spanish, "Manos arriba!"

Two men jumped on deck, both wielding MP-5 machine guns. The first had black, uncombed hair covering his forehead and ears. He wore a thin, scraggly beard and a blood smeared Smiley Face T-shirt with SMILE NOW, CRY LATER printed above the yellow circle, black jeans, and green Crocs. The second man, thin, wore only torn brown shorts, revealing facial, neck, chest, arm, and leg tats. He gestured with the short barrel and spoke English. "Back! Back!"

Steven, pale and shaking, looked at his uncle. "I'm sorry about this. I really didn't think they'd... Uncle Ron, I didn't think..."

Borland's gaze was hard. "Stay quiet, Steven. I have an ace."

Steven's eyes widened, his voice a sharp whisper. "No. Don't do anything—"

Borland cut him off, calling out to the men in Spanish with an icy tone. "We're on a fishing trip. What do you want?"

The shirtless gunman narrowed his eyes and spoke in broken English. "You mess with Pacheco. I kill you, culeros."

The other, wearing the Smiley Face T-shirt, held his hand in front of his compadre. "Wait."

Steven stammered, face flushed. "This wasn't supposed to happen...I didn't want it to be like this."

Borland turned back, staring down the man in the lead while continuing to speak in Spanish. "We're just a charter boat for fishing. There are no drugs. Go check for yourself."

Steven's hand found his uncle's arm, squeezing it in a desperate warning. "Please, Uncle Ron. Don't let them search. Please."

Borland glanced at the captain, who was inching his fingers around the emergency channel button.

"Alto!" the thin gunman's voice roared.

A deafening burst of gunfire shattered the air, and sharp cracks ricocheted off the boat's deck. The captain's body jerked before slumping back against the wheel, his blank stare fixed on nothing as blood seeped through his clothes.

Steven stumbled over his words. "Oh, oh, G, God," His face drained of all color as he choked back a cry, his gaze riveted on the captain's vacant stare.

With calculated control, Borland's hand moved and aimed his pistol from inside the pocket of his jacket and fired. The shot hit the shirtless attacker square in the chest. He grabbed Steven's collar, pulling him down as bullets tore through the bridge. Borland felt something like a sledgehammer hitting his shoulder. On his back, Borland fired again, his return shots forcing the gunman to duck for cover. A sharp, burning pain shot through his shoulder as he squeezed the trigger again, his body moving even as the deck blurred in and out of focus.

Borland and Steven hid behind the edge of the cabin, impairing the gunman's line of sight. Someone jumped onto the deck. Borland pushed himself up, teeth gritting against the pain. Blood ran down his arm, staining the wooden planks. By studying their chatter, Borland calculated a row for a shot aimed at their knees. Tossing the two protein bars over the intruder's heads surprised them. When they looked up, Borland fired. He heard the men scream and drop to the deck. Borland fired again until the screaming stopped.

Steven whispered, "We're gonna sink, Uncle Ron!"

"Help me up. We need to take their boat."

The two crept around the left side of the wheelhouse.

"When I say so, run and jump in the back of their boat."

"No. I don't think I can do that. I'm, I'm too scared to go."

"You have to, Steven."

Borland aimed his pistol with one hand and held his cap with the other. "Ready?"

Two more men jumped on deck, making the boat wobble. Borland flung his cap out toward the water, hoping to get the men's attention away from them, but the cap spun in the air and plopped into the sea.

"Besame el culo." A shotgun blast blew a hole through the wheelhouse. Shards of wood sprayed Borland and Steven.

Another bandit yelled in Spanish, "Saca tu maldito culo de aqui!"

Steven stood with his hands raised. "Okay, okay. I'll give you the drugs. Just, just let us go."

One man stepped around the damaged wheelhouse, his plain gray T-shirt covered in blood splatter, and leveled his gun at Borland. "Dejalo, cabron!"

Borland pitched the pistol on the deck, grimacing as he raised his hands, blood seeping through the shoulder of his shirt.

A third man stepped aboard, wearing clean clothes and nice boat shoes, and spoke in English. "We'll send your boss a message. He only deals with us." He tossed heavy chains and shackles onto the deck, and the metal clanged in the tension-thick air.

Chapter 42

The temperature dropped several degrees as dark clouds rolled into the Gulf. The rain increased, leaving no dry spots on their boat. Marla glanced at Borland's phone as the boat stopped at the green dot. She asked again, hoping for the same answer. "It has to be in one of those waterproof pouches, don't you think?"

"That's the only way it could still work," Standish said. "Come on, let's get your tank."

With their scuba gear on, both rolled backward off the rail and into the ocean. Marla froze for a second, then a low sound of bubbles blew past her head, as she heard herself breathe underwater. The crystal blue water was serenely still. Rays of sunlight filtered down, illuminating scattered particles suspended in a watery sky. She focused on her instructor's guidance from San Antonio by keeping her hands and arms in front while pedaling the fins. After just two minutes, pressure built in her ears, signifying this was deeper than any depth in a swimming pool.

To Marla's left, a lone, red and white striped fish drifted with the current—an easy meal for a larger creature. She hoped she wasn't the same for a shark. Twenty feet in front of her, a dozen dark, sleek fish rushed across her sight, ignoring her.

Marla worried about claustrophobia, with the tight suit, the surrounding water, and not breathing real air—the opposite happened. The silent sea engulfed her in isolation, and the weightlessness felt like a bird coasting through the sky, leaving the hordes of human life behind.

Standish tapped Marla's shoulder, pointed at her regulator, and exhaled, blowing bubbles out. Marla needed to breathe. She nodded and took a breath.

When they reached the bottom, specks of sand and particles kicked up around their fins. The water nudged Marla to one side. Forty-seven feet down, the visibility was sharp and hauntingly eerie about an unfamiliar world below the surface.

When Standish gestured to follow, Marla pushed away, using her fins to propel herself forward.

A dark outline appeared, moments later becoming clearer. A boat sat submerged on the ocean floor, tilted, with six rows of chains hooked to a metal rail. Bullet holes riddled the deck and hull. The shattered wheelhouse looked as if it had been through a battle.

An empty black shoe lay on its side several feet away. A strange, iridescent haze encased the boat, rising like smoke in a windy sky. Marla found fenethylline, but questioned its rapid dispersal in the calm waters, and why was the drug still there? It had to be in packages.

As they slowed their approach, Marla grasped Standish's forearm and waved her hand not to get any closer. They eased upstream, avoiding the haze, and found the end of a twelve-inch pipe with murky water flowing toward the boat. That was why the tiger sharks had high salt in their blood. It had to be the brine solution coming from the outflow pipe of the desalination plant. Unlike standard discharge pipes, this one stretched twice as long as any other. Marla wondered why. Was the plant trying to hide the discharge? Poisons, toxins, excess salt content? Even at this distance, the effects were undeniable.

Standish took the jar out of the mesh bag, opened it, and stuck it against the opening of the pipe. She closed it and dropped it back in the bag.

When the sand swirled near their fins, Marla noticed a scattering of bones between her legs. Bones picked clean of everything, but they didn't look like fish bones. She stooped, chose one, and measured it against her forearm—slightly longer. She dropped it in the mesh bag.

Standish gestured at the boat's stern with excitement. Jackpot! A black backpack lay sideways on the deck near the stern. Marla took an extra breath as her heart raced. She pulled the regulator out of her mouth and smiled, but realized the bag was at the heart of the white cloud, and toxic. They dared not risk getting too close, as the drug would cling to their wetsuits and equipment. She couldn't enter the haze, which rose like a deadly phoenix. Two sharks three times her size were dead, and she didn't want to join them.

Standish unclipped the retractable rod from her belt and extended its length. Marla's eyes locked onto the haze as Standish maneuvered the rod closer to the backpack. With her arm fully extended, the tip played with the backpack's shoulder strap, careful not to disturb the underwater cloud. A sudden cold current passed through with a shift in the water. The toxic cloud changed direction, and Standish dropped the rod and spun around, swimming as quickly as possible. Marla held her breath as she grabbed Standish by her shoulder and dragged her farther away.

The current abruptly shifted again. They checked each other for any white particles on their suits and equipment. Marla pushed off the ocean's bed, and a bone that looked like a finger flipped in the water. She watched it hit the sand and gazed at bits of bone and cartilage close to it, stripped clean of all flesh. Standish bent down and dropped it in her bag. She motioned for Marla to try with the rod.

Marla grasped the extended rod and held it up at an angle. It wavered up and down and side to side from the slow, steady current pulling against her. She edged closer until the tip slipped under a shoulder strap. It took all her strength to lift it. A shadow swept over her, darkening the water. She looked up just in time to see a blue-green tail vanish into the distance—a shark circling them.

Her pulse hammered as the backpack slipped off the pole and settled back into the sand. The massive shark, with dark charcoal stripes and a white underbelly, reappeared, its powerful body coasting through the water, no more than a dozen feet away, its eyes black and fixed in her direction. She held her breath, trying to steady her nerves. The creature glided forward, its sleek, muscular form cleaving the ocean, its head leveled straight at her.

With a surge of adrenaline, Marla swung the rod and struck the beast square on the nose. The impact sent a jolt up her arms, and the shark whipped to the side, its body twisting so forcefully that it split the toxic haze like a parting curtain. For a moment, the backpack floated free, suspended out of the cloud. Marla seized the opportunity, thrusting her hand out to snag the strap.

Her fingers tingled, her mind raced at the thought of the fenethylline that might cling to the bag. She dropped it and unzipped it to reveal a waterproof pouch. Inside lay the iPad intact. She gripped the pouch and held it out to Standish, expecting a grin. Standish's eyes were wide, her hands flailing.

Before Marla could even react, a blunt force hit her in the back, knocking the pouch from her grip and sending her sprawling. A surge of icy fear rushed over her as she swiveled to see the predator circling back, its powerful tail churning the water. It turned, moving in a deadly, rapid arc. She pressed herself flat on the ocean floor, hands covering her head, as the shark surged past, its massive body creating a strong current. Seconds later, another powerful blow sent her sprawling over the sand. It spun around faster than Marla ever imagined. All she saw were dozens of sharp, white teeth protruding from its wide-open mouth. On her back, in a frenzied last chance, she grasped a handful of sand and threw it at the shark. She ducked and shielded her head again.

Standish appeared by her side and thrust the rod under the shark's jaw. The rod snapped in two. The shark whipped its head away, and with a single powerful stroke of its tail, it disappeared.

Standish tapped her regulator. Marla exhaled the breath she had been holding. Once more, bubbles formed around her. With the pouch firmly in her grip, Marla gave Standish a brief, exhilarated look. They kicked upward and raced toward the safety of the boat above, praying for positive closure.

The clouds had opened, with a torrent of rain cascading off the deck. The captain huddled near the wheelhouse, the driest spot on the boat. After climbing back onboard, Marla slipped her scuba gear off and eased it onto the deck. The captain handed her a towel, but there was no need for it in the middle of a rainstorm.

With an ecstatic smile, she said, "I hope this will reveal...something."

Standish laid her gear next to Marla's, snatched the other towel, and dried her face and hair for a few seconds. She had never seen Marla euphoric before now. "Be careful what you wish for. We don't know why it was down there...at least not yet."

Marla pressed the power button on Borland's iPad, and the screen lit up white. She used the same password as his phone when prompted, and it opened. Her excitement at finding the tablet and beating a shark attack was short-lived. She dropped onto the bench. With rain pounding her back, she read Borland's texts while protecting the iPad from the water.

Predators, above or below the water's surface, hunted fear, drawn to it like a beacon in the dark. Fear was the scent of death, and predators feasted on it with insatiable hunger.

Borland's texts told a sickening story. After reading his last text, she felt their horror. Panic would suffocate their lungs long before the water could, with an unforgiving ocean devouring their screams. Six chains snaking like sea serpents, each locked tight around an ankle, dragged Borland and whoever else to the bottom.

Sharks, ravenous from the feverish scent of fear above the surface and the smell of blood below, triggered a feeding frenzy on the sunken craft. A blur of teeth ripping into muscle and flesh, leaving remnants for the scavengers to pick clean. Were the bones she found his? Marla pitched the tablet on the padded seat.

When Marla's phone rang, she cracked a sad smile. It was David Weidman from the San Antonio Crime Lab. Desperate to change her mind and heart, she answered, "Hi, David."

"I got it and ran it. The blood and urine from Nico Palermo's body tested negative for amphetamines and theophylline. There were no other stimulants at all, but here's the interesting part, hemlock and nicotine were present in both samples. A very low level of hemlock. Maybe not enough to kill, but enough to sicken. This is even crazier. Heavy on the nicotine, like a five-pack-a-day level."

"Five? How can anyone smoke that much?"

"The guy must have had serious lung damage if he smoked that much. I suggest you ask the medical examiner about the guy's lungs."

"On my way. Thanks."

The rain stopped, and the clouds vanished in a moment. The hull bounced against small waves, and the motor hummed in her ears. She dropped her phone on the bench pad and couldn't wait to get off.

Chapter 43

Marla exited the medical examiner's office, the sharp tang of formaldehyde and disinfectants clung to her clothes. The doctor finished a preliminary external exam and planned to cut into the body later. Her mind churned with as many questions as answers. Nico Palermo's body lacked needle marks, no broken bones, and no apparent physical trauma besides being thrown out of a van. If the cartel had anything to do with the killing, they would brutalize him before killing him. What was the random white powder on his face? Amphetamine? With David's unofficial illicit drug tests negative, where did the hemlock and nicotine come from? Though Marla urged the examiner to evaluate for toxins, he responded that a complete drug and tox panel required several weeks. Marla didn't reveal her source, but asked to add nicotine and hemlock to the analysis, and was relieved when the doctor agreed. This didn't feel like a quick, heated crime of passion or a simple overdose. Someone was slow and deliberate—a long-term poisoning—a prolonged hatred.

Yet one detail gnawed at her, the presence of nicotine in his system.

Marla's thoughts turned to Harlow, the girl she'd met at the sandwich shop—Nico's sister. The young woman had played a game of hide and seek with her brother. What other games did she play? Marla needed answers, and the girl seemed like a good place to start.

◆

Harlow sat in the control room, her eyes darting between screens. With a tap of the keyboard, she opened the aperture for the amphetamine, which was two feet wide. The powder cascaded into a waiting tilt truck, filling it in seconds. A worker pushed the apparatus into the mixing room and was ready to start a new batch in one of the four heating containers.

Her phone rang, displaying an unfamiliar San Antonio number. Could it be one of Nico's connections? The word about his demise must have spread fast. She hesitated before answering.

"Hello?"

"Harlow? This is Marla Adams," came the measured voice. "I heard about your brother and wanted to check in. Are you okay?"

"Um, yeah, I'm fine. I mean, it's tragic about Nico, but I don't know what happened." Harlow's tone was careful. She needed to concentrate on Pacheco as if her life depended on it, and keep the production smooth. After pressing another key, the aperture for the theophylline silo opened, filling another tilt truck in seconds. A different worker pushed it into the mixing room.

"I'd like to stop by and talk, if that's okay," Marla said. "Maybe bring you something? Anything you need?"

Before Harlow could answer, a sharp knock startled her. Slats stood outside, beckoning her to come to the door.

"I have to go." Harlow abruptly hung up before Marla could respond. She opened the door. "What is it?"

"Two detectives are here."

Harlow swallowed before answering. "What do they want?"

"They didn't say. Only they wanted to talk to you."

"You didn't let them in, did you?"

"No. Told them to wait out by the gate."

Harlow stepped into the glare, heat pressing down from the sun. The two plainclothes detectives stood just outside the gate, stone-faced, while the guards inside gripped their rifles in defiance. She forced a polite smile, though her fingers tightened into her palms. Something in their stance told her they weren't here for casual conversation.

"Miss Harlow Palermo?" the taller one asked, flashing his badge.

"Depends. Who's asking?"

"I'm Detective Leake, and this is Detective Bell. Need a word with you about your brother, Nico Palermo. Mind if we come inside?"

Her stomach dropped, but she kept her expression smooth. "Of course." She turned to the guards. "Give us some space." Once out of earshot, she opened the gate. "What?"

"May we come inside the building?" Leake asked, already drifting toward the front door.

"Sorry, not happening." Harlow rushed ahead of him and blocked the entrance. "We're in production, and company policy says no visitors. What is this about?"

With Harlow paying attention to Leake, Bell opened the door. His gaze lingered on a shadow moving in the hall.

Harlow quickly turned. "Hey! Back away."

Bell's eyes wandered past the door behind her. "What kind of production?"

"Water," she said smoothly as she closed the door. "A desalination plant."

"Desalination?" Bell repeated, as if it were a foreign concept.

Leake leaned in, tone low. "Miss Palermo, we're here to talk about your brother. A little cooperation would go a long way."

Harlow stood between them and the door. "And why wouldn't I cooperate? My brother's dead. I want to find out what happened, too."

"Then let us in," Leake said, "or better yet, come down to the station where it's quiet."

"Quiet?" Her voice turned sharp. "What exactly are you implying? Am I a suspect now?"

"No one said you were," Bell interjected with a practiced calm. "But refusing to answer questions in a straightforward way does raise concerns."

Harlow dropped the fake smile. "Detective, I'm busy and don't appreciate you insinuating anything. If I need to, I'll call my lawyer right now."

Leake scoffed. "Funny. You brought up lawyers, not us."

Her eyes narrowed. "Are you here to harass me, or are you actually looking for answers about Nico? Because standing here grilling me isn't helping anybody."

Leake shifted his weight, clearly unfazed. "A visit to the station might help sort things out."

Harlow glanced at her wrist as if checking an invisible watch. "Fine. Gimme an hour, and I'll come. Satisfied?"

Bell stepped back, his tone softened but still firm. "One hour, Miss Palermo. If you're not there, we'll have to come back, and we will come inside."

The warning hung in the air. Harlow held his gaze for a moment before giving a curt nod. "I'll be there."

Leake turned to go, then paused. "Oh, one more thing—Jax Whitmore. You know where he is?"

Harlow swallowed before answering. "Haven't seen him."

"All right, Miss Palermo," Leake said. "One hour, right?"

The detectives headed for the gate where an armed guard had already stepped up to let them out. Harlow stood still until they drove away. Once they were gone, she spun on her heels, opened the door, and stormed inside. "Slats!"

He appeared from around the corner, holding an AR-15. "What now?"

"We gotta finish production today and get everything out of this building. Wash it all down. If they come back, I don't want a single trace left behind."

Slats frowned. "Cleaning this place will take days. There's too much powder everywhere, walls, floor, machines, everywhere."

The intercom crackled above them. "Boat docking."

Harlow slapped the doorframe. "Tell them to leave and come back later."

Slats hesitated. "You really think Pacheco's gonna let them sit out there waiting on your say-so? He'll have your head."

Nico's phone buzzed in Harlow's pocket. Her voice clipped. "What?"

The captain's voice came through tense. "We've connected, but nothin's movin'. ¿Qué chingados pasa?"

"Hold on!" she snapped back before shoving the phone into her pocket.

Slats stepped closer, lowering his voice. "You can't keep the guy waiting. He's probably already in contact with Pacheco."

Harlow's mind ran through scenarios, none of which were good. "Fine. Get the crew upstairs and ready for the shipment." She stormed into the control room, her fingers flew across the keyboard, and the generator kicked on, causing the floor to vibrate beneath their feet. Seconds later, the vacuum pipe engaged, creating a deep suctioning sound that echoed through the walls.

Overhead, packages thudded through the pipeline as workers tore into the plastic wraps dumping powder into the first silo. On her screen, bar graphs for amphetamine climbed fast.

Slats was already waiting at the door when she came out. "You understand the cops are coming back, right? Since you ain't going there."

She gritted her teeth. "Got it. That's why this whole place needs to be cleared. Don't care what it takes."

Nico's phone buzzed again. "What?"

The captain's voice was sharp and frustrated. "What's the holdup?"

"It's working," Harlow snapped, her tone razor-edged. "Pressure too low."

"Then take five extra minutes and just keep sending."

"¿Cinco minutos? And wait for the Feds to show?" His voice rose, irritation crackling through the line. "Pacheco not gonna be happy about this? How 'bout I call him and tell him this is your mess?"

Her jaw clenched so tight it hurt. "Don't you dare call Pacheco! I'll handle it."

"Mas te vale, puta. I ain't sittin' here like a pendejo waitin' for you to get your shit together."

Harlow glanced at the security monitor, which showed the vessel tethered to the dock, a vacuum tube connected to the porthole, and the captain slapping his hand against the wheel. "Give me two minutes," she said.

"Dos minutos," he growled. "No mas."

The line went dead.

Harlow pitched the phone onto the console. The dull thud did nothing to calm her nerves.

Behind her, Slats appeared in the doorway again. "The packages stopped, and the men upstairs are getting itchy."

She shot back. "Let's get this moving before that jackass does something stupid."

She hammered at the keyboard, and the system booted up with an ominous hum. Moments later, the vacuum pipe roared to life, creating a powerful suction through the underwater connection.

She redialed. "Fixed."

Seconds later, she heard the thuds of packages hitting the floor overhead. She eyed the bar graph on her screen as it climbed: twenty percent, forty percent, sixty percent.

Her phone buzzed again. She didn't look. "What now?"

The irritation in his voice was palpable. "Still slow. Something's clogging the flow."

"Then fix it," she clapped back.

"How am I supposed to fix a clogged pipe in the water? You're supposed to be runnin' this show, remember?"

"And I'm telling you, it's working. My silos are filling."

"Yeah? Then why do I still have packages to send? Better get it together, Palermo, 'cause I ain't waitin' with my culo in the wind!"

The graphs now almost stalled at sixty-nine percent. Harlow calculated the risk. The system had an automatic shutdown if the flow slowed too much. She couldn't afford that.

"Give me one more minute!"

"Una. No mas! And then I'm out."

"Just keep unloading." Harlow ended the call before he could reply. "Slats," she grabbed a flashlight from a drawer. "Come with me. We need to check the intake valve."

They rushed to the reinforced metal and opened it, where the suction system's intake valve connected to the pipe. The dull thrum of the vacuum was uneven. Harlow killed the electric motor, crouched, and unlatched the small square plate covering the intake.

"Here," she shoved the flashlight into Slats' hand. "Hold this."

The moment she pulled the plate aside, she found a cluster of shredded plastic and thick packing tape jammed tight against the intake.

"Dammit," she uttered, reaching in and yanking it free.

Slats shifted. "Think Pacheco's gonna be okay with this kinda delay?"

"Are you planning on telling him?" she snapped.

He raised both hands. "Not me."

With a sharp yank, she freed the last of the tangled mess, tossed it aside, and reconnected the plate. She flipped the power back on, and the intake devoured a rush of air, with the pump above them humming to life again.

"Problem solved."

Slats pointed at the mess on the floor. "That had to come from the boat."

Harlow wiped her hands on her pants. "Yeah. The Mexicans are sloppy. Too much tape and shredded plastic." She grabbed the phone from her back pocket.

"You got it?" the captain barked.

"It's fixed," she said. "Your guys need to stop wrapping the product like amateurs. I just pulled half a roll of packing material out of the system."

"Noted," the captain replied, his tone easing. "Unloadin' now."

"Hurry it up!" She hung up before he could retort.

Harlow watched the graphs resume their ascent. The tension in her chest eased, but not by much. Slats lingered by the open control room door. She no longer cared whether he was inside.

"We good?" he asked.

"For now," she replied, staring at the monitor. The bar for amphetamine crept past ninety percent. "But if the cops show up again, we're dead meat."

"By who?" Slats asked. "The cops or Pacheco?"

Chapter 44

Marla had just returned to her rental after a run with Festus on the beach when her phone rang. David Weidman's name came on the screen. "Hello?"

"Marla? You sound out of breath. You okay?"

"Yeah. Finished a run with my dog. Whatja find?"

"You are not going to believe what my buddy said regarding the Palermo autopsy. That outrageous nicotine level didn't come from cigarettes." Disbelief filled David's voice. "The lungs were clear. He was not a smoker and had nicotine all over his arms and torso."

Marla closed her eyes and shook her head in confusion. "Do you mean on the skin? How did it get there?"

"I'm not a medical examiner. You'll have to ask the doctor about that."

Her mind reeled with questions and theories as she tried to make sense of the situation. "Is this self-inflicted?" She hoped for a logical explanation.

David just said, "No clue. Best you call the doc and ask him."

"Thanks, David." Marla ended the call and stepped inside the house to grab a bottle of water. After taking several sips, she poured half into Festus' bowl. Needing more information to solve this strange puzzle, she called the Medical Examiner's office.

"Hello, this is Dr. Sanchez speaking."

"This is DEA Special Agent Adams. I'm contacting you about the autopsy results on Nico Palermo."

"Yes. I recognize your voice. So far, I only have preliminary results, and those could change."

Marla had to be careful not to get David's connection in trouble. "Did you run the nicotine and hemlock analysis?"

"I did. Both positive blood and urine. How'd you know?"

"Not quite ready to reveal my sources."

"Understand," Dr. Sanchez chuckled. "I have not completed a full toxicology screen, but the hemlock was low-dosed. The levels in the blood, tissues, and urine for an acute high dose versus long-term poisoning are different. Because we found nicotine in the circulatory system and the lungs were clear, we concluded it was applied dermally."

"Like someone rubbed nicotine on his skin?"

"Yes. I've looked a little closer and found a few small globs of cream around the neck and waistline. It appears someone added the nicotine to the cream."

Marla settled in the chair near the table with the ancient television and sipped from the water bottle. "Like sunscreen? Was the body tanned or sunburned?" Marla tried to understand the doctor's findings.

"Neither," Dr. Sanchez responded. "The skin had little pigment from post-sun exposure. It will take quite a while to get the full ingredients of the cream, but it looks more like a thicker hand cream than a thin sunscreen lotion."

"And what part of the body did you find this lotion with nicotine?"

"So far, the skin from the hands, arms, chest, abdomen, and upper back was all positive. Below the waistline, everything was negative."

"Could the person have applied the cream on himself?"

"Not on his back. Someone had to do that part. And by the way, the white powder around the face and inside the mouth was positive for amphetamine. I ran a quick test, not the full tox. That will take longer. I found none in the nasal passage, trachea, or esophagus. Someone planted this after the death."

"This definitely points toward murder," Marla concluded.

"It's still preliminary, but that sounds accurate," Dr. Sanchez agreed. "Poisoned with hemlock, receiving a fatal dose of nicotine, and amphetamine powder on the face...I don't believe this was self-inflicted."

Two hard knocks on Marla's front door startled her. "Gotta go, Doc. Thanks." With her hand on her holstered pistol, she turned the knob, and the door clicked open.

Junior stood alone in a sheepish stance. "Can I talk to you?"

Marla stepped out to the porch. "Sure. What's your name?"

"Junior."

"Junior what?"

"Just Junior."

"Okay, Junior. What can I do for you?"

"I know where Jax Whitmore is."

"You do? How do you know him?"

"We're fishing buddies."

"Why do you think I'm interested in his location?"

"Cause he claimed he killed you, and I was goin' to the cops to tell 'em he said that, but I heard you had a dog, so I was going to come over and maybe...help it, take it and feed it...and stuff." Junior looked for the dog. "But when I got here, heard you inside, so I guess you're not dead and all."

Marla threw out a little slang to make him feel better. "Well, that's right nice of you. How you know where Jax Whitmore is?"

"Just do. I'm really mad at him. He don't go fishin' with me like he used to, and he made me do somethin' really stupid. I like this girl...his girl, but he said it was okay to ask her out. She said no. Made me feel stupid, so I ain't likin' him no more."

"I see." Marla waited.

Junior pointed north. "He's at the Palermo place."

"You mean the desalination plant?"

"Yeah. You gonna arrest him? Need him outta my way, so's I can ask her out again."

"I appreciate you telling me all this. How about you coming with me to the police station and tell Sergeant Standish what you said?"

"No, no. I don't never want to go to where the cops are. I...I'm not going."

Marla patted Junior's shoulder. "That's fine. That's something I can do for you."

Marla's phone rang in her back pocket again. "Listen, I got to take this. Thanks for the info."

"Yeah...yeah...okay. Hey. Want me ta keep the dog fer ya?"

"No, thanks."

"Okay." Junior trudged through the sand back toward town.

Marla closed the door as she answered the call.

"Three things, one good, one not so much, the last, I don't know," Standish said.

"Give me the I don't know one."

"The sheriff's department found Jax Whitmore's body five miles out of town. The body is already at the medical examiner's office."

So, Junior had no idea Jax was dead. "All our suspects are dying off. Who's next?"

"The county commissioners are going crazy. They see the possibility of no tourists coming to the island for the summer."

"Right about that. What's the good news?"

"The judge signed the warrant for the desal plant."

"I can help you form a team to hit the place. The bad news?"

"Found out what BHH Cleaning is, and you're not going to like it."

"Okay."

"It stands for Borderline Hog Hunter Cleaning Service."

Leo Searcy, you're nothing but a bottom feeder. "You're right, I don't."

Chapter 45

At four in the morning, the world was thick and heavy on the island. The wind had kicked up, bringing the soft hiss of small waves lapping at the shoreline. In the backseat of a police cruiser, Marla Adams adjusted her tactical vest, feeling its weight on her shoulders. The tang of saltwater made her throat dry and scratchy as she caught her reflection in the side window. Above her, the clouded sky was an unbroken black, contrasted against the harsh glare of the nearby desalination plant. No guards were patrolling the fence line at this time of night.

Beside her, Sergeant Standish ran a finger along her pistol barrel, her jaw set like granite. The Harlow Palermo arrest warrant and the desalination plant search warrant lay folded in her pocket. Nearby, Special Agents Miller and Allison sat watch in their vehicle, flanked by two police cruisers and a Sheriff's SUV.

Standish's fist tapped Marla's knee once, trying to break the tense silence. "You good?"

Marla nodded. "Good as I'll ever be. Ricky? What about you?"

He sat in the front passenger seat, his face lost in shadow, only the faintest silhouette visible against the glass. His uniform collar, damp from sweat, he didn't answer right away. Just stared out the windshield toward the plant, then finally said, "Hope y'all know what you're walking into."

Standish glanced at him. "We're walking in with a plan—Marla's plan."

Ricky's mouth twitched, not quite a smile. "Plans work, 'til they don't."

Marla narrowed her eyes. "Are you still in this?"

He turned to meet her gaze, unreadable. "I said I was, didn't I?"

Marla studied him a second longer. His tone hadn't been defiant, but it hadn't reassured her either.

Ricky added, "Just sayin'...Harlow ain't stupid. Folks like her always got a back door—and someone willing to hold it open."

Marla's jaw tensed, unsure whether that was a warning or a confession. She glanced at Standish, who didn't look convinced either.

Her phone rang. When Marla answered, Dr. Sanchez, from the Medical Examiner's office, was clinical. He had run a limited tox on the Jax Whitmore body, given the history of Nico Palermo. The results were positive for marijuana and nicotine—a smoker of both. But also strongly positive for hemlock, and no cream detected on the skin. Marla's thoughts raced. Hemlock? From where? She thanked the doctor and ended the call without a word to either Standish or Ricky. She had enough to think about without Jax Whitmore on her mind.

When Marla opened her door, the others on the team spilled out of their vehicles. Both DEA agents wore black shirts, pants, and tactical vests. Each vest displayed "DEA" in large yellow lettering. One held a Remington 870 pump-action shotgun while the other held a Ruger Mini-14 semi-automatic rifle. All the others held an AR-15 along with their sidearms. The local officers are more nervous than the others. As Standish told Marla once, they had practiced, but none had been in a major shootout in years.

Marla turned to the assembled group. "Listen up! Harlow Palermo's inside, and we suspect there are several men with assault rifles. We know the building has multiple access points and is likely booby-trapped. Does everyone have multiple handcuffs with them?"

Everyone nodded.

"Good. Watch your corners, and no one moves alone."

The team responded with a chorus of affirmations before breaking into groups. An armored vehicle drove around the vehicles, barreled into the fence, and tore down a section.

Marla, Standish, and Ricky rushed toward the eastern perimeter and stopped at a rusted service entrance with corroded hinges. Standish held a battering ram—*The Master Key to all locks*. "Been waiting all day for this."

Marla's pulse pounded in her ears as she gestured to Ricky. "Check it."

Ricky wiggled the knob and gave a slight shake of his head. "Locked."

Standish didn't wait for confirmation, planted her feet, swung the ram, and caved the door in with a loud crack, the sound reverberating into the hallway. She jumped back, expecting gunshots that never came.

Ricky whispered, his voice almost inaudible over the increasing sound of waves crashing against the pier behind them. "No resistance?"

"Could be a trap," Standish said.

Wind whipped Marla's hair. Was a storm coming in the middle of this? She signaled them to fall back as she pulled a small mirror from her vest to check the vicinity. The open room was dimly lit, and to her surprise, instead of the expected desalination equipment, most of the space was empty—a hollow front, a façade. Nothing but a paper-thin cover for drug production. She waved them forward. "Let's move."

They slipped inside, with the harsh buzz of overhead lights casting stark shadows on cold concrete. They reached a junction where the corridor split in two directions. Marla hesitated.

"Standish...you and Ricky take the left. I'll cover the right and loop around." She pointed at the mic on her vest. "Call if you need me."

"Copy that." Standish led Ricky down the left passage.

Marla had barely advanced twenty feet when a staccato of gunfire echoed through the building.

Marla's radio blared. "Shots fired!" Standish's voice clipped. "We're pinned down. Southwest quadrant!"

Marla sprinted back, cut the corner low and fast, and spotted Standish and Ricky crouched behind steel drums, bullets sparking off metal. Across the floor, two men fired behind desalination machinery, muzzle flashes lit the room. Marla dropped to one knee, took aim, and fired two shots. One man collapsed. The other ducked and bolted. She charged after him.

A third man lunged from the side, tackling Ricky. His gun skidded across the concrete. A boot slammed into Ricky's ribs. He grabbed the leg, twisted hard, toppling the man. But the guy was fast, jumping up and swinging a looping punch into Ricky's jaw, splattering blood across his face. Ricky kicked his attacker in the groin and delivered a hard right hook into the man's jaw, staggering him and crashing against a steel drum. Clenching his hands together, Ricky slammed his fist down on the back of the man's neck.

Surprising Standish, another one of Pacheco's men grabbed her from behind, locking his arm around her throat. She rammed her elbow into his ribs, then stomped her foot hard enough to hear a crunch. He yelled and loosened his grip when Standish drove the back of her head into his nose, splattering blood across his face.

Ricky kicked his attacker in the groin and delivered a hard right hook into the man's jaw, staggering him and crashing against a steel drum. Ricky blocked a punch, then twisted his opponent's arm and drove a knee into his gut, doubling him over. With Ricky clenching his hands together into a fist, he slammed down on the back of the man's neck.

Standish's attacker lunged with a knife. She caught his wrist mid-swing and wrenched it sideways. Twisting his arm, she shoved her hand against his face. Pushing him backward and slamming his skull against a metal drum. He collapsed as his head bounced on the concrete with a thud.

After Ricky cuffed his attacker, he wiped sweat from his forehead and asked Standish, "Is he dead?" He reached down and grabbed his gun from the floor.

Standish checked him. "No. Just out."

"You should handcuff him."

"Save 'em for the awake ones." Standish pointed across the building. "Look at those silos marked AMPHETAMINE and THEOPHYLLINE. We are definitely in the right place."

Ricky pointed to a door on the left labeled MIXING ROOM. "Let's go there."

When they entered, the harsh odor hit them. A cocktail of chemicals burned the back of their throats. Ricky went straight for the tablet-press machine, shoving it onto its side before firing twice at a nearby computer tower, then kicking it across the room like a trash can.

"Wait!" Standish yelled. "This is evidence."

"This is bullshit." Ricky fired into each of the four chemical vats. Liquid gushed from the puncture holes, pooling across the floor. "I'm going to make sure no one uses this stuff anymore."

The man Standish fought earlier staggered into the room, bloodied but not beaten, and lunged at Standish, tackling her to the floor in the chemically slickened sprawl. Standish threw a punch, but he ducked, driving his shoulder into her midsection, shoving her against a leaking vat. He pulled a knife out from his belt and swung it wide at her face. Standish leaned back, then using the man's forward motion, she slammed the back of his head against another vat. He slipped on the liquid, grunting in pain, and dropped the knife. Standish didn't wait and stomped his ribs. On his back, he threw a feeble swing. Her elbow slammed into his face, knocking him unconscious again. This time, she cuffed him.

Another man burst from behind a row of drums and charged Ricky, wielding a metal pipe. Ricky dodged the first swing. The second caught his shoulder, sending him stumbling, gun sliding across the floor again. The attacker raised the pipe, ready to swing, but Ricky bull-rushed him into an empty tilt truck. They both fell and rolled on the concrete, the man clawing at Ricky's face. Ricky caught the guy's throat with an uppercut, making him fall on his back, choking and wheezing for air.

After cuffing another assailant, Ricky reached for his gun on the floor a second time. He asked Standish, "Are you all right?"

She wiped blood from her cheek. "Had worse." She pointed at Ricky's service weapon. "Hang on to that thing, wouldja?"

A sharp crack of a gunshot split the air. Standish stumbled forward, falling to her knees.

Slats stepped into the mixing room with his pistol aimed at her. He fired again. Ricky spun and shot him twice in the chest. Slats fell hard, the gun clattering on the concrete.

Standish groaned, rolling onto her side. Ricky grabbed her arm and hauled her up, his hand tracing the impact points on her body armor.

"Damn, that hurts," she muttered, wincing as she climbed to her hands and knees. Her finger dug into the vest. "Kevlar."

Ricky scanned the room, his pulse hammering in his head. "Where's Adams?"

Before Standish could answer, a metallic clang echoed from outside the room. Ricky spun, gun raised. A scrawny figure darted between the reverse osmosis equipment—a runner trying to slip away.

Marla vaulted over a knocked-over table and tackled the man. They hit the floor hard, with her landing on top, grappling for control. She threw an elbow into his face. A right hook stunned him. She flipped the guy onto his stomach and snapped on the cuffs.

Ricky and Standish leaned against each other as they left the mixing room. "Adams, are you good out there?" he asked.

She brushed a strand of hair from her face. "Never better."

A rush of boots echoed down the hall, officers shouting commands that bounced off the walls. One by one, the DEA agents and police dragged Pacheco's men from their hiding places; some cowered behind machinery, others made desperate, last-ditch attempts to fight. A scrawny runner lunged at an agent, only to be slammed against a worktable and cuffed.

Another rushed toward the side door before being tackled to the ground.

Standish wiped a sleeve over her face, exhaling with a heavy effort, while Ricky kept his gun raised, scanning for movement. "Looks like things are wrapping up."

As authorities hauled the last of the handcuffed men outside, one thing was glaringly obvious—Harlow Palermo was nowhere to be found.

Chapter 46

Standing near the control room, Marla glared at the metal mesh stairs that led to an upper level above the silos and a metal walkway heading to a wooden door.

"Harlow Palermo is up there. I can feel it," she said to herself.

Weapon trained on the door, Marla climbed the stairs, with each silent step grinding against her nerves. The hum of machinery mixed with a faint voice came from inside. With a swift kick, the doorframe splintered, and Marla burst inside.

The chemical stench hit her like a slap across her face. The room was in chaos, with hunting knives and waterproof polypropylene bags strewn across the floor. Long strips of black and blue duct tape ripped and coiled like dead snakes. A twelve-inch-wide pipe jutted out from the floor, with an electrical box on the wall nearby, reading "VACUUM ON-OFF."

Marla knew this was how they were smuggling the drugs in the building—the fishing boats on the dock sending everything through a pipe underwater.

Harlow stood across the room. Gone was the once-helpless girl from the sandwich shop. Her green hair was replaced with a searing fire-red dye, and a look cold enough to freeze bone. One hand gripped a phone and the other a hanbo staff.

Marla aimed her gun at her suspect. "You're under arrest, Harlow Palermo."

Harlow hurled her phone like a fastball. Marla dodged—it bounced off the wall and fell to the floor. The distraction was fleeting. Harlow spun the wooden staff in her hand, then swung it, slapping it against the side of Marla's armor vest. The blow knocked Marla sideways. Harlow lunged, kicking Marla in the chest and slamming her against the wall. The hanbo swept her legs, landing Marla on her hands and knees. Harlow jumped on Marla's back, shoving her onto her stomach.

Pain shot up Marla's head as the staff pressed into her neck. She twisted her arm enough to fire her pistol into the wall with a deafening noise inside the tight room. Harlow recoiled just long enough for Marla to shove her off and climb to her hands and knees. Spotting the phone's screen gleaming with "LEO," Marla hissed, "Knew it."

The staff slammed against Marla's back, pain shot down her spine like fire, and dropping her flat on her stomach again. Harlow kicked the gun out of Marla's hand into a tall pile of empty bags. She spun away, but Marla's sweat-slicked fingers latched onto Harlow's ankle, sending her sprawling. Harlow flipped on her back and kicked at Marla's face.

A KA-BAR knife used to open the drug packages lay inches away from Harlow's hand. She reached for it, stretched for it. Marla yanked hard, but Harlow twisted and kicked her away, snatching the blade and slashing without hesitation. Marla's arm exploded with pain, blood spraying across her face.

Harlow bolted for the doorway, then froze at the sound of footsteps climbing the stairs. She turned around to find Marla clutching a foot-long two-by-four with a bloodied hand like a war club.

"Give it up," Marla growled. "You got nowhere to go."

At the door's entrance, Harlow tightened her grip on the knife in one hand and hanbo in the other, wildfire in her eyes. "I'd rather die than rot in your prisons."

"Don't give the bastards the satisfaction. Stay alive and make them pay for what they did to you."

"Who? Pacheco or the cops dogging me my whole life?"

Marla took a step closer and raised the board in her hand. "It's over!"

Harlow sneered, tilting her head with a pretentious innocence that felt more menacing than genuine. "Over? Do you really think I'm scared of you? Taking me in won't stop this. The cartel will replace me before you can reload." She edged backward on the walkway, stopping where one silo stood below, its open top revealing a sea of dry, powdery chemicals.

Marla glanced past Harlow and saw the top of Standish's head as she eased up the stairs. "There's no way out, girl."

Harlow's smile faltered, transforming into something dark and determined. She leaned the wooden staff against the wall, dug into her pocket, and held something in her fist. "All right," she held her wrists together with one hand still holding the knife, "come cuff me." Her tone dripped with mock compliance.

"Drop the knife!" Marla yelled.

Harlow stuck it in her back pocket. "How about there?"

Marla winced from the pain in her arm. Blood dripped from her fingers as she eased her handcuffs out of her back pocket. "Hands on your head."

Harlow eased one hand higher and placed it atop her head before lifting the other in a fist. "Like this?"

"Turn around," Marla ordered.

An unsettling smile formed on Harlow's lips as she licked them. "Don't think I will. Shame, you know. I was gonna make you breakfast," she said in a satirical voice. "Saved six quail in the cage just for you." She opened her fist, revealing tiny seeds in her palm.

"What's that?" Marla asked.

Harlow's hand hovered momentarily before answering. "Hemlock." In one fluid motion, she shoved the seeds into her mouth and chewed.

The word clicked in Marla's head like a puzzle piece locking into place. Nico and Jax. Harlow had killed off her competition. The poison in their stomachs, the slow agony for one, the rapid death of the other. Harlow wanted Marla to know there was no saving her now.

"We have an ambulance outside." Marla stepped closer. "I can help you."

"I don't want your help!"

Harlow grasped the hanbo and swung it. Marla raised the board to block the rod from hitting her head. The force shoved her off balance. Her feet slipped, tumbling over the railing.

The fall was silent. She hit the powdery chemical with a muffled thud, swallowing her in a dense cloud of particles. She couldn't get traction. Couldn't see. Her body sank deeper with every movement.

Her limbs thrashed, kicking up a blinding storm of white dust. Every breath pulled chemical grit into her mouth. Feet touched nothing, arms flailing for anything. Each movement dragged her deeper.

This is it. This is how I go. Not in a shootout. Not a sting. But drowning in a vat of drugs.

She coughed and gagged…tried shouting, but choked instead. The chemical burn stung her sinuses. Lungs on fire. *No, I am not dying in this tomb.*

Her hands clawed at the slick metal walls. Heart thundered. Her chest screamed for air.

"Adams!" Ricky's voice echoed from below. His eyes darted around the room. Remembering the large aperture at the base of the silo, he grabbed the emergency release handle and yanked. Nothing.

"Hold on!" His voice cracked as he slammed his shoulder into the jammed mechanism. Metal groaned. He threw his weight again and again—until the handle gave with a violent snap.

The hatch burst open.

A thick torrent of powder exploded out, flooding the floor. Marla tumbled out, gasping and coughing, her body coated in pale dust like a corpse rising from ash.

Ricky dropped to his knees beside her, grabbing her shoulders. "Marla? Look at me!"

Dazed but alive, she hacked up another lungful of powder and nodded, dazed but alive. Reading the name on the silo, she grinned through grit and pain. THEOPHYLLINE. She could live with that covering her. She pointed at the walkway upstairs. "Standish."

Harlow barreled toward Standish over the narrow walkway, knife in one hand, hanbo in the other.

"Drop it!" Standish fired. The shot rang out, but it didn't stop Harlow from charging.

Harlow's footfalls clanged against the metal grating. She yelled and flung the hanbo at Standish.

Standish ducked as the wooden staff flew past her and hit the ground two stories below. She fired again.

Harlow lunged forward with brute force, plunging the knife into Standish's vest, the force shoving her backward.

"No!" All Ricky could do was watch the momentum carry both women over the railing of the walkway, arms flailing as their bodies slammed to the concrete floor.

He skidded to a halt at the base of the stairs, his heart pounding, refusing what his eyes saw.

Harlow lay sprawled a few feet away. Blood seeped from a bullet wound in her abdomen and a gash on her forehead.

"Standish!" Ricky shouted. "Come on, wake up! Say something!"

She lay on her back, her head tilted to one side, eyes half-open and still. With the knife embedded in her chest, blood pooled beneath her, painting the concrete dark red.

"No, no, no, no, no, no." Ricky holstered his pistol, his trembling hands pressed against her neck, searching for a pulse. Nothing. "Adams!" Ricky's voice cracked as he yelled over his shoulder.

Marla ran to him. "What happened?" She took in the sight. Her gaze locked on Standish with the knife speared in her chest, then glanced at Ricky, who was shaking his head.

"She's gone." Ricky's voice was a mere whisper. "The girl stabbed her." He gestured toward the stairs. "They fell, and...Standish didn't make it."

Marla steadied herself, forcing her emotions down. She stepped closer, kneeling beside Standish's body. The sight of her friend lying lifeless sent a surge of fury and grief coursing through her veins. Her ribs tightened with rage and sorrow. Another person close to her—gone. Everyone close to her was gone. She cleared her throat before asking Ricky, "Where's Standish's pistol?"

"I heard her shoot the girl," Ricky said. "Standish must have let it go during the fall. I'll look around for it."

"Handcuff Harlow. I'll look for the gun."

He nodded, rising to his feet and removing the handcuffs from the belt.

Before Ricky reached her, Harlow rolled with a grunt, Standish's gun clutched in her trembling hand. She fired point-blank. The bullet slammed into Ricky's vest.

It all flashed in his head—the gun range, Marla's help, the fast draw, hitting the center of the target. Ricky drew and fired.

Marla spun around, drawing her weapon, but it was already over. She kicked Standish's pistol away and rolled Harlow onto her stomach. Glancing at Ricky, she knew he was okay. "Come on. Cuff her!"

After Ricky checked the bullet lodged in his armor vest, he cuffed Harlow's wrists behind her back and rolled her over to look at her wounds. Harlow gasped for breaths as the EMTs arrived. After stabilizing their patient, they loaded Harlow onto a gurney and rushed her to an ambulance.

The overhead lights cast a harsh glow over the scene as more EMTs with gurneys entered the building. Standish's stillness told them there was no need to hurry for her.

Marla stayed beside Standish for a moment longer and pressed her forehead to her friend's shoulder. "You didn't deserve this," she whispered as she remembered the last two years of her life. "None of them did."

Ricky returned to her side, his expression heavy with guilt and sorrow. "We'll get Standish the justice she deserves."

"Justice isn't enough." Marla holstered her weapon.

The facility was silent as the team processed their only loss. The dawn's first light crept through the high windows, illuminating the blood-streaked floor.

"I should have done more," Ricky said.

Marla looked at him with exhaustion in her eyes. "You saved my life, Ricky."

He nodded, pride flickering in his gaze, and his face hardened with a sense of relief.

Marla patted Ricky on his back. "If Harlow pulls through and is willing to talk, we can burst this drug bubble."

"Think this is the end of it?"

Marla shook her head. "No. There's one more target."

"Who?"

"Leo Searcy."

"I can't go. His house is not within the city limits."

"I'm going with the deputies to his house and arresting him. Come with us. You've earned it."

His lips tightened into a sad smile. "If it's okay with you, I'll stay with Standish a little longer."

When Marla left, Ricky pulled out his phone and made a call. He held Standish's hand as the phone rang.

Leo answered, "Hello?" He repeated the hello before saying, "That you, Ricky? Why are you calling me?"

Ricky said nothing. He stared at the blood-covered concrete and disconnected the call. "I'm with you, Standish. A hundred percent from now on...I swear."

◆

A line of vehicles flashing red and blue emergency lights sped across the Queen Isabella Causeway, weaving through morning traffic. Marla sat in the back seat of the lead vehicle, her gaze fixed on the lagoon's shimmering blue waters.

To her, Leo Searcy, her so-called uncle, knew of her childhood kidnapping and never said a word. A man who helped move drugs across the Gulf and into people's veins—he was nothing but a common criminal in her eyes.

Sunlight streamed through her window, and she squinted at the brightness hitting her face. Maybe the first rays of morning sunlight promised a new beginning. Maybe it meant the last black sheep in her family would be out of her life forever.

Six SUVs turned off the pavement onto a long dirt road leading to a house. As soon as they stopped, Marla rushed to the front door. It stood open.

Her hands wrapped around her weapon, aiming straight ahead as she entered. Deputies and DEA agents fanned out behind her, searching the residence.

The first time Marla came to the house, she focused on the man. Now, she couldn't help but notice Leo's house was spacious, clean, almost elegant. Artwork adorned the walls, and a luxurious chandelier hung from the ceiling. A stark contrast to the outside.

She stopped in the kitchen where the stolen DEA file and her cap from the beach house lay on a polished granite counter. After holstering her weapon, she picked up a cream-colored notepad, the expensive kind, with words written in beautiful cursive, Not Today.

A deputy approached Marla. "The house is empty."

A sickening pit opened in her stomach as she realized Leo had slipped through her fingers.

A deafening roar shook the ground behind the house. Marla dropped the note and sprinted to the back door. The others followed, boots pounding against the floor.

Outside, a helicopter sat on the helipad, its blades churning at high speed, kicking up dirt and debris in a chaotic spiral. Leo occupied the passenger seat, while the pilot gripped the controls, ready for takeoff. The blades spun faster, the engine louder. The aircraft lifted inches off the helipad, seconds from disappearing into the sky.

Marla raised her weapon and fired at the engine until the magazine emptied. With each shot, a scream from her stolen childhood.

The roar stuttered. Thick black smoke poured from the exhaust, and the engine coughed. The helicopter's landing skids bounced back onto the concrete pad.

The pilot threw open his door and jumped, tumbling to the ground before scrambling away. Leo twisted in his seat, pistol in hand. The side window exploded outward as he fired. The others returned fire. Leo grunted, body jerking as rounds struck his leg and abdomen. He reached for the controls. The helicopter bucked and slid forward.

Marla reloaded another magazine from her back pocket and fired at the tail rotor, shattering the blades. The machine let out a deathly groan.

The rotor blades slowed, their deadly spin easing as they approached the helicopter. Gun lowered but still tight within her hands, she kept her eyes locked on the wreckage. Leo had slumped in his seat, with blood dripping to the floor.

Marla couldn't decide on the verdict of what her heart wanted. Her uncle, who wasn't her uncle, was still alive. Was this finally the end of a family that was never hers?

Chapter 47

The wind ruffled green leaves from the tall trees in the cemetery. A row of South Padre Island uniformed officers stood at attention, their badges adorned with a single black stripe as the six pallbearers carried the flag-draped casket from the funeral home vehicle to its final resting place. Beside the six-foot deep hole, a large poster displayed Standish's official police photograph, capturing the essence of her strength and determination.

Beyond forty-five officers and their spouses, few locals attended. Heartbreak etched Chief of Police Womack's face as he stepped forward to deliver the eulogy. He stood stoic as he addressed the crowd. "I pray every day that there will be no cop funerals, but even in small towns like ours, it still happens. The death of Sergeant Melissa Standish shook our very being. It brings doubt and our mortality to the forefront. Any day of the week, any of us could be lying in a casket. I hope it never comes.

"Standish's life was here, protecting and helping citizens for sixteen years. She was a leader, a mentor to people, and a friend to all its citizens. She dedicated her life to serving this city and gave the ultimate sacrifice. Today, we honor her as we lay her to rest, but her impact will live on through every person she touched."

A twenty-one-gun salute shattered the silence, and the bugler played the mournful notes of Taps.

Marla stood in the last row, holding back a tear, hiding her emotions from the world, but inside, her heart burned. The world felt quieter, emptier, as the officers dispersed, but her resolve burned brighter than ever. Standish would have expected nothing less.

❖

On the other side of town, wearing scrubs, a surgical cap, gloves, and a mask, Raylene held several items against her chest. "I'm here to change a dressing."

The police officer standing at the doorway nodded and allowed her to enter.

Inside the room, Raylene dropped all the stuff in her hands on the bed between Harlow's legs before sitting in a chair next to the hospital bed. The police had handcuffed Harlow's wrists to the side rails.

Raylene's gloved fingers intertwined with Harlow's. "Are you awake?"

Harlow half opened her eyes and turned her head toward Raylene. "Hmm."

"This isn't how you wanted it to go, was it?"

"Hmm."

Raylene held a handcuff key between her fingers. "Do you realize they sell these keys at the old hardware store? They do. Can't figure out why, but...they do." She inserted the key into the lock and turned it until the cuff released. "Want the other one free?"

Harlow barely shook her head. "No. You bring it?"

"Yeah, sure." Raylene stuck the key in her pocket before reaching for a white jar of cream. "Are you certain about this?"

"Mmm hmm." Harlow sighed. "Don't want to go any further."

Raylene unscrewed the cap and placed the jar next to Harlow's free hand. With a muted whisper, she said, "I'm going to go now."

Harlow snickered. "Still wearing gloves?"

"Yeah, but this time to cover my fingerprints, not to keep the nicotine off my hands. Want me to come by later and check?"

"No need." Harlow dipped her fingers into the thick cream and smeared it on her cuffed arm. "I'll use every bit of this on me. Hope to be gone in about twenty minutes."

Lingering for a second, Raylene's eyes traced the shape of Harlow's face for the last time. She gave a slight nod. "I'll let you be."

Harlow didn't look up. "Bye," she said, the word heavy and final.

Raylene walked out past the officer and slipped down the hallway. She turned a corner and disappeared.

❖

Later that afternoon, Marla found herself in the sterile, fluorescent-lit hallway of the hospital. She stared through the observation window at Leo Searcy, his face pale and lined with defeat as he lay on the bed. Marla's mind lay heavy with the weight of the information. Not the plant's complex systems, but Harlow's consuming ambition to control everything astonished her. Marla felt herself slipping. Did she know her job? Maybe Leo was right—just be a cattle rancher. She should have known more, should have guessed what Harlow was doing...what Leo Searcy was doing. She missed it all.

"You're sure about this?" Marla asked the assistant US attorney standing beside her.

"He has information we need," the attorney replied, "and requested to speak only to you. I offered him witness protection if he gives enough info."

Marla entered the room, pulling up a chair. Leo's tired eyes gazed at her, a trace of his old defiance still lingering.

"You don't look happy to see me, niece," his voice raspy from the tube previously down his throat during surgery.

"I'm here for answers, Mr. Searcy," Marla replied evenly. "You're not getting Wit Pro unless you give us everything."

"No more, Uncle Leo?" His lips twitched into a weak smirk. "You want everything? That's a tall order."

Without emotion, she pushed the RECORD button. "Start talking."

"Turn that off."

Marla hesitated before pushing the PAUSE button. "What?"

"Before we start, you need to understand my perspective." He lifted a hand from the bed and circled a finger in the air. "You realize I was not near you when you were a child. You lived hundreds of miles from me, and I hardly ever saw you. Visited you once or twice a year, and when I did, you didn't look abused, so I let things go. You had a good childhood, happy most of the time, friends, college, got a job as a cop, worked with your dad—"

"Wasn't my father, and you knew it."

"Partly. He recounted the entire story to me after the last time he got the local cops to release me, but you were, I don't know, ten or eleven. Am I surprised my brother lost it and killed people? Yeah, but just for the record, I never put cops on pedestals. They fuck up, just like everyone else. And some...go way off the deep end. That *is* something you understand. Are you the first kid who was unaware of what their father did? No, am I sorry for what happened to you? Yes. Why didn't I do something about it? Did you want me to destroy your family when you were ten? I think you'd be even more fucked up in your head than now."

Marla stared at him, not sure whether to reject everything or accept and forgive. The one sure thing she planned to do was treat him like any other perp she questioned. "Start talking about the reason I am here. Your Wit Pro." She pressed the button on the recorder again. "Speak."

"And one more thing. Turn that off."

Marla took a deep breath. "I've heard enough about why you couldn't save me from my kidnapper."

Leo pointed at the recorder. "Off."

Marla pushed the button again. "What?"

"I'm not talking to the IRS about where my money is, but I will tell you."

"I'm DEA. Same thing, a federal employee."

"I told you before, I have money...had plans to use it. Use it to benefit you...your ranch...your livelihood. A way to make up for my faults with the family."

Marla continued to stare at him.

"I won't say where, but it's all in offshore accounts, safe, drawing a nice income. Involved with private and conservative agencies. Many of those companies are Fortune 500. It's a board game, bouncing money from one to another. Whoever gave the best advice for me and the best returns. Offshore, so no income tax, a hundred percent income into my accounts."

"Why are you telling me this?"

"Because when I go into Wit Pro, Leo Searcy disappears. Gone forever. Without a family, no wife, no children, no real family except you."

"I'm not part of your family."

"To me, you are. So, how is Leo Searcy going to maintain all those accounts if he's not around? That's where you come in."

"What are you talking about?"

"I added you as co-owner of all my accounts and investments."

Marla stood. "Are you nuts? I'm a federal employee. A DEA special agent. I am not a co-owner of any offshore drug money accounts!"

"Yes, you are. I called my lawyer an hour ago," he pointed at the phone on the bedside table, "and had your name added to every account. Congratulations."

"Nope. I refuse."

"Then all the money will go to questionable governments of several little islands. More likely in the hands of people willing to grow the drugs you want to stop. Does that make you an accessory?"

Marla plopped down in the chair again.

"Do what you want with it," he said. "Keep it, buy land, buy cattle, give it to the Girl Scouts, whatever strikes your fancy."

"Where are these accounts?"

"The usual places: Virgin Islands, Dominica, the Caymans, others."

"Who's your lawyer? Your accountant?"

"Well, that's where you have to earn my trust. I'll tell you later...maybe later."

"In the meantime, who manages all of it?"

"My lawyer watches over everything. I suggest that to keep from going to jail, you keep your mouth shut about this. How could you ever begin to prove your innocence? Okay, I'm ready for the recorder. Are you?"

Marla turned on the recorder, and for the next several hours, Leo revealed every detail of the operation. He disclosed the intricate web of connections within the cartel, explained how they used an underwater vacuum system to transport drugs from fishing boats to the desalination plant, and even revealed their methods of funneling payments through offshore accounts. As far as Pacheco was concerned, Leo expected him to be dead or deep inside Mexico, never to be found by the United States government.

Marla focused back on Leo. "You're still going to pay for what you've done," she said, her tone cold. "But I'm hoping you'll get what you deserve from somewhere that you think is a safe place."

Leo's smirk reappeared. "Then you will own it all. How might that look? A DEA agent owning millions in offshore accounts. You need to keep me alive for a lengthy time."

Marla stood and glanced out the hospital room window and then turned back to Leo. "The good news is, I'll never see you again, talk to you again, and when you die, that will be the last time I hear your name."

Chapter 48

DEA agents discovered hemlock plants beside the birdcage filled with quail. A local poison expert explained the birds were immune to hemlock seeds and leaves but had it in their meat. The slow feeding caused Nico's illness, while the quick death of Jax resulted from a belly full of meat. But where did the nicotine in the cream come from? Nico had a massive amount in his system and on his skin. Did Harlow put that on him? Marla had to wait for Harlow to awaken from the coma to answer.

The city's demolition crews arrived at the desalination plant the same day as the funeral. Once a looming symbol of corruption and moral decay, the plant was nothing more than rubble. The DEA and local police watched demolition crews dismantle and destroy the underground pipelines and the underwater vacuum system.

Stepping away from the dock, where her boss, Assistant Special Agent in Charge Ronald Borland, once stood, Marla watched the final demolition of the cartel's infrastructure crumbling into dust.

"We did it, Standish," Marla whispered as the sea breeze carried her words away.

An automobile almost ready for the wrecking yard drew near Marla's truck. The trunk unlatched with a pop, and Raylene exited the car, opened the back door, pulled a child out, and held it close to her.

"Can I help you?" Marla asked.

Raylene stopped beside Marla. "Yes. I have something that belonged to Jax. Well, probably not really his, but something I don't want. It's dirty, and I feel bad about keeping it."

Marla gave the beat-up car a once-over. "What's that?"

"Follow me." Raylene lifted the trunk lid to reveal two large sacks of money. "This is not mine. I don't want it. Do you mind taking it?"

Leo's money flashed through Marla's mind. She should do the same as this girl. "What's your connection to Jax Whitmore?"

"We were...I lived with him in that garbage dump on the spoil island that the cops raided and ripped apart. I'm the baby mama, the girlfriend, the bitch. Whatever he wanted to call me that day."

"I'd call you honest. What's your plan without money and not living in the garbage dump?"

"I...we don't have one. I'll figure something out."

"Would you move?"

"From nothing? In a second."

"How about moving near San Antonio?"

"Never been there. I've lived my entire life on this island."

"Time to see more of Texas." Marla lifted the sacks from the trunk and placed them on the ground. "Ever seen a cow up close?"

"A cow? Like on television? Four legs, horns, and a tail?"

"That could describe many animals. I need another ranch hand. There's a hundred head of cattle on my ranch, and one more person sure could help."

Raylene shifted the baby to her other hip. "The woman who killed my Jax? What about her? Where is she?"

"Harlow Palermo is in the hospital under tight security. After being shot twice and trying to kill herself with hemlock, the girl is miraculously still alive."

Raylene's secret never needed to come out: nail salon, nicotine, cream. She looked around at nothing specific. "Hmm. When do you need help?"

"If I ran a security check on you, what might pop up?"

"Do you mean, have the police ever arrested me? No, they have not."

"You have a phone?"

"Yes," Raylene answered.

"Hand it to me, and I'll put my head ranch hand's number in there. Text her your full name and birthday tomorrow morning, and Cassie will call you. If you're clear, she will find a place for you and the baby."

"Where's that?"

"She'll give you all that information once you're cleared."

Raylene smiled. "Thanks."

Marla's phone rang. "Hello?"

Ricky was firm. "Harlow Palermo is dead."

"When?"

"About thirty minutes ago. The doctor said she went into convulsions and stopped breathing. I'm here now, and she's naked, with most of her body covered with cream. Next to her is a plastic jar with a little of the cream still inside."

"Aren't her hands cuffed to the rail?"

"Right side wasn't."

"How?"

"Don't know."

"Is it a white cream?"

"Yes."

"Like what Nico Palermo had on him?"

"Just like it," Ricky said.

"Does it look like she put it on herself?"

"Looks like she did herself in. It's all over her face, arms, chest, and stomach...and her right hand."

"Where'd the jar come from? You got an answer for that?"

Ricky paused before speaking. "I, um...I'll look into it."

"Send a sample of the cream and the jar for prints and toxicology. Has to be nicotine."

When Marla ended the call, Raylene asked, "More problems?"

"Harlow Palermo is dead."

Raylene held back her smile. "Oh, no. That's terrible."

"Where were we? Oh, yeah. Tomorrow. Send all that in tomorrow."

"Thanks," Raylene said. "I will."

✦

The next day, Marla sat in the precinct conference room as Chief Womack returned from his extended leave. His wife's recovery had gone well, though his eyes carried the weight of recent losses.

"Thank you all for stepping up in my absence," he said, his voice warm but commanding. He paused while scanning the room. "Ricky Roberts, front and center," Chief Womack pulled a badge from his pocket. "You've proven yourself to be a leader under the toughest circumstances. Standish would be proud. Effective immediately, you're promoted to sergeant."

Ricky's eyes widened in shock as he stepped forward. "Chief, I—"

"Don't make me regret this, son," Womack interrupted with a grin.

The room erupted in applause. Marla clapped along, a genuine smile breaking through her usual guarded expression. As the clapping subsided, Ricky caught her eye as he used his hand for a playful fast draw. She did the same.

"Guess I've got big shoes to fill," he said quietly.

"You'll do fine," Marla replied. "Just keep her in mind, and you will be the sergeant she knew you could be."

As the meeting ended, Marla lingered for a moment, letting the noise of the precinct wash over her. The fight wasn't over—always another battle, another challenge. But for now, they'd won a sliver of the war.

Marla's phone rang. It was the DEA office calling.

THE END

Acknowledgements

South Padre Island is a wonderful place to visit, vacation, and eat fresh seafood. As in every book, I expand on the scenery. The police department is not a small white building. It's inside a large brick building that holds many government offices, but that would be no fun. There is no small beach house where Marla stayed on the north side of the island.

Following research on dead sharks and whales left on the beach, authorities often choose to let many decay instead of spending resources on removal. Dumping the carcasses elsewhere only brings the predators and scavengers to another location. Nature takes care of things.

For those not familiar with feral hogs, they can be devastating to farmers, destroying and eating thousands of pounds of crops in a night. In Texas, these animals are hunted year-round.

Thanks to my two critique groups, Write Right Critique Group and All Writers Online Workshop. Thanks to all the people I asked a thousand questions to: Jan Elliott, a member of Texas CattleWomen Inc., Scott Hilburn, Luci Hanson Zahray (The Poison Lady), Texas Department of Public Safety Crime Laboratory, Crimescenewriter2 forum, Caprock Writers and Illustrators Alliance, NOAA Southern Regional Office, and the South Padre Island Chamber of Commerce and Police Department.

A special thanks to KJ Waters for the marketing, publishing, and business end. Jody Smyers for the fantastic and suspenseful book cover design.

Without editors, any book would be a mess. Cameron Chandler's innovation has been inspirational. His vision, critiques, ideas, and edits are astounding. I am lucky to have him hanging around. Audrey Mackaman is excellent at line editing. I call her my English teacher, but without the ruler to slap my hand when I write incorrect sentences.

About Patrick Hanford

Patrick Hanford has lived in Texas most of his life. He graduated from the University of North Texas, Texas College of Osteopathic Medicine and recently retired from family medicine after more than thirty-five years. He interjects his past experiences of daily medical clinic life throughout his stories.

He lives with his wife, plays golf, walks in West Texas wind, and travels the world to find new inspirations. You can find out more at patrickhanford.com.

www.ingramcontent.com/pod-product-compliance
Lightning Source LLC
Chambersburg PA
CBHW070511310726
48976CB00002BA/410